Also by Carl Hiaasen

SQUIRM

Also by Carl Hiaasen

Hoot

Flush

Scat

Chomp

Skink—No Surrender

Carl Hiaasen

SQUIRM

EMBER

With special thanks to Timothy P. McCleary, PhD, and Raphaelle He Does It - Real Bird of Little Big Horn College, Crow Agency, Montana, for their helpful comments and expert advice.

Visit us on the Web! GetUnderlined.com

Educators and librarians, for a variety of teaching tools, visit us at
RHTeachersLibrarians.com

Library of Congress Cataloging-in-Publication Data is available upon request.

ISBN 978-0-385-75300-5 (tr. pbk.)

Printed in the United States of America
10 9 8 7 6 5 4
First Ember Edition 2020

For all those who stand up

ONE

This one kid, he got kicked out of school.

That's not easy to do—you need to break some actual laws. We heard lots of rumors, but nobody gave us the straight story.

The kid's name was Jammer, and I got his locker.

Who knows what he kept in there, but he must've given out the combination to half the school. Kids were always messing with my stuff when I wasn't around.

So I put a snake inside the locker. Problem solved.

It was an Eastern diamondback, a serious reptile. Eight buttons on the rattle, so it made some big noise when people opened the locker door. The freak-out factor was high.

Don't worry—the rattlesnake couldn't bite. I taped its mouth shut. That's a tricky move, not for rookies. You need steady hands and zero common sense. I wouldn't try it again.

The point is I didn't want that rattler to hurt anyone. I just wanted kids to stay out of my locker.

Which they now do.

I set the diamondback free a few miles down Grapefruit Road, on the same log where I found him. It's important to exit the scene fast, because an adult rattlesnake can strike up to one-half of its body length. Most people don't know that, and why would they? It's not a necessary piece of information, if you live a halfway normal life.

Which I don't.

"What does your dad do?"

I hear this question whenever we move somewhere new.

My standard answer: "He runs his own business."

But the truth is I don't know what my father does. He sends a check, Mom cashes it. I haven't seen the guy since I was like three years old. Maybe four.

Does it bother me? Possibly. Sure.

I've done some reading about this, how it can mess up a person when his parents split, especially when one of them basically vanishes from the family scene. I don't want to be one of those screwed-up kids, but I can't rule out the possibility.

Mom doesn't say much about Dad. The checks always show up on time—the tenth of the month—and they never bounce. We might not be rich, but we're definitely not poor. You wouldn't believe how many pairs of shoes my sister owns. God, I give her so much grief.

The way I look at it, Mom doesn't get a free pass just because she doesn't want to talk about my father. That's not what you'd call a healthy, open approach to an issue. So I stay on her case, though not in a mean way.

"What does he do for a living?" I'll say, like I've never asked before.

"Well, Billy, I'm not exactly sure what he does," she'll begin in the same tight voice, "but I can tell you what he *doesn't* do."

Over time, based on my mother's commentary, I've scratched the following professions off my Phantom Father list:

Astronaut, quantum physicist, lawyer, doctor, heavy-metal guitarist, veterinarian, architect, hockey player, NASCAR driver, jockey, plumber, roofer, electrician, pilot, policeman, car salesman, and yoga instructor.

Mom says Dad's too claustrophobic to be an astronaut, too lousy at math to be a quantum physicist, too shy to be a lawyer, too squeamish to be a doctor, too uncoordinated to play the guitar, too tall to be a jockey, too hyper for yoga, and so on.

I don't like this game, but I'm making progress, information-wise. Mom's still touchy about the subject, so I try to take it easy. Meanwhile, my sister, Belinda, acts like she doesn't care, like she's not the least bit curious about the old man. This fake attitude is known as a "coping mechanism," according to what I've read.

Maybe my father is a psychiatrist, and one day I'll lie down on his couch and we'll sort out all this stuff together. Or not.

At school I try to keep a low profile. When you move around as much as my family does, making friends isn't practical. Leaving is easier if there's no one to say goodbye to. That much I've learned.

But sometimes you're forced to "interact." There's no choice. Sometimes staying low-profile is impossible.

The last week of school, some guy on the lacrosse team starts pounding on a kid in the D-5 hallway. Now, this kid happens to be a dork, no question, but he's harmless. And the lacrosse player outweighs him by like forty pounds. Still, a crowd is just standing around watching this so-called fight, which is really just a mugging. There are dudes way bigger than me, major knuckle-draggers, cheering and yelling. Not one of them makes a move to stop the beating.

So I throw down my book bag, jump on Larry Lacrosse, and hook my right arm around his neck. Pretty soon his face goes purple and his eyes bulge out like a constipated bullfrog's. That's when a couple of his teammates pull me off, and one of the P.E. teachers rushes in to break up the tangle. Nobody gets suspended, not even a detention, which is typical.

The dorky kid, the one who was getting pounded, I didn't know his name. The lacrosse guy turns out to be a Kyle something. We've got like seven Kyles at our school, and I can't keep track of them all. This one comes up to me later, between sixth and seventh period, and says he's going to kick my butt. Then one of his friends grabs his arm and whispers, "Easy, dude. That's the psycho with the rattler in his locker."

I smile my best psycho smile, and Kyle disappears. Big tough jock who likes to beat up kids half his size. Pathetic.

But lots of people are terrified of snakes. It's called *ophidiophobia*. The experts say it's a deep primal fear. I wouldn't know.

During seventh period I get pulled out of class by the school "resource officer," which is what they call the sheriff's deputy who hangs out in the main office. His name is Thickley, and technically he's in charge of campus security. He's big and friendly, cruising toward retirement.

"Billy, I'm going to ask you straight up," he says in the hallway. "There's a rumor you've got a snake in your locker. A rattlesnake."

"A live rattler?" I laugh. "That's crazy."

"Can we have a look?"

"No problem. Who's *we?*"

"Me. Just myself."

"Sure, Officer Thickley. You don't need to ask first."

"Oh, I always ask," he says. "See, if I show respect for the students, they'll show respect for me. It's a two-way street."

"Be my guest," I tell him. "You can just pop the lock, right?"

"I'd like you to come along with me."

"But I really can't miss this class," I say. "Mrs. Bowers is reviewing for the final."

"Please, Billy. I'm not a fan of snakes."

We walk down the hallway to my locker. Thickley stands at least ten feet behind me while I open the door.

"Here you go," I say.

"Holy crap!"

"It's not real, man." I dangle the rubber snake, its tail jiggling. "See? Just a toy."

The color returns to Thickley's face. I bought the joke

snake for like three bucks at a party store. It's black and skinny, and doesn't look anything like a diamondback rattler. They had it on the same aisle with the fake vomit and dog poop.

"Billy, why have you got that thing in there?"

"Because other kids keep breaking in and messing with my stuff. You knew Jammer, right? This was his locker before he got expelled."

"Oh," says Thickley. "Then we should get you a different one."

"*No necesito.*"

"But the locker still smells like Jammer's . . . stuff."

"Is that what stinks so bad?"

Thickley says, "I'll get you a can of Febreze."

You're probably thinking: *This is a disturbed young man.*

Based on what happened with me and the rattler, right?

But I've been catching snakes since I was a little kid, and I know what I'm doing. Usually I don't handle the poisonous ones, because a split-second mistake will put you in an ambulance, speeding to the E.R. You might not die from the bite, but from what they say, the pain is extreme.

Right now at home I've got a corn snake, a king snake, two yellow rat snakes, and a banded water snake, all nonvenomous. I can't say "harmless" because the water snake is mean and nasty. Honestly, the rattler was way easier to handle.

I never keep a snake for more than a week or two. They stay out in the garage, inside dry aquarium tanks with lids that screw down tight. My mother isn't thrilled about the arrangement, but she's gotten used to it. She says it's safer than wakeboarding or BASE jumping, neither of which is on my list of future hobbies.

A wild snake won't hurt anybody, as long as you give it some space. That's true for rattlers, same as the others.

"What is *wrong* with you," my sister often says. This is never a question. "These aren't normal pets."

"They're not pets, Belinda. I don't *own* them."

"At least a puppy gives you love. A snake gives you nothing but a blank stare." My sister, the comedian.

In a few months she's leaving for college—Cornell University in Ithaca, New York. Big-time school. Good for her.

Belinda says she's looking forward to northern winters, but she hasn't got a clue. Like me, she has spent her entire life in Florida, the place everybody up north wants to be every January.

She didn't know about the rattlesnake, of course. Neither did Mom. They steer clear of my aquarium tanks in the garage.

I'm holding the king snake when Mom pokes her head out the door and says, "What happened at school today, Billy? Put that creepy thing away and come inside."

Turns out the dorky kid—Chin is his last name—he friended my mother on Facebook. Who does that? He sent her a message thanking me for saving him from the beat-down in D-5. He said nobody's ever stuck up for him before.

See, this is why I'm not on social media. Way too much human contact.

"Why didn't you tell me about this?" Mom asks.

"'Cause it was no big deal."

"Fighting is too a big deal. You've got a week left of school before summer. Can you please try not to get kicked out?"

"They won't kick me out, Mom. I've got straight A's."

"But what if you'd hurt that other boy?"

"Only thing I hurt was his shiny blond ego."

She sighs. "We've had this discussion, Billy."

"What—I'm supposed to turn the other way when I see something bad going down?"

"No, of course not, no. What you should do is immediately report it to a teacher. Or run to the office and tell somebody. That's how cases of bullying are supposed to be handled. It says so in the school Code of Conduct."

I have to chuckle. I'm not trying to disrespect my mother, but seriously—the Code of Conduct? Kyle the lacrosse star was punching that poor kid in the head. Come on.

Next day, I notice Chin eating by himself in the cafeteria. He's got a bruised eye and white gauze taped over one ear. He never looks up from his lunch tray, so he doesn't see me.

I walk straight to the lacrosse kids' table, sit down next to Kyle, and start eating my ham-and-fried-egg sandwich.

He just glares at me. It's not what you'd call a bonding moment.

One of Kyle's jock friends tells me to move to another table.

"Aw, but you guys are so cool," I say. "I want to be just like you. Talk the same cool way. Wear the same cool clothes. Hang with the same cool girls. It's truly an honor to sit with you here at your special cool table. Seriously, this lunch is the high point of my entire life."

And they thought *they* were pros at sarcasm.

"Move it, Snake Boy!" the kid barks.

I can't help but laugh. Is this what they're calling me now?

"So, you guys are into reptiles, too?" I put down the sandwich, whip out my phone.

Kyle's angry, but nervous at the same time. Doesn't say a word.

I google a picture of a wild-hog hunter who got bitten by a diamondback over near Yeehaw Junction. That's a real place, you can look it up. The hog hunter's arm is swollen thick as a pine stump. His fingers look like boiled purple sausages. I hold up the phone so that Kyle and his all-jock posse can see the photo.

"That's what can happen," I say, "when you're not careful."

Kyle goes pale and edges back his chair. "Dude, you *are* a total psycho."

"Can I have the rest of your Doritos?" I ask pleasantly.

They all get up, snatch their trays, and walk off, Kyle in the lead.

FYI, that hog hunter didn't die from the snakebite. He was back in the woods a month later—but way more careful.

Kyle won't bother Chin again. That's my guess.

The night before the last day of school, Mom's in the kitchen working on the household budget. She has a yellow notebook, two sharpened pencils, and a calculator. I notice the monthly check from my father on the table. His name is printed on it, but no address.

Mom doesn't care if we see the check, but she always cuts up the mailing envelope and throws away the pieces— which I later dig out of the garbage can and try to tape back together.

Usually it's impossible, because the snipped pieces are as small as confetti, but on this particular night she must have been in a hurry with the scissors. When she's not looking, I collect the fragments of the envelope and smuggle them to my room. This time they fit together like a miniature jigsaw puzzle, and it's easy to read the return address printed in the upper left-hand corner.

So I walk back to the kitchen and say, "Mom, how much is a plane ticket to Montana?"

"What are you talking about?"

I show her the taped-together envelope.

She frowns. "We can't go anywhere this summer. I've got a brand-new job here, remember?"

"They've got Uber cars in Montana."

"I doubt that," Mom says. "Uber tractors, maybe."

My sister and I don't approve of her working for a car-service app, because it's so dangerous on the roads. Florida has possibly the worst drivers in the universe. Also the most trigger-happy.

But Mom said she was bored with accounting and wanted a job where she could meet new people every day.

"Let me fly out there by myself," I tell her. "I can pay for it from my savings."

"And where would you stay?"

"With Dad. Where else?"

"But he didn't invite you, Billy."

"I'm inviting myself."

Mom looks sad. "He's got a whole new life now, honey."

"That's bull," I say. "Just because you get a new zip code doesn't mean you get a new life. Look at *us*."

She closes her eyes for a moment, then says: "I wish I could let you go, but it's not a great idea. He got remarried."

"Doesn't he still ask about me and Belinda?"

"I send him pictures."

"That's it?"

"Let's not talk about this now, Billy."

Back in my room, I go online to check the balance of my bank account: $633.24. This is what I've saved up from Christmases and birthday presents, and also from working at Publix for five weekends until I couldn't stand it anymore. Bagging groceries requires friendly conversation with strangers, which I'm not especially good at.

Truthfully, I'm surprised I've got so much cash in the bank. There's a travel site offering $542 round-trip tickets from Orlando to Bozeman, Montana, so I write Mom a check and slip it into her handbag after she goes to bed.

Then I "borrow" her credit card to order the plane ticket off the airline's website.

The last day of school is short because I've got only one final exam, in algebra. I'm done at noon, and Mom is waiting in the parking lot. She found my check in her purse, and she's angry.

"You are *not* going to Montana," she declares.

"It's a nonrefundable ticket."

"Don't be a smart-ass, Billy. I don't even have your father's phone number!"

"Then how do you know he's married?"

"He told me in a letter. This was a few years ago."

"Were you mad?"

"I'm mad he doesn't call you guys. That's all."

"And you seriously have no idea what he does for a living?"

Mom sighs. "He says he's working for the government—whatever that means."

"How come you never told me?"

"Because I was embarrassed I didn't know more."

I reach over and squeeze her arm. "If he doesn't want to see me, I'll come straight home. That's a promise."

She says, "This is all my fault."

"Please don't cry. It's just a plane ride."

But she knows better than that. So do I.

Too much time has passed. I need to talk to the man.

That evening, I take the snakes out of their tanks and put them in pillowcases, which I knot snugly at the open ends. My mother drives me down Grapefruit Road until I find the right place to stop. She stays in the car, as any normal person would, while I walk into the trees, open the pillowcases, and free the snakes.

I'd waited until dark so they could crawl away safely. Most hawks don't hunt at night, another piece of information you'll probably never need.

The next morning, Mom takes me to the airport. I've told her I spoke to my father and he's excited about my visit.

Not true. I'd spent an hour on the internet but couldn't find a phone number anywhere. All I have is the return address on that envelope.

And now I'm getting on an airplane, flying across the country to meet a man who might not even want to see me.

Brilliant.

TWO

My family moves around so much because Mom has a weird rule:

We've got to live near a bald eagle nest, and by "near" my mother means fifteen minutes, max. She's totally obsessed with these birds, which I agree are pretty impressive. Still, it's a strange way to arrange your life.

You can go online and look up all the active nests in the state. Mom always picks one close to a good school district, and that's the neighborhood where she buys a house.

Sunday is our eagle-watching day. The nests are usually at the top of a tall dead tree. Mom, Belinda, and I each carry our own pair of binoculars—like I said, we're not poor—and for an hour or two we'll just sit on the hood of the car, looking up at the birds.

"They mate for life," Mom often whispers.

Many do, but some don't. I leave that subject alone.

Florida baldies usually don't migrate north once they find a mate. After the babies grow up and leave, the mother and father birds sometimes fly off. I've explained to Mom that they often build more than one nest, but she always starts worrying if they don't show up again after a few days. She thinks they got sick from eating fish in polluted water, or somebody took a shot at them. Those things do happen, but there are times when eagles go away just because they're in a mood to explore.

Then the nest starts to crumble, and pretty soon you're staring up at an empty heap of sticks and dead branches.

Before long, Mom starts tap-tapping on her laptop again, searching for a new nest to adopt. Next thing I know, the house goes up for sale, a moving van appears, and we're on our way to another eagle town. In the time since my father left, we've lived in Key Largo, Clearwater, Everglades City, Punta Gorda, and now Fort Pierce.

Of all those places, Everglades City was my favorite, because it's surrounded by wilderness—or the closest thing to wilderness that's left in Florida. We stayed there two years and three months, until the nest was blown down by a funnel cloud, which is basically a tornado over water. The nest was a short boat ride from our house, and on Sundays a neighbor would loan us his skiff to go see the eagles. They usually had two babies, both fledged and gone by midsummer. It was the first weekend of October when the funnel cloud dropped out of a thunderhead on Chokoloskee Bay and shredded the nest.

After that we didn't see the mother and father birds again, though I doubt they died in the storm. Baldies are tough. They probably just made a new nest somewhere else. Mom didn't want to talk about it—she was so bummed.

I thought of a plan to cheer her up so we could stay in Everglades City, but it sort of backfired and she sold the house anyway. The night we took down the FOR SALE sign, I bagged up my snakes and let them go near a gravel road off the Tamiami Trail.

Mom waited in the car with the doors locked. That's our routine.

On the morning I'm leaving to see my father, the last thing she says at the airport is: "Billy, please don't bring back anything alive."

"You mean like snakes?"

"I mean anything that needs a bag or a cage," she says, and kisses me on the cheek.

You can't fly straight from Florida to Montana, so I've got to change planes in Atlanta. A skinny guy wearing a Delta name tag is waiting to walk me to the new gate, even though I tell him I can find my own way (which isn't true, because the airport is ridiculously huge and confusing).

The jet going to Montana is larger than the first one. Sitting beside me is a woman who smells like the bacon cheeseburger she gorped while we were waiting to take off. Her husband is reading a book about World War II on his tablet.

I spend the entire flight with my face at the window. It feels like I'm gliding through an IMAX movie. We pass directly above the Mississippi River, winding and broad and muddy. After that it's the Great Plains, checkerboards of gold and green. Some of the farm fields are cut in humongous perfect circles.

But the best sight, by far, is the Rocky Mountains. From the sky, the first thing you notice is the foothills, which look like the bony brown knuckles of a giant. Then suddenly these amazing peaks appear, bright and jagged, with clouds wisping along steep ridgelines. Even in June the mountaintops are still white! I'm totally jacked because I've never seen snow before.

The Bozeman airport is laid out next to a towering row of white-capped crests. After we land, a flight attendant asks me to stay in my seat until the other passengers get off. I can't figure out what I've done to get myself in trouble. Once the plane is empty, the flight attendant leads me down the jet bridge into the terminal building.

"Your uncle's waiting right there," she says, pointing to a young bearded dude wearing black jeans and a hoodie. I've never seen him before in my life. She hands him some papers to sign, then nods goodbye to me.

I look at the bearded guy and say, "I didn't know I had any uncles."

He grins. "Just go with it."

Apparently, kids my age aren't allowed to travel alone unless an "approved" adult is meeting them when the plane lands. My mom has a friend whose nephew attends Montana State, and that's who was waiting at the airport. Mom didn't tell me ahead of time, probably because she didn't want me to arrive with an attitude. I sure don't need a babysitter.

The guy's name is Kurt and he tells me he's majoring in middle-childhood education.

"Perfect," I say.

"So, I'm giving you a ride to Livingston?"

"Is that far?"

Kurt chuckles. "In Montana there's no such thing as far. People drive six hours to a Little League game and it's no big deal. Livingston's only thirty minutes on the interstate."

The first part of the car ride is almost as unreal as the flight, the highway climbing and dipping through valleys of bright green timber. Every third word out of my mouth is "wow," so it's obvious to Kurt that I've never been out of Florida. We zigzag through a steep pass called Bear Canyon, and like an idiot, I ask him if it has any bears.

"Uh, yeah. Lots of 'em," he says.

"I'd love to see a grizzly."

"Ha, you and two jillion other tourists. I know lots of people born and raised here that have never laid eyes on one."

"How about you?"

"Nope."

"Maybe I'll get lucky," I say.

Kurt tells me about a roadside attraction that features captive grizzlies. The biggest of the show bears has appeared in major movies. "The place is just a few miles ahead," he says. "They're amazing critters. You want to stop?"

"Thanks, but I'd rather see a wild one."

"Well, they don't hang out in Livingston."

"They do in Yellowstone Park," I say.

"For sure. Major griz country."

"My dad's gonna take me there. We see any bears, I'll text you a picture."

"Yeah, right," says Kurt.

The house is on Geyser Street. It's pale gray with navy-blue shutters. There is a genuine picket fence in front, a neatly planted garden, and a porch with a wooden swing. I'm a long, long way from Florida.

Two bicycles are propped against the fence. I wonder if Kurt dropped me at the wrong place, so I double-check the address on my father's envelope. It matches the number on the mailbox.

I wheel my suitcase up to the front door and knock. A girl answers. She has long, straight brown hair and matching eyes, and she's a little taller than me.

"I'm looking for Mr. Dickens," I say. "Dennis Dickens."

The girl sighs. "Oh brother. Come on in."

"What's wrong?"

"I said come in, *brother*."

I drag my bag inside. The girl's name is Summer Chasing-Hawks. It turns out I'm actually her stepbrother. She says my dad "sort of" married her mother a few years earlier.

"He's not here," Summer informs me.

"When will he be back?"

"You want some lemonade? Mom's floating the river over near Billings. She won't be home till dinnertime."

Summer goes to the kitchen and returns with two cans of Pepsi. "No more lemonade. Sorry," she says, tossing me one of the cans. "We're Apsáalooke Indians, which you probably never heard of. Nowadays they call us Crow. My mom met your dad on the rez. His drone crash-landed on our trailer."

"Aren't the Crows the ones who nailed General Custer?"

"Nope. Our tribe was on the other end of that deal—we sent scouts to help the U.S. soldiers." She shrugs. "Back then we had major issues with the Lakotas."

I sit beside an orange tabby on a chewed-up sofa. The cat is old and twitchy, with a bald patch on its rump. There's also a weird-looking mutt sniffing around. It looks half Labrador and half greyhound, a bad combination of goofy *and* fast. Summer says the dog's name is Satan.

"It used to be Sparky," she adds, "until he ate Mom's favorite boots."

"I'd really like to see my dad. Do you know where he went?"

"I predicted you'd show up here one day, Billy."

"Is that why he took off?" I ask. "Because he found out I was coming?"

"He travels for his job. Something came up, short notice." Summer finishes off her Pepsi and crumples the can.

The windows of the house stand open, and the air feels cool and dry. On one wall hang some framed photographs of my father and his new family. Dad's hair looks lighter than mine, and in some of the photos he's got a scraggly goatee.

I don't think I look anything like him, but Summer says she definitely sees a resemblance.

"I knew who you were the minute I opened the door," she says, nodding.

"It sucks he's not here. I flew all the way from Florida."

"Then your arms must be really tired." She shrugs and smiles. "Old joke. Bad joke. Sorry about that."

"Can I hang out until your mom gets home? I need to ask her some questions."

"Of course you can hang here, Billy. Where else would you go?"

We walk down to the Yellowstone. I can hear it from blocks away, which is wild. Florida rivers are so lazy and quiet that you can barely tell the water's moving. Summer says the Yellowstone is running high and dirty because of heavy snowmelt from the mountains. Standing on the bank, I see the pure power of the racing current. I toss a stick and watch it vanish downstream.

The sun is dipping behind the mountains and the air's getting colder. Back at the house, Summer stacks a few logs in the fireplace and lets me light the kindling.

"What exactly does my father do?" I ask. "His job description, I mean. My mother said he does something for the government, but she's not sure what."

"You never asked him?"

"I haven't seen the man since I was little. Or talked to him."

Summer looks honestly surprised. "He's never once called?"

"Nope. But he always sends a check."

"Which arrives by the tenth of every month, right? Five thousand bucks."

It feels weird talking about this kind of stuff—about the money my family gets—with a girl I hardly know.

"So, Dad must've told you," I say.

Summer Chasing-Hawks sits forward and holds her hands close to the fire.

"Billy Boy," she says, "I'm the one who writes those checks."

I hadn't wanted to leave Everglades City. Belinda said she was ready for a change, ready for a town with an outlet mall.

Not me. There weren't many snakes in the salty mangroves, but I could ride my bike to plenty of places that were loaded. Once I went fishing in a canal where I saw a python and an alligator trying to eat each other. The battle went on for like three days, until finally they both gave up and swam away.

True story. I got video to prove it.

After the funnel cloud trashed the eagle nest, I came up with a scheme to calm my mother so we wouldn't have to move. This was the plan that backfired.

One afternoon I asked to borrow her laptop.

"Why, Billy?"

"You'll see."

A couple of clicks later, we're watching a mother eagle feed tiny pieces of gnawed catfish to her baby. It was live-streaming from a nest at the National Arboretum in Washington, D.C. The website said the nest was on top of a poplar tree.

Suddenly the father baldy showed up with another fish, which he dropped into the nest beside the mother. The baby eaglet was small and fuzzy, a ball of gray lint.

"Hey, look, there's another egg!" Mom exclaimed.

There were tears on her cheeks, she was so excited. We spotted a hairline crack in the other egg.

"That one's starting to hatch, too," I said.

"I know, I know! This is so amazing!"

"See, Mom, we don't have to keep moving. They've got these eagle-cams all over the country. You can watch 'em anytime you want."

"Really?"

"And you can see way more on the video than you can with a pair of binoculars. Right? I mean, this is like being *inside* the nest. It's like being one of the birds!"

Her eyes were riveted to the screen of her laptop. "Billy, I'm worried about that other egg."

Oh no, I thought. *Here she goes again.*

"Eagle eggs don't always hatch at the same time," I reminded her. "Sometimes one is late. Relax, Mom, I've read up on this."

She didn't sleep or leave the house for days. You couldn't

pry the laptop from her hands. Belinda did the cooking, I took care of the laundry. Mom chewed her fingernails down so far that she needed Band-Aids.

I was at school on the morning the second eaglet finally hatched. When I got home, my mother was snoring on the sofa, hugging the laptop. Belinda and I helped her to bed. That night she bought fresh stone crabs and threw a little party, just for the three of us. We toasted the baby eagle with Gatorade.

The next afternoon, Mom was crying again. She said the big eaglet was being mean to the newborn.

"That's totally normal. They're just fussing," I said. "Don't worry—the momma bird won't let anything bad happen."

"But, Billy, she's not in the nest all the time! When she's out hunting with the poppa bird, she can't keep an eye on those babies."

"Here, let me see." I took her laptop and walked to the kitchen, where, accidentally on purpose, I dropped it on the floor.

My clever plan had flopped. I should've known Mom would get totally obsessed. After her laptop came back from the repair shop, I rigged the parental controls to block out all eagle-cams. I did this for her own peace of mind. Otherwise she would have been glued day and night to those websites—basically, a bird-watching zombie.

Soon afterward we moved to Fort Pierce, where we live now. The nest she'd found here was in a half-dead Australian pine on the shore of the Indian River Lagoon. The good thing was, from the ground you couldn't see the eaglets until they grew taller than the edge of the nest. By then they were fairly big and strong, so Mom couldn't get too worried about them. Best of all, the mother and father birds stayed in the area after the young ones fledged and flew off in the spring. That means we won't have to leave again for a while, unless the nest gets wrecked by another storm.

"You've got bald eagles out here, right?" I ask Summer Chasing-Hawks.

"Sure. Goldens, too. They're even badder than baldies."

"I'd like to get a picture of one, for my mother."

"Maybe you'll luck out."

"Also I want to see a wild grizzly bear."

Summer chuckles and says, "Montana ain't Disney World. You don't just buy a ticket and stand in line for the show."

"You ever seen one?"

"A griz? Yup."

"Really? Where? In Yellowstone?"

"He was dead in a creek," she says with a glum shrug. "There wasn't much left."

She places another log on the fire.

"What happened to him?" I ask.

"Who knows," Summer says. "Maybe a bigger bear got him, or maybe it was old age. Survival of the fittest, Billy."

Right now I'd rather talk about bears and eagles than about my father. Summer told me he'd put her in charge of his checkbook because she was good at math. She said he's got plenty of money and he's very generous to her and her mom.

He told them he works for a security agency of the government, a drone program he's not allowed to talk about. To me, it sounds like baloney.

And even if it were true, why would you let a kid sign your name on all your checks?

I don't share these doubts with Summer, but my mind is buzzing with sketch theories about what Mr. Dennis Dickens actually does for a living. He could be a bank robber, for all they know, or a cyber hacker. Maybe even a dope dealer!

"Where do golden eagles live?" I ask Summer.

"High on cliffs. They eat gophers and jackrabbits."

"Snakes, too?"

"No doubt." In the fire's glow she looks a lot younger than me, her face as smooth and round as a doll's. The patchy old cat jumps in her lap, and the goofy-looking dog curls up at her feet.

"Stop worrying," Summer says. "Your dad's a good guy. If he wasn't, my mom would've dumped him a long time ago."

"Did he say where he was going on his trip?" I ask.

"He never does. His missions are always, like, top-secret."

"But doesn't that make you wonder?"

"He always comes home. That's all that matters."

THREE

Summer's mother says her Crow name is Little Thunder-Sky.

"But everyone calls me Lil," she adds. "Have some more mashed potatoes."

I'm starving, so I basically inhale everything on the plate. My stomach is still on east-coast Florida time, which is ten-thirty at night. For dinner Lil grilled buffalo sliders, possibly the best burgers ever.

At the table not a word is spoken about my father. Lil wears her long hair in braids, and her face has a permanent raccoon stripe from wearing sunglasses all the time. She looks about the same age as my mom. Summer told me she's a professional trout guide, rows a drift boat down the rivers.

"Did you catch anything today?" I ask.

"Six nice rainbows and a fat old cutthroat."

"Wow. Are they good eating?"

Lil laughs. "They're all swimming in the river. I'm strictly catch-and-release."

"Fly-rodders only," Summer adds proudly. "No worm-slingers allowed."

I don't know how to cast an artificial fly, but I've watched lots of videos and always wanted to learn.

"The sports I had on the boat, they couldn't hit the water with a brick," says Lil. "It's a miracle we landed anything.

They're from Indianapolis—one's a dentist and the other owns a chain of funeral homes. But, hey, it's a payday. And they had some funny stories, believe it or not."

"You're in the funeral business," I say, "you better have a sense of humor."

"So true." Lil cuts up the last remaining slider and feeds it to Satan the dog. The creaky old cat shows no interest at all.

It's almost embarrassing to admit that Lil and Summer are the first two Native Americans I've met. They don't seem so different—not that I was expecting them to live in tepees or stitch deerskin moccasins. I haven't read up on the Crow Nation yet, but I know what happened to most Indian tribes in the Old West. That's not a subject for a guest like me to bring up.

After Summer and I clear the dishes, we join Lil by the fireplace. She says, "I'm sorry Dennis isn't here. You came a long, long way, Billy."

"Last time I saw him, I was three years old. Maybe four. I don't even remember what his voice sounds like."

"Doesn't it make you mad he hasn't called?" Summer asks.

"It makes me curious, that's all." And, okay, maybe a little angry.

Lil folds her hands on her lap. "Well, here's the story of how your dad came into our lives. It was a Saturday morning, springtime, a few years ago. I was home tying some trout flies—"

"And I was finishing an art project for elementary school," Summer cuts in.

"—when all of a sudden, *bang!* The whole trailer shook, so I knew it was too big to be a bird. Sometimes robins get confused and crash into the windows, but this was a different kind of bang. So I run outside, and there's a major dent in the wall and this broken . . . *thing* . . . on the ground. I didn't know what the heck it was. There were four little propellers and plastic wings—"

"And a camera," Summer says. "Like a GoPro, only bigger."

"I'd never seen a drone before," Lil goes on. "Anyhow, we pick up the parts and take 'em inside the trailer. Before long, there's a knock on the door. It's Dennis, your dad. Blue jeans, flannel shirt, hiking boots. He's holding something that's beeping, which turns out to be the remote control. He says he lost his 'aircraft.' That was the word he used! And I say, 'Aircraft? You mean that silly toy helicopter?' His face gets all serious and he goes, 'It's not a toy, ma'am.' So I point to the kitchen table, where we'd laid out the plastic pieces of his wrecked drone, and he says, 'Oh no!' I mean, the poor guy looked like his heart was shattered."

Summer says, "Cut to the hot romance part, Momma."

"So I invited him to stay for lunch. Pork sandwiches and coleslaw. He asked me out. I said no thanks. Afterward, he kept calling and calling, until finally I ran out of excuses. We dated a few months, and then he asked us to move in with him here in Livingston, me and Summer."

"Was it hard to leave the reservation?" I ask.

"I've always liked this town. And the school's good."

Summer says, "Life on the rez can be . . . challenging?"

"What did my dad tell you about his actual job?" I ask Lil.

"Some sort of surveillance work for the government. They bought him a new drone right away. Dennis says the less we know, the better. As you can imagine, Billy, after all that's happened, our tribe doesn't have a whole lot of trust in your government. Originally they left the Crow Nation with thirty-eight million acres. Know what it is today? One-tenth that size. They stole back the rest and paid us five lousy cents an acre."

"That sucks," I say, possibly the understatement of the century.

"But we don't see your dad as the 'government,'" Lil adds. "He's a good, honest man."

Summer nods. "He'd never hurt anybody."

"Nice to know. I'd really like to see him," I say.

"He checks in every few days to let us know he's okay," says Lil. "He's never gone long, Billy. A week at the most."

"Can we try to call him now?"

"I already did. His phone's off. That's not unusual."

I've got lots more questions, but I'm tired. The fire is beginning to die, the embers popping and hissing. Lil says I should take the spare bedroom. Satan follows me through the door, flops down on the rug, and farts.

Before saying good night, Summer comes in and turns on the baseboard heaters because, she says, "you Florida boys have thin blood." The temperature tonight is supposed to drop to 45 degrees—and it's June.

Lying in bed under a homemade quilt, I wait for Mom's goodnight phone call. I texted her after the plane landed, but we haven't had time to talk. She's been out on Uber jobs all day.

First thing she asks: "So, how's your father?"

"I haven't seen him yet. He's off on a business trip."

"But you told me he knew you were coming."

"He got called away at the last minute," I say.

When you're not used to lying, it's easy to get tripped up. I can't tell whether Mom believes what I'm saying.

"What kind of business trip?" she asks.

"The usual, I guess."

"There's nothing 'usual' about your father. Did you find out what his actual job is?"

"I met his family. They're really nice."

A beat passes before Mom says, "You mean 'family' as in children?"

"His wife and stepdaughter," I say. "They're Crow Indians."

"Oh wow."

"I know, right?"

Another beat. Then: "So, you like Montana?"

"It's a great big place," I say. "That's for sure."

Mom hasn't remarried after the divorce. She's gone out with a few guys, and as far as I could tell, none of them were total jerks. Belinda's favorite was a piano teacher named

James, who could play jazz, rock, and classical. One night he brought his electric keyboard to the house and put on a show. My mother clapped politely, but we could tell she wasn't exactly enchanted.

The guy I liked best drove an airboat, taking tourists through the Everglades. One time he gave me a ride up and down the Lopez River. His name was William, and he only had eight fingers. He'd lost both thumbs in the propeller of his airboat, in separate accidents. Mom informed us she wasn't in the market for a clumsy boyfriend.

These days she doesn't go out on many dates. I've asked her if it's hard being single with two kids, and she says Belinda and I are a blessing, because we scare off the men who are selfish and shallow. "The last thing they want is an instant family," she says.

I don't mind not having a stepfather, though I know Mom gets lonely at times. She'll never admit this, because in her mind loneliness is a sign of weakness.

You might be wondering: *What kind of mother lets her son fly 2,000 miles to meet a man he doesn't even remember?*

To be honest, I was surprised Mom didn't put up more of an argument. But here's my theory: she's still looking for answers about what went wrong with their marriage. Letting me go to Montana is the next best thing to going there herself, which her pride wouldn't allow.

At midnight she calls back to chat some more. It's two a.m. Florida time.

"Did I wake you, Billy?"

She did, but I say, "No. Whassup?"

"Listen—at the first sniff of trouble, you grab a cab to the airport and come home."

"Yes, Mom." Like they have flights every hour.

"I don't care how nice his new family might be. If you don't get the straight story from Mr. Dennis Dickens, I want you out of there. Is that understood?"

"Don't worry," I say.

After she calms down, Mom tells me that my sister landed a summer job as a cashier at T.J. Maxx. We talk about how weird and quiet it will be around the house after Belinda goes off to college.

"I went out to see the eagles today," Mom says.

She sounds wide awake. Unbelievable. I can barely hold my eyes open.

"One of them caught a fish. I think it was a snook."

"Yummy," I try to say, but the word comes out like a caveman's grunt.

The wind is rattling the window of the bedroom, and the baseboard heater is making a ticking noise.

"I should let you go to sleep," she says.

"Yeah, I'm beat."

"First I need to ask you something, Billy. What does she look like? Your dad's new wife."

I'm not really comfortable with the question. "She's brown," I say.

"Don't be a smart-ass. She's Native American, so of course she's brown."

"No, I mean really brown. She's out on the river all the time."

"What for?" Mom asks.

"Because she's a fishing guide. She's got her own boat and everything. She rows ten, twelve miles every day. Sometimes more."

For a couple of moments my mother doesn't say anything. Then: "That's pretty cool, I've got to admit. What's her name?"

"Little Thunder-Sky."

"No way! How beautiful is that?"

"She wants everyone to call her Lil."

"A request you will honor. Is she young?"

"Same age as you," I say, "so, yes, she's young."

My mother likes that answer. "'Little Thunder-Sky.' Wow," she says. "That's mountain poetry."

"Mom, I need to ask you something. Why'd you always cut up the envelopes that Dad's checks came in?"

"Because that's not how I wanted you to find out where he was. I wanted him to be the one to tell you," she says. "I wanted him to *want* you to come see him, but he never asked."

"I'm going to find out why."

"Call me tomorrow. Love you, Billy."

I lie there listening to the low whistle of the wind outside. Satan jumps in bed with me, and I don't have the heart to kick him out. Both of us are sound asleep in about two minutes.

*   *   *

The next morning, Summer makes cheese omelets and bacon for breakfast. Lil packs a lunch. We load the cooler in her boat, which is hooked to her SUV, a blue Ford Explorer. It's chilly outside, so Summer loans me a fleece that belongs to my dad. The arms are too long, but I don't care. It's warm.

Lil drives to a ramp called Mayor's Landing, where she backs the boat into the water all by herself. She tells me to get in the bow except I'm not sure which end is which, since there's no motor. Summer finds this hilarious.

Before we shove off, Lil gives me a quick lesson with a fly rod. She makes casting look incredibly easy, but when it's my turn, I promptly snag myself in the back of the head with the streamer fly. It doesn't hurt at all when Lil tugs the hook from my scalp because she'd already bent down the barb, to do less harm to the fish. She tells me to keep casting. I'm expecting a sarcastic comment from Summer, but she restrains herself.

The river is a breathtaking obstacle course—gravel beds, boulders, snags, stumps of massive dead trees. We glide through all of it, untouched. Lil rows from the middle seat, and she's totally pro with oars, steering the boat with one dip at a time. Summer lounges in the stern, reading a book.

"Can we try calling Dad again?" I ask Lil.

"Sure. Summer, would you dial for Billy?"

Summer puts down her book and takes out her phone. "Straight to voice mail," she reports, and lets me listen.

It's an automated recording, not Dad's voice. I end the call without leaving a message.

"Does he do this on all his trips?" I ask.

"Ninety-nine percent of the time there's no cell service where he's at," Lil explains.

I cast the streamer fly snug to the shoreline and something grabs it underwater. I jerk back hard—too hard—and the thin monofilament line snaps.

"Major brown trout!" Summer says.

I bow my head and reel up. Lil beaches the boat on a gravel bed and ties another fly on my rig. Overhead I hear a familiar cry—an osprey, just like the ones we have in Florida. Lil points out a second bird perched high in a cottonwood tree. Like eagles, ospreys often work in pairs, and they hunt by sight. It's hard for them to find fish on days like today, when the water is cloudy.

I'm casting like a crazed robot again, hoping for a strike from another big fish. "I need to figure all this out," I say to Lil. "Who does Dad work for? The CIA? FBI?"

"Don't think we haven't asked, Billy."

After an hour I finally catch something—a slippery little rainbow trout, as bright as chrome. The splashes of rosy color on its sides look hand-painted. I've never seen anything like it, and all I can do is stare. Lil gently unhooks the fish and it's gone in a flash, literally.

Later we stop to eat lunch on the shady side of the river. A flock of white pelicans floats past. This species—possibly the very same birds we're watching—migrates all the way to Florida Bay every winter. Summer and her mother smile at each other when I tell them that.

"Look it up," I say, "if you don't believe me."

After lunch the wind starts gusting, which makes it way harder to cast. Still, I manage to land two more small rainbows and a nice cutthroat, a fish that gets its name from orange gashlike markings below the gills. In the treetops we count several more ospreys and hawks, but no bald eagles. Lil points to a pale rock bluff where she spotted a golden a few days ago, but the bird isn't there now.

She rows effortlessly, even in the swift water. One careless stroke and the boat could crash against a boulder and flip. The stretch of the river leading to the takeout is flat and slower, so Summer asks for a turn on the oars. She aims the bow toward a bare notch on the shore and beaches the boat perfectly. Lil's Explorer is already parked at the ramp, thanks to a shuttle service that the trout guides use. Summer and I steady the boat in the current while Lil backs the trailer down the slope. I get the feeling she can do this with her eyes closed.

On the drive back to Livingston, we pass a herd of pronghorn antelopes standing in a field watching the cars on the interstate. This blows me away. Summer says the pronghorns always disappear before the first day of hunting season.

"They've got a survival calendar in their brain," she adds, tapping her head. "Same goes for the elk and deer."

When we arrive back at the house, there's a Montana state patrol car parked out front. The trooper steps from the car and asks Lil if her name is Little Thunder-Sky.

"Am I in trouble?" she asks.

"We found a vehicle that's registered to you. A red Chevy king cab?"

Summer leans close, whispering: "That's what Dennis drives."

"He doesn't have his own car?"

"Oh, it's totally his. He put it in Mom's name. Everything's in her name, including the house."

Lil tells the trooper that the truck is used by her husband, who's away on a trip.

"A camping trip?" the trooper asks. "Because the vehicle was left on a dirt road way up the Tom Miner Basin. It's been there a week, at least. Two of the tires are flat."

Summer blurts, "What! How did that happen?"

"A sharp object is how."

"Like a broken bottle?"

"No," the trooper says. "Like a knife."

"Oh no," Lil murmurs.

"Have you spoken to him lately?"

"His phone's off. He's in a dead zone," Summer cuts in.

The trooper frowns. "I'm afraid we'll have to tow the truck if your husband doesn't show up soon. Meanwhile, you should get somebody to go up there and take some new tires."

Lil says, "I'll do it myself, first thing tomorrow."

"When is he due home, ma'am?"

"Honestly, I'm not sure."

"Is he alone?"

"I believe so," Lil says.

The trooper glances uneasily at me and Summer, like he's got something else to ask Lil but doesn't want to do it in front of us.

Then he says it anyway: "If you don't hear from your husband soon, you should call the sheriff's office. They're in charge of search-and-rescue."

"Thanks for your concern," says Lil, "but I'm sure he's all right."

After giving us directions to the location where the red king cab was found, the state trooper drives away. Lil hurries into the house.

Summer and I unpack the drift boat. We lower our voices to discuss this unexpected news about Dennis Dickens—her stepfather, my father.

None of the possibilities are good.

FOUR

Everything I know about my dad is what my mother has told me, which isn't much.

He was born in South Miami, no brothers or sisters. His parents died while he was away at college in Gainesville, but Mom doesn't seem to know the details. When she and Dad first met, he was the assistant manager of a Foot Locker store in Pembroke Pines—he fitted her for a pair of cross-trainers. She said he loved the outdoors, like she did. Their first date was a trip to the Corkscrew Swamp looking for otters.

In their seven years together, my father held thirteen or fourteen different jobs. All the people he worked for liked him, she said, and he never once got fired.

He would just quit, for no apparent reason, always on a Thursday.

"Time for a new life direction!" he'd announce to my mother as he walked through the door.

"What happened now, Dennis?"

"Oh, the job wasn't so bad" was his usual reply. "But I didn't see the right future for me. I felt like I couldn't breathe there anymore."

"If you don't stop this nonsense," Mom would say angrily, "you're gonna have some serious breathing problems around *here*, too."

This is strictly her version of the conversation, but I bet it's pretty accurate.

The day Dad moved out of the house was also a Thursday. Mom ripped up his goodbye note, and now she regrets it.

"I didn't know he was serious," she told us, much later.

After my father left, Mom began referring to him as "the serial quitter." I wasn't old enough to realize what was going on, but Belinda did. She's totally on my mother's side, and who can blame her? She says only a loser walks out on his family.

Mom was surprised when the first check arrived.

"Where'd he get all this money?" she exclaimed, according to Belinda.

The older I got, the more I wondered about my father— where he'd gone and why he'd left. Was he running from us, or searching for something?

As Summer and I put away the fly rods and gear, I ask her if it's unusual for a person to get his tires slashed in Montana.

"I never heard of that happening," she says. "Not around here, anyway."

"Where's the Tom Miner Basin?"

"Way down in Paradise Valley, on the way to Yellowstone Park. A long time ago it was a hunting ground for the Crow."

"Who lives there now?" I ask.

"Ranchers, rich white people, and bears."

*   *   *

By the time Mom calls, I'm already in bed.

"Have you seen your father yet?" she asks.

"Tomorrow's the big day."

"Please don't get your hopes up, Billy. Tomorrow's a Thursday. You know his track record on Thursdays."

I don't tell her about the visit from the state trooper. Instead I give her a fishing report. She's proud that I caught a trout on my very first day using a fly rod.

"Did you spot any eagles, Billy?"

"No, but Lil says several pairs live along the river between here and Big Timber. Some goldens, too. They're even cooler than baldies."

"I never told you this," Mom says, "but your father was the first one to show me an eagle nest. It was up on a power pole in Key Largo. I'm sure it's gone by now."

"So he's a birder, too?"

"He's got darn good eyes. At least he used to."

It sounds like she considers this a nice memory. Sometimes I wish she'd share more of them.

"How was your day, Mom?"

"Not so wonderful. I'm in hot water with Uber."

"What did you do?"

"A passenger was being super-rude, so I kicked him out of the car."

"I hope you hit the brakes first."

"Very funny."

"Where did this happen?" I ask.

"On top of the Barber Bridge, in Vero Beach."

"Seriously, Mom?"

"He emailed the company to complain! Can you believe that?"

"Yes," I say. "I totally can."

My sister and I had predicted something like this. I ask Mom what the rider did that was so rude.

"He asked me out for a drink, and I very politely said no. A few minutes later I hear him talking to his wife on the phone, pretending to be the perfect husband. Some loud real-estate shark from Miami. Supposedly he was up here looking at properties. Anyway, as soon as he hung up, I stopped the car and told him to get out. Then he had the nerve to call Uber and say I was abandoning him on a dangerous highway. That bridge has a perfectly fine pedestrian lane!"

"Maybe you should try a different kind of job," I say to Mom.

"Why? Usually I get along with everybody."

"I'm going to sleep now, okay?"

When I walk out of the house the next morning, the temperature is in the forties. I'm wearing every stitch of clothing I brought, plus a down parka belonging to Dennis Dickens. We're bringing a ten-gallon container of gasoline, a backpack with some food, and a couple cans of a chemical pepper spray specially invented to discourage a charging bear. Summer calls shotgun, so I take the back seat.

Lil stops at a repair shop in town to buy two new tires mounted on secondhand rims, which we load in the Explorer. The main road south leads through a narrow pass into the world-famous Paradise Valley. Right away I see how it got its name—snowy peaks rising on both sides of a wide green plain, the Yellowstone River winding like a silver-blue vein through the middle. If someone had shown me a painting, I wouldn't have believed such a place was real.

Summer and her mom are quiet on the ride, probably because they're worried about my father. I'm worried, too. Even though I barely remember the man, there's still a connection.

Eventually we come to a highway sign for the Tom Miner Basin. Lil turns down a watered dirt road that runs along a bowl-shaped valley framed by slopes of the Gallatin Mountains. Below us is a sprawling patchwork of cattle ranches and farms, half a dozen shades of green. Crossing one high crest, we can see all the way back to Livingston, and seemingly beyond.

"The view is fifty-two miles," Summer reports, "on a clear day."

Which it is right now. Not a cloud in the sky.

Soon the dirt road gets narrow and gnarly. Lil says it leads to a campground near a petrified forest, where some of the trees are fifty million years old. She says that's when the Tom Miner Basin was covered with ash and lava from an erupting volcano.

I wouldn't mind hiking through an actual petrified forest, but we don't make it to the end of the road. Rounding a bend, we spot my father's red truck, a jumbo pickup with four doors, pulled halfway onto the shoulder.

Lil parks behind it. Neither she nor Summer gets out.

"You don't see many of those up here," says Lil.

She's pointing at a large prairie rattlesnake. It is the only venomous species in Montana, and normally it's found on—duh—prairies. This one must have traveled to these woods from a dry, craggy hillside across the valley.

The snake is minding its own business, sunning beside one of the flattened tires on Dad's mud-caked pickup.

Summer says, "He'll crawl off in a few minutes. Let's wait."

Not me. I hop out for a closer look.

The rattler's scales are dullish gray and tan, with a mottled pattern meant to blend with the dusty habitat where it usually lives. It's not as thick around as its Florida cousins, but I count six rattles on the muscular tail.

"What on earth are you doing?" Summer calls from inside the Explorer. "We are *not* impressed."

Although snakes don't have earholes, they're able to sense the smallest movements of nearby animals. Rattlers also have tiny pits near their nostrils that help them track warm-blooded prey. When I was researching the solution to my school-locker problem, I found a video online that shows a blindfolded rattlesnake striking a balloon filled with hot water. Its aim is dead perfect.

The prairie rattler lounging by the truck's deflated tire

has realized it's no longer alone. The triangle head rises slowly, exploring for scents with slow flicks of a forked black tongue. I'm crouching safely out of striking range.

Lil's voice has an anxious edge: "Billy, get back here, please."

Sensible advice for a normal person, but I don't want to sit around waiting for the snake to crawl away. I want to look inside my father's pickup for clues, right now.

So I toss a handful of pebbles in the dirt near the rattler, which immediately uncoils, zips across the road, and vanishes down the hill.

Lil steps from the SUV saying, "Most white folks love to shoot those things. You are definitely your father's son."

The doors on Dad's truck are locked. I wipe the dust from a side window. On the floorboard I see a Rockies baseball cap along with a jumble of empty water bottles and soda cans. On the passenger seat sits an open box of shotgun shells.

"Do you have a key?" I ask Lil.

"No, Billy, I don't."

She and Summer get to work using Lil's jack and wrench. After the lug nuts are unscrewed, I lift off the slashed tires. While Summer and Lil begin bolting the new ones on Dad's Chevy, I poke around trying to figure out which direction my father walked.

I locate an uphill path leading toward the thick timber. There are no boot prints, though I didn't expect to find any. Lil says it rained hard here last night. I walk back to the road, where Summer and Lil are still at work.

"I found a trail. I'm going to get a head start," I say.

Lil glances up. "Why don't you wait for us, Billy?"

"I won't go far. Promise."

Summer hands me the backpack and both of the bear-spray canisters.

"Make lots of noise," she advises. "Clap, shout, hoot, sing—that way you won't surprise any grizzlies. They'll run off as soon as they hear you."

Into the woods I go. It feels stupid to be shouting all by myself.

"Whoa, bear! Hey, bear! Don't eat me, bear!"

After a few minutes I sit down on a tree stump to wait. I take out my cell phone to check in with Lil and Summer, but there are no bars, no signal. Any second I expect to hear them coming up the path.

The woods seem too quiet, and my nerves start to buzz. Unfortunately, like my mother, I have basically zero patience. I just can't hang around doing nothing.

So I get up and move on, confident that Lil and Summer will catch up soon.

Except they don't.

FIVE

My sister has this boyfriend. She claims to be madly in love.

The kid she's dating is a total tool, but I keep my mouth shut. Belinda is sick of moving from town to town, and this is her way of telling Mom enough's enough.

I know Belinda isn't wild about the guy. His name is Dawson and he goes to a private school, but that's not where he got his high opinion of himself. Anybody who goes out of his way to tell you his haircut cost fifty bucks? A serious tool.

Belinda knows. I don't need to say a word.

She tells Mom she can't possibly imagine her life without charming, handsome Dawson, which is another way of saying she doesn't care what happens to the eagle nest here in Fort Pierce—she doesn't want to pack up and move now, not with college on the horizon. She's made a few good friends at school, and she wants to hang with them the rest of the summer. Simple as that.

The issue hasn't come up yet because Mom's happy right where we are. However, that could change tomorrow if the birds disappear.

One time, as a favor to my sister, I actually took Dawson fishing in the Indian River Lagoon. He caught a little crevalle that magically grew to ten pounds when he retold the story. The best part was I had to unhook his fish because Dawson wouldn't touch it. He wouldn't bait his own hook, either—he said he didn't want the shrimp to bite him.

"Shrimp don't bite," I pointed out.

"Everything bites!" Dawson declared.

What made me think of him now is that I'm hiking through a place where a person could get seriously bitten by something way bigger than a shrimp, something with actual teeth. Dawson would be wetting his pants.

The trail winds back and forth before forking into twin paths. I choose the one that veers right, hoping that Summer Chasing-Hawks and Little Thunder-Sky can track me. The ground is too hard-packed to leave any footprints, so I place a dime in the middle of the path to show them which way I went.

Hiking the swamps of the Everglades is completely different from hiking the high-timber country of the Rockies. For one thing, Montana bears grow much larger than Florida bears. When I said I wanted to see a grizzly, I meant from a safe distance—not nose to nose in the deep woods. That's why I'm holding a can of pepper spray in each hand.

And shouting: "Whoa, bear! Hey, bear! Don't eat me, bear!"

A porcupine the size of a tumbleweed scuffles past, slow enough for me to snap a picture with my phone. Farther down the trail I spot a white-tailed deer, a buck with a major rack of antlers. He bolts from sight before I can get a photo. I hear him crashing through the trees.

Maybe the noise will scare off the bears, or maybe the bears are used to nervous deer.

I'm a little nervous, too—though not really scared. More humans get chomped by gators and sharks in Florida than attacked by wild bears in Montana. I looked it up on the internet last night while I was lying in bed listening to a train rumble through town. Statistically, you're a hundred times safer hiking through grizzly country than driving a car to the supermarket. That's what I keep reminding myself.

After a while I emerge from the tree line and enter a rocky meadow spangled with wildflowers—yellow, purple, crimson, and white. The magpies start to yap, and I figure they're annoyed by my shouts interrupting their sleepy afternoon.

"Whoa, bear! Hey, bear! Don't eat me, bear!"

Between chants I hear an odd noise—a high-pitched hum, somewhere in the sky. The sun is bright and of course I forgot my shades, so I set down both cans of bear spray and use my hands to block the glare. The humming grows louder and louder until it sounds more like a mechanical buzz.

Leaning back, I spot something hovering no more than fifty feet in the air, straight above my head.

A remote-controlled drone.

I wave both arms.

"Hey, Dad, it's me! Billy!"

The drone draws closer. It's a gray quadcopter—four propellers and a red stripe on the bottom. I can see the shiny black eye of the camera lens.

I keep waving. "It's okay! You can come out!"

I'm not sure how long it's been since Mom sent any photos of me to my father, but I've grown about three inches in the last year. I hope he recognizes me on the video feed. Maybe he can read my lips, since most drones don't come with microphones.

Unless it's a super-high-tech military spy drone.

"Yo, Dad, can you hear me?" I yell.

The quadcopter flutters for a moment, spins slowly, then begins rising.

"Wait! Wait!"

It keeps going, up, up, up, until I can barely hear the motor. Still, I keep waving like a fool.

"Wait, it's only me!" I holler at the shrinking speck. "Billy Dickens!"

But the drone speeds away above the rocky field, heading for distant treetops.

I chase after it until I enter a stretch of timber so dense that I can't see any blue patches of sky. There's no trail to follow, so I'm forced to slow down and thread my way through the tree trunks.

Not far ahead I hear something make a deep-throated noise. It sounds large and not particularly human. I fumble to pull out the bear spray—a major swing and a miss. I've left both canisters back in the meadow.

All I can do now is shout: "Whoa, bear! Hey, bear! Don't eat me, bear!"

Slowly I begin backing away. If you run from a grizzly,

then it thinks you're dinner—at least that's what it said online. But, actually, who else but the bear could possibly know what it's thinking?

Exiting the forest in reverse seems to take forever. Finally I feel the sun on my neck, and once again I'm out in the exposed meadow. Hurriedly I retrace my steps to where I dropped the bear spray, hunker down next to the canisters, and unzip the backpack. Inside are a pair of binoculars and four peanut-butter-and-jelly sandwiches, one of which I stuff in my mouth and wash down with a bottle of water. I also devour an apple and a power bar that tastes like a roof shingle.

Clouds are skidding in from the northwest, and the temperature is diving. There's still no sign of Summer and Lil. I lie down to wait using the backpack as a pillow. Overhead, shiny black crows circle in odd silence.

I can't stop wondering what my father's doing way out here and why he hasn't come out of the woods to meet me. I also wonder if any hungry bears have picked up the tasty aroma of my PBJ.

A normal person could never fall asleep in such a sketchy situation, but that's what I do—doze off, clutching a can of bear spray in each fist. If Mom saw me now, she'd have a nervous breakdown.

The crows begin to caw excitedly, and that's what wakes me up. Or maybe it's the humming.

I open my eyes and see the gray quadcopter staring down at me. This time I don't bother to wave.

A small object drops from the craft and lands near my head. It's a small round rock, wrapped in white paper. Still flat on my back, I put down the bear spray and read the message on the paper. It's written in blue ballpoint ink, the letters small and extremely neat:

> Billy, please get away from here as fast as you can. I'll explain everything later, when I see you.
>
> Love,
> Dad
>
> P.S. I apologize for all the lost years. Be sure to tell your sister, too.

I glare up at the camera, spread my arms, and shout: "Are you kidding me?"

The drone spins around and flies off.

Watching it fade into a pale dot, I realize my father could be hiding with the remote control just about anywhere in this wild countryside. There's no point trying to find him, because he obviously doesn't want to "interact."

A mix of sadness and anger tells me not to move—to just lie here in the middle of the meadow until the man feels guilty enough to show his face. I assume the drone is still airborne, aiming its faraway eyeball at me.

The minutes drip by. I remain outstretched and motion-less. From the sky it must look like I'm unconscious, maybe even dead. I wouldn't be surprised to attract some hungry buzzards.

"Come on, Dad," I mutter. "Do something."

I strain to listen for footsteps, or the call of a man's voice. But there's nothing to be heard except for those obnoxious crows. Once again I feel seriously restless.

So much for the sunny summer day: a light cool rain has begun to fall, and bugs are chewing my ankles. I brush something off of my cheek, but now it's clinging to my hand—a lanky brown spider.

That's it. I'm done.

I flick the spider into the wildflowers, grab the backpack, and stand up. Dad's lame note is folded in my pocket where I'd put it. I think about that open box of ammunition on the front seat of his pickup. What does he need a gun to protect himself from? Bears? Wolves? Or something else?

We might never end up being friends, but I intend to find out what's going on.

The wind howls, and it's getting colder by the minute. My plan is to hike back toward the road, where the truck and the SUV are parked, and wait for Lil and Summer to return. Obviously they took the other path where the trail forked.

While crossing the meadow, I sense I'm being watched, though not from the air. Carefully I step around an impressive mound of fresh animal poop—seriously, it would take the world's biggest dog a year to make a pile so huge. The poop is full of chokecherries, the favorite snack of a certain hump-shouldered mega-predator.

The tree line is only a hundred yards away, so I jog to the place where I first came out. Or where I *thought* I came out.

But where's that trail? Usually the compass in my head is reliable, but not today. There are no easy landmarks to use for direction. The trees, mostly lodgepole pines, all look about the same size.

As I search back and forth for the slim opening into the forest, I feel a pair of eyes locked on me. My hands tremble as I grope through the backpack for the binoculars. They're not super-fancy—just your basic 7 × 35—but they'll work fine at this distance.

Standing erect on the far edge of the meadow is something tall and cinnamon-colored. It takes me a moment to dial in the focus.

Now I can see her perfectly, watching me watching her.

I know it's a she because two chubby cubs are rolling around in the wildflowers nearby.

"Griz" is what I whisper to myself. "Wow."

I don't realize I'm inching backward until I trip over a rotten log and end up on my butt. I scramble to my feet and snatch up the fallen binoculars. Breathlessly, I scan the border of the clearing, but the mother bear's not there anymore.

If she ever really was.

I can't rule out the possibility that I'm imagining things. Somehow I find my way to the main dirt road. It still feels like there's a jackhammer in my chest. The first thing I notice after leaving the forest is that the rain has stopped. The second thing I notice is this:

My father's red pickup truck is gone.

"What's his problem?" I say aloud, to nobody.

Who drives off and leaves his son alone in the middle of grizzly country?

P.S. I apologize for all the lost years.

Yeah, Dad. Whatever.

The third thing I notice, the one that worries me the most:

Lil's blue Explorer is gone, too.

I've never hitchhiked before, but I assume there's no point sticking out your thumb when there aren't any cars in sight. Basically, I'm hiking without the hitching.

A night in the Tom Miner Basin with no tent or sleeping bag isn't an ideal option. I don't even have any matches for starting a campfire.

So I move at a fast clip down the dirt road. The highway leading back to Livingston is miles away. I can see it from here—a gray ribbon snaking through the foothills. At this point I'm mad at almost everybody—my father, Lil, Summer, but especially myself.

Coming all the way to Montana thinking Dad would be happy to see me was foolish. I should have listened to my mother.

Right now she'd be saying: "Hydrate yourself, Billy. *Hydrate!*"

So I take a water break, and that's when I hear a car engine. Someone is speeding up the hill, opposite the way I'm going, but I don't care. A ride's a ride.

A pale green pickup rounds the bend, churning dust. I thrust out one arm, thumb extended.

The driver slows to a stop. It's a ranger with the U.S. Forest Service. He says somebody phoned in a report of a gunshot in an area where deer poaching has been a problem.

"I can't take you with me," he says, "but I'll give you a lift on the way back, if nobody else comes by before then. You got a phone?"

"No bars," I say.

"Keep walking and you'll get a signal."

"I didn't hear any shots."

"You wouldn't if you were standing upwind. It's blowin' twenty-five, maybe thirty, miles an hour out there," he says. "Stay on the road, son, okay? No shortcuts. I'll keep an eye out for you on the way down."

So at least I won't be stuck way out here until morning, which is a relief.

A little while later I hear another engine, also speeding uphill. The blue Explorer comes around the bend—this ought to be interesting.

Little Thunder-Sky slams on the brakes as soon as she spots me. Summer Chasing-Hawks is in the passenger seat wearing a worried expression.

"Nice of you guys to come back," I say.

Summer leans her head out the window. "Come back *where*? We've been looking all over for you."

So . . . it turns out the trail I followed out of the woods wasn't the same one I followed in. That's why I didn't see Dad's pickup or Lil's SUV when I reached the road. I was in the wrong place.

"Did you find Dennis?" Lil asks.

"Nope. He sent his stupid drone," I say. "A touching father-son moment."

Lil sighs. "Hop in, Billy."

She makes a three-point turn, aiming us back toward the highway.

"Your father's got more than a cell," she tells me. "He's got a full-on satellite phone."

"That's handy."

"It means he can contact us from basically anywhere, anytime he wants," Summer explains, "even from a dead zone."

"Isn't science amazing," I say.

"He called Mom, totally freaked because he spotted you with the drone. He asked what the heck you were doing out in the bear meadow. She told him we drove up to fix the flat tires on his truck."

Lil takes over the story: "I explained that you came all this way because you want to see him. He kept saying he wasn't allowed to leave his 'surveillance post.' He said he couldn't come out of the woods because he's working 'undercover.'"

"That makes no sense," I say. "Why would the government be doing a secret mission out here in the middle of nowhere? What are they spying on—terrorist chipmunks?"

Summer's eyes narrow. "You think he's lying?"

"Something's weird about his story is all I'm saying. He's working 'undercover' in the middle of a forest? What—disguised as a pinecone?"

Lil looks perplexed. "I don't know what's going on, but his tires definitely got slashed."

"That doesn't mean he's on a dangerous government assignment," I say. "It just means he pissed somebody off."

I tell Lil about my encounter with the ranger. She doesn't seem concerned by the report of gunfire in the area. "Lots of people poach deer out of season," she says with a shrug.

We pass Dad's empty pickup, parked in the same place we found it. Lil doesn't bother to slow down. What would be the point? He's not coming out of the woods.

I take out two peanut-butter-and-jelly sandwiches and hand them across the seat.

Summer grabs one, but Lil isn't hungry.

"Summer and I tried to find you," she says. "We must've taken a different path."

"You didn't see my dime?"

Summer spins and fixes me with a scalding look. "First of all, Mom and I were practically running, trying to catch up.

Second, you never told us to look for a dime. And, third—that's the best you could do for a clue? The smallest coin they make?"

Lil waves a hand. "Just tell us what happened out there, Billy."

"Dad sent me a note taped to a rock. The drone delivered it."

"A note?" Summer says. "What did it say?"

"Basically, not much."

Lil is plainly irritated with my father. She apologizes to me about sixteen times. "You came all the way from Florida. I really wanted this to work out."

"It wasn't a wasted trip. I'm pretty sure I saw a momma grizzly."

"No way!" Summer exclaims.

"With two cubs. I swear."

Thinking about the bears makes me smile.

Thinking about my father doesn't.

SIX

The next morning, Lil and Summer announce we're going to Yellowstone National Park. I guess they feel bad about my father snubbing me and they think a road trip would be a fun distraction.

Southbound on the highway, I'm doing okay until we pass the Tom Miner Basin, where I find myself scanning the sky for the sparkle of a drone.

And thinking: *What's your story, Dad?*

In the town of Gardiner, Lil gasses up the Explorer while Summer and I grab three subs for lunch. At the park entrance there's a line of cars and RVs, which turns out to be a preview of the whole day. This time of year, the Yellowstone experience is basically a traffic jam with incredible scenery.

The park fills with thousands of tourists determined to see actual wildlife, which is fine. I get that. But too many of these pilgrims get crazed, rushing up to the animals and snapping pictures so they can show everybody back home.

The bigger the critter, the bigger the traffic mess. Bear jams are the worst.

Summer fills me in on the scoring. Number one on the tourist hit-the-brakes list are grizzlies, then black bears, wolves, moose, bison, elk, antelope, and deer, in that order.

But any four-legged creature—large or small—draws

a crowd. Our first traffic jam is caused by a gopher, of all things.

A van with a Florida license plate skids to a halt when the driver spies one of the chubby rodents munching grass by the edge of the road. Gophers are the biological opposite of an endangered species. There are jillions of them out west, digging tunnels and holes in yards, pastures, and hayfields. Stopping to photograph a gopher in Yellowstone is like stopping in downtown Miami to take a picture of a rat.

Yet now, unbelievably, throngs of people are streaming from their cars to surround one of these bewildered rodents. So we sit in the long line of traffic, waiting and waiting. . . .

"Oh, this is nothing," Lil says.

It's not a terrible place to be stuck. The brisk mountain air smells like Christmas trees. Eventually the rock-star gopher gets bored and crawls down a hole. The cars and RVs begin rolling onward again.

The next traffic jam is what Summer calls a tourist IQ test.

A group of buffalo is grazing in a vast field. The vehicles ahead of us aren't moving, because a woman in flip-flops has hopped from a camper and is now striding toward the largest, gnarliest-looking bull in the herd.

Once you see something like this in person, you'll never need to look up the word *moron* in the dictionary.

Signs are posted all over the park warning visitors not to approach the wild animals, because they are . . . duh, *wild*. Still, every summer a startling number of nitwits decide it would be cool to get a selfie with an American bison, a creature that has no sense of humor and weighs as much as a Toyota sedan. Sometimes these photo adventures end badly, with tourists getting gored.

Which is something I don't want to witness with my own eyes. Neither does Lil. She jumps out of the SUV and starts hollering for the woman in flip-flops to come back. Other motorists are yelling at her, too.

"Stop! Stop!"

"Stay away from that thing!"

"Are you crazy? Leave him alone!"

The woman ignores the uproar and approaches the shaggy horned giant.

Buffalo have poor eyesight—one reason they nearly went extinct back in the 1800s. White settlers shot them by the thousands, sometimes out of hunger but often just for cruel fun, even firing from passing trains. The buffalo didn't run away because they couldn't see what was killing them.

The government finally outlawed the slaughter, and the bison herd in Yellowstone gradually made an amazing comeback. Yet because the animals are now protected from hunting, they've got basically zero fear of humans.

Which doesn't mean they actually *like* us. They just tolerate us, and barely.

The woman in flip-flops starts clicking pictures of herself in front of the buffalo, which turns its boulder-sized head and paws a hoof on the ground. This is a signal that the bull is getting annoyed. The woman might think the animal is dull-witted and slow, but it could chase her down and trample her in like five seconds flat.

Lil keeps yelling, though the other onlookers have grown quiet, as if waiting for something awful to happen. Several of them are now shooting videos of their own.

The wayward tourist appears to be speaking to the bull buffalo as if it were a stray dog. Maybe she's coaching it on how to pose for her photos. All I know is that the humongous old bison looks like it's had enough.

Me too.

I slide out of Lil's Explorer and start running across the field toward the bozo in flip-flops.

The woman gets mad when she sees me coming. "Get outta here! You're gonna ruin my selfies!" she cries.

The people up on the road think I've lost my mind. They're shouting at me, too, and even in the clamor I can make out Summer's voice.

But I keep on running, closer and closer, until I feel the cold stare of buffalo eyeballs. The animal pivots from the clueless tourist to confront a new rude intruder—me.

By the time I stop, I'm near enough to smell the bison's nappy coat and feel its steamy heat. Gnats and flies are buzzing around its somber face.

"What are you doing?" shrieks the woman in flip-flops.

"Saving your life," I say.

"Leave me alone!"

The buffalo bobs its head and snorts. You don't need a zoology degree to know what's coming next.

I grab the angry numbskull around the waist and start pulling her away. She accidentally drops her phone, and now she's trying to wriggle free, so she can dash back and get it. No matter how fiercely she struggles, I hang on.

Over my shoulder I watch the buffalo unhappily watching us. It's pawing the ground again, deciding what to do. The woman continues squawking, squirming, calling me names, but I'm stronger than she is. I don't let go until we're safely back on the road.

Instead of thanking me, she threatens to have me arrested. I point across the open plain to where the bull buffalo is now stomping her precious phone to pieces. "Lady, that's what was going to happen to you," I say. "Maybe worse."

Her red-faced husband leads her to their RV, and off they go. I get back in the Explorer expecting a lecture, but all Lil says is: "Well done."

Summer is grinning. "Billy, has anyone ever told you that you're different?"

We don't see any bears, moose, or wolves, but it's still an excellent road trip. Lil and Summer take me to some mind-bending waterfalls in the Grand Canyon of the Yellowstone. We follow a zigzag walkway to a viewing platform, where I stand half-hypnotized by the roar and rumble in the gorge below. The mist from the crashing waters feels cool on my cheeks.

Signs warn visitors not to climb over the rails, which

seems obvious because you could easily slip from the rocks and fall hundreds of feet into the raging currents. Summer says it's happened before. Some people forget to pack their brains when they go on vacation.

There's also a sign saying no drones are allowed in the park. I can't help wondering if my father's so-called surveillance job ever takes him this far up the river.

On the ride back to Livingston I pretend to nap until we're past the Tom Miner Basin. Once we reach town, Lil makes a late-lunch/early-dinner stop at Mark's In & Out, where I destroy two cheeseburgers and a small mountain of fries. Mom would not approve. I didn't call her last night because I didn't want to talk about what had happened with my father.

"Can we reach him on the satellite phone?" I ask Lil.

"He leaves it off because he doesn't want to drain the battery."

"But I could still leave a message, right?"

"If you want to, Billy."

Summer says, "Leave him a message. Definitely."

Back at the house, Lil gives me the number of my dad's satellite phone, which has so many numerals it would be hard to remember. I go into the bedroom to make the call, which doesn't take long. There's no answer on the other end. When the voice prompt beeps, I say what I have to say. It's a brief message.

The next number I dial is Mom's.

"Nice of you to check in," she says sarcastically. "Please tell me you've heard from your father."

"Sort of."

I describe the odd encounter with Dad's quadcopter, omitting the part about the note he dropped by remote control. Still, she's ticked off.

"He didn't even walk out of the woods to see you?"

"Lil and Summer couldn't believe it, either."

"I'm gonna call that jackass and give him a piece of my mind!"

"It's all good, Mom. I got to see a grizzly bear with two cubs."

"From way far away, I hope."

"Oh, at least a mile," I lie, because I don't want her to worry.

"Any eagles?" she asks.

"Not today. But I'll text you video of some epic waterfalls."

"You okay?"

"I'm fine, Mom, just fine."

"I'm sorry about what happened with your dad. I don't know what's going on in his head. Maybe I never did."

Afterward, I slip out the back door alone. Satan the dog trails me down to the river. A dark wedge of cloud looms over town. The wind is kicking and the temperature is chilly. It doesn't look, or feel, much like summer.

I sit on a big flat rock. The Labrador half of the dog

wants to leap in the water, but the greyhound half is nervous about the weather. A coal train whistles, and I close my eyes. Satan pokes his soft nose against my hands. Cold raindrops pepper my arms.

The storm is charging down the Yellowstone through Paradise Valley. The worst of it is nine miles away—I calculate the distance by counting the seconds between the lightning flashes and thunderclaps. If my father is still holed up in the Tom Miner Basin, he's soaked to the skin. I hope he's got a waterproof case for that drone.

At Lil's house I found a program for last year's Livingston rodeo, listing all the cowboys. Their names were absolutely perfect—Shane, Wyatt, Josh, Heath, Logan, Morgan, Garrett, Thor, Tooter, Pistol, two Coles, and three Codys. From the day they were born, these guys were destined to grow up and wrestle steers or ride wild bulls. It was a done deal.

Mine isn't a bad name for a cowboy, although the rodeo announcer would probably call me Billy the Kid.

If I lived here, I'd pick something different. Trace would be a good one. Or maybe Dusty—that's even better.

"Now riding Spleen Crusher, the baddest bull between here and the Dakotas, is Dangerous Dusty Dickens! Let's give him a big ole Montana welcome!"

It's pouring so hard that I'm shivering. I feel sorry for the dog. There's another white burst of lightning, and this time I only reach the count of two before thunder rocks the hills. That's way too close.

Even a cowboy called Dangerous would scramble to get

out of a storm like this, but for some reason I stay where I am, sitting on the flat rock by the river. My arms are wrapped around the drenched dog. When I whisper to him, I call him Sparky, his original name, instead of Satan the shoe-eater.

Another lightning bolt makes both of us flinch, and the thunder breaks instantly. Glancing at the sky, I see an enormous brown bird tracing graceful circles over the winding river. It's twice as big as an osprey, bigger than a buzzard, maybe even bigger than a baldy. From the tip of one wing to the other must be seven feet.

Raindrops are stinging my face, but I can't take my eyes off the bird. The next time it sails over me, I notice bushy feathers on its legs, all the way down to the talons. That leg plumage is the clincher, the key clue—and another piece of information most normal kids wouldn't know.

The huge bird that's riding the gusts of the river storm is a golden eagle.

Maybe that's why I didn't move from the rock. Part of me must have sensed that I'd miss something magical if I ran for cover.

Suddenly a zigzag bolt zaps a cottonwood tree on the bank across the water. The crash of the thunderclap is ear-splitting. I flatten myself, shielding the miserable dog. The surface of the rock is wet and slick.

When I raise my head to peek at the sky, the eagle is gone.

Soon the thunder fades, the rain quits, and the clouds

roll on. The dog rises and shakes hard, trying to dry off. I stand, too, craning my neck to see where the golden went.

It's hard to believe it was really up there, soaring between the lightning bolts, but it was.

I'm almost positive.

Here's the message I left on my father's satellite phone: "Hey, it's Billy. Your son? I came a really long way to see you. What's the problem?"

He still hasn't called back. After so long without contact, I shouldn't be surprised that he's dodging me.

"We used to have thousands of horses," Summer is saying. "Not us personally, but the Crow as a tribe. We were famous for our horses."

"Still are," says Lil.

Summer grabs a cookie from a jar. "There's a cool rodeo show at the Crow Fair, but it's not the same as running herds of wild mustangs across the plains."

I've been so fixated on finding my father that I haven't spent much time asking his new family about their lives, their stories. How often do you get a chance to hang with people named Little Thunder-Sky and Summer Chasing-Hawks?

Lil says, "Leave the past upriver. That's what my great-grandfather used to say. But it's hard to do."

Summer looks over at me. "Some of the family wasn't

too happy when Mom hooked up with your dad. They let us know, too—"

"Dennis is solid." Lil cuts in. "A good man."

I keep my mouth shut, but what I want to say is: *Good guys don't hide from their kids*.

Summer tells Lil about the golden eagle I saw down by the river. Lil smiles and says, "Oh, I know that bird."

"Why was he flying around in that terrible weather?" I ask.

"Because it's smarter than sitting up in a tall tree during an electric storm."

She asks how I want to spend tomorrow, my last day in Montana. I tell her I want to go back to the Tom Miner Basin. She shakes her head and says that's not a great idea.

"I wouldn't know where to start looking," she says. "He could be anywhere."

Later, when I'm lying in bed, listening to my playlist, Summer enters the room, followed by the dog and the crusty old tabby.

"Mom and I came up with a name for you," she says.

I pull out my earbuds. "A Crow name?"

"Well, it's not official or anything. More like honorary."

"All right, let's hear it."

"'Big Stick.'"

I'm wondering if the name means what it *sounds* like it means. My face must be turning red, because Summer laughs and says:

"Relax, it's a river thing. When a fishing guide takes out a new sport who turns out to be super-good with a fly rod, the real deal, they call him a Big Stick."

"But I'm just learning how—"

"It's not all about the fishing. The name is about who you are as a person."

"So it's a compliment?" I say.

"Uh, yeah?"

"Then thanks."

"You're welcome, Billy Big Stick."

I guess it's better than Snake Boy.

"I've got a question," I say to Summer, "and don't get mad. But do you really sign those checks my mother gets every month?"

"I wouldn't make up something like that!"

I still can't get my head around it. "So you forge Dad's signature?"

"He's the one that taught me how," she says. "It's not really forgery, if it's his idea."

"But why?"

"Because somebody's got to pay the bills when he's not here, and Mom's busy most of the time. So he put me in charge of the checkbook. Dennis isn't exactly a math whiz, and he's also kind of scattered. He doesn't always remember when the tenth of the month rolls around, but I do. He knows I'll never forget to send that money to Florida—and that's the only check he ever asks about. He *is* a good person, Billy."

"Let's not take a vote," I mutter.

Summer gets why I feel the way I do about my dad. She's not making excuses for him. "He's got some major explaining to do," she says.

"Let's go back to Tom Miner."

"Billy, it's like looking for a microscopic needle in a super-giant haystack. A needle that doesn't want to be found."

The next morning, we head the opposite direction of where I wanted to go. We get off the interstate at Springdale and put Lil's boat in the Yellowstone, which seems slower and wider here. There's a faint drizzle, with low clouds, and the river's surface is the color of flattened tin.

Lil rows, Summer reads her book, and I sit in the bow casting a fly rod. Once I find the right rhythm, my technique improves. In only a couple hours I land seven rainbow trout and three cutthroats.

Lil is chuckling when she nets the biggest fish. "I'd say Billy Big Stick is living up to his name."

From the back of the boat comes Summer's voice: "Ha! Beginner's luck."

By noon the sun is shining bright. Lil anchors under the boughs of a big lush cottonwood. Rising on the opposite bank is a rock cliff honeycombed with holes that are filled with swallow nests, the sleek birds swarming like moths.

For lunch Lil brought pasta salad and turkey wraps. Summer baked some oatmeal-raisin cookies, and I eat way more than I should. She and I swap seats so she can fish the next stretch of river, while I zone out in the back of the boat. I'm not surprised to see how well she casts, and it's a pretty thing to watch. Her first catch is a nineteen-inch brown trout that fights like a pit bull. Once the fish is shining in the net, Summer blows it a kiss before Lil sets it free.

We float beneath a tall craggy tree that has a bald eagle nest at the top. I take like ten pictures, which I text to Mom. I don't expect a response right away—today's an Uber day, and she doesn't check her messages while she's driving.

Which is good. Mom does okay when she can focus.

"Did you tell her what happened when you went to find your dad?" Lil asks.

"Of course he told her," Summer cuts in. "*I* would."

"She was bummed," I admit, "and ticked off at him, too. She'd said she didn't want me to come out here, but I think secretly she did. I think she wanted us to reconnect."

The eagle nest sits so high that we can't see over the rim. The babies could be hunkered down low, waiting for their parents to bring them a fish.

"Whatever happens with me and Dad, this has still been a cool trip," I say.

Lil pulls back on the oars. "It's not over yet."

After catching a few more trout, Summer asks to switch seats again. She wants to finish her book, and it's only two miles until we reach the takeout ramp. I'm happy to be back in the bow, concentrating on making good casts and not thinking about my father. That's another great thing about fly fishing: doing it right requires your complete, undivided attention.

Lil says lots of her customers are successful big-city business executives who are desperate to escape the grind of their jobs. She mutes their phones before they step into the boat, and she says they always thank her at the end of the float. I believe it.

All day long a warm downstream breeze has nudged us along, but now we turn a bend and the air goes dead still. Here the river is broad and lazy. Something that looks like a shaggy brown coconut pops to the surface—Summer says it's a beaver. Once he spots us, he whacks his flat tail—*pow!*—and dives.

I watch for his face to poke up again, but Lil says he's probably hiding in his den, a mud-packed heap of branches at the mouth of a small creek. Summer explains that the entrance to the den is underwater.

Lil rows closer, and as the current sweeps us past, I snap another picture for Mom. There are definitely no wild beavers in South Florida.

The fish have quit biting, and I don't mind. There's nothing boring about being here. It's nice to be the only humans in sight.

Summer is the first to hear the humming, because I'm tuned in to a bunch of squabbling redwings. She slaps her book shut and says, "I can't believe this."

Lil lets go of the oars and stands up, hands planted on her hips. "All this drama," she murmurs, frowning.

"What are you guys talking about?" I say.

Then I hear it, too.

The drone.

It's hovering downriver, pointed our way, watching us. This is why the blackbirds are so riled.

Lil shakes a finger at the quadcopter. "Knock it off, Dennis!"

If I were my father, I'd pay attention.

As the drone comes closer, Summer rises from her seat. "Yo, up there, is that really you?"

"Of course it's him," snaps Lil.

The little gray quadcopter tilts back and forth, as if nodding.

So I guess it's my turn. I speak extra slowly, in case he's lip-reading from the video feed.

"DAD! WHY . . . ARE . . . YOU . . . DOING . . . THIS?"

The drone glides forward until it's directly above the boat, so low I can practically poke it with the tip of the fly rod. I'm tempted to try, but I don't. If I touch just one of the moving propellers, the aircraft will go haywire and fall.

Probably on top of my head.

"Dennis, have you lost your mind!" Lil hollers. Now that the drone is so close, the buzzing of the blades is annoying. Summer plugs her ears with her fingers.

I stare at the unblinking eye of the quadcopter's camera, imagining my father staring back at me from . . . where? Depending on the strength of the signal, he could be operating the flight controls from high on a canyon rim, or the middle of a hayfield, or even the back of his truck.

One thing is certain: he's not far away.

"WHERE ... ARE ... YOU?" I call to the invisible pilot.

The drone wobbles slightly, and a small shiny packet tumbles from a compartment on its underside. I reach up to catch the falling object, but I miss.

Splash.

"No!" Stretching over the side of the boat, I try to grab the packet before it disappears underwater.

But it doesn't sink. It floats.

"Bubble Wrap," Lil grumbles, rowing quickly downriver in pursuit. Dad's quadcopter follows us by air.

I scoop up the little package and unpeel the wrapping. Inside is another neatly written note—and what looks like somebody's molar.

It's yours, Billy, the note informs me. *The first one you ever lost.*

"Seriously?" Summer says. "Now he's the tooth fairy?"

I lock eyes on the hovering spy craft and wonder how my father expects me to react. The yellowed nub in my hand is small enough to be kid-sized, but so what? I drop it in my pocket and read the last line of the note.

See you in Florida, it says.

SEVEN

So here I am, bagging groceries at Publix again.

After returning from Montana, I tried to find a job out-doors, where I could mostly be by myself. No luck. A golf course in our neighborhood had openings on the landscape crew, but the manager said I wasn't old enough to drive the riding mowers. He said their insurance policy didn't allow them to hire kids.

Which is why I ended up back at the supermarket. Belinda's working at T.J. Maxx, and Mom's still driving for Uber. She didn't get fired for kicking that creep out of her car, but the company put her on probation. They said one more "incident" and she's gone.

Publix gives me twenty hours a week, which leaves plenty of free time to go snake hunting west of town in the dead orange groves and ranch scrub. Mostly what you find out there are banded water snakes and garter snakes, but on the dry patches you'll sometimes luck into a speckled king snake or a corn snake.

What I like best about hunting snakes is the peace. All you hear are wild birds and your own footsteps. It's a long bicycle ride from where we live, so sometimes Mom gives me a lift. She downloaded the Uber app to my phone, so I can call her to come get me when she's between customers.

One afternoon I'm walking back toward town along Highway 70 when an old junker pulls off the road. The engine sounds like a washing machine full of chipped rocks. It clatters and shakes for a minute, then conks out.

A young driver emerges. He's wearing a faded black hoodie and dragging on a cigarette, which raises the possibility that he's not a genius. There's a neon-blue skull tattooed on his bony right arm. The skull is smoking a cigarette, too.

"What's in the bag?" he asks me.

I open the pillowcase and show him.

"Oh #!$*&!" he cries, scrambling to the other side of the car.

"They're harmless," I say.

"I hearda you, bro! You the Snake Boy."

The kid isn't exactly a model of good hygiene. His teeth are stained brown from the tobacco, and his pale skin looks blotchy and pitted. He's got small brown eyes and a home-made buzz cut.

I can't stop staring at the skull tattoo. Everyone at school still talks about it.

"Hello, Jammer," I say.

He looks pleased that I know who he is. "You the one got my old locker, bro?"

"Yeah. Can I ask why it smells so bad?"

"Dirty laundry and stuff," he says.

"Oh, come on."

"Yo, I was livin' in the boys' bathroom at the F Building.

The one next to where the band practices. That was my crib for, like, half the year."

"How'd you end up there?"

"'Cuz my stepdad threw me outta the apartment. Everything I owned got put in that locker. Socks, shirts, jockstraps. Some of it got washed, some didn't."

Jammer offers his own version of why he got expelled from school. "Some dude's Jeep got jacked after a football game. The cops found it, but they said they's a laptop missin' from under the seat. They said it was me that stole it, but, see, I was at my girlfriend's house when all that #@&$ went down. She was gonna testify for me, too, but then her family moved back to Dallas. So I copped a plea and went to juvie. Yo, they's no way to fight back when the whole system's rigged against you."

"Rigged how?" I ask.

"Hell, I'd still be in school if I was a rich boy like you. They wouldn'ta gone and kicked me out."

"We're not rich. Where'd you get that idea?"

"Yeah, right," he says.

I check to make sure I'm wearing what I think I'm wearing: a dirty T-shirt, board shorts, and nasty mud-splattered sneakers.

"Does this look like I shop at Vineyard Vines?" I say.

Jammer shrugs. "The cops set me up is all. Know what I'm sayin'? I bet they never mess wit' you."

"What's wrong with your car?"

"Fan belt. Can I use your cell, bro? Mine's dead."

I toss my phone to Jammer because he won't come anywhere near me and my snake bag. He dials a number and tells—not asks—somebody to come pick him up. Afterward he slides the phone back to me across the hood of the junker.

"Why'd you give out your locker combination to so many people?" I ask.

"Just friends. They messin' with your stuff?"

"Not anymore."

"You put a badass snake in that locker is what I heard. That's ultra-sick, man."

"Nobody got hurt."

"Yo, can I have, like, five bucks?" Jammer's gaze drops again to the pillowcase in my hand. "Know what? Never mind."

"Did the police ever find that missing laptop?"

"I ain't sure they ever *was* a laptop. Know what I'm sayin'?"

"See you later, man." I start walking away.

"Bro, what's your true name?" he calls after me.

"Billy Big Stick."

"What's *that* mean?"

"Ever heard of the Crow Indians?"

"Is that, like, a baseball team?"

I turn around. "FYI—cigarettes choke off the arteries to your brain. You should really quit."

Jammer waves lightheartedly and blows a circle of smoke.

I walk way down the road before stopping to call my

mother. Minutes later, a rusty SUV with bald wheels honks as it speeds past. Jammer grins at me from the passenger seat. The driver is looking down, totally texting on his phone.

My feelings aren't the least bit hurt when they don't stop to offer me a ride. In fact, I'm relieved.

When Mom finally arrives, I get in on the passenger side. A middle-aged man sits in the back seat. He's wearing a short-sleeved uniform shirt from Taco Bell. I've never laid eyes on him before.

"Billy, this is Mr. Randolph. I'm driving him to work."

"Hi there, Billy," says Mr. Randolph. "My wife's sister borrowed my ride. That's why I'm Uber-ing."

I look sharply at Mom, who pretends to be concentrating on the traffic. She's not supposed to transport family members while she's driving a paying customer.

"What's in the sack?" her passenger asks me pleasantly.

"Nothing," my mother cuts in. "His lunch. That's all."

She doesn't want poor Mr. Randolph leaping from her car at fifty miles per hour, which might very well happen if he learns the pillowcase is full of squirming reptiles.

I play along. "Yeah. It's just my lunch."

After we drop Mr. Randolph off at the Taco Bell, I remind Mom about the importance of sticking to the Uber company's rules. She acts like she's agreeing, but I know better.

"I just don't want you getting in any more trouble," I say.

"You're a good kid for worrying about me so much."

"But you're still gonna do things your own way, right?"

She says she spotted a small drone flying above the house today. "I swear it followed me to the post office!"

"What did it look like?"

"Gray," she replies, "with a dark stripe on the bottom."

"You're sure it was gray?"

"It made me think about your father."

"Lots of people have drones," I say.

"Right, I know, but why would this one follow *me*?"

"Mom, it's probably just some neighborhood kids foolin' around."

I still haven't told her about Dad's Bubble-Wrapped note that said he was coming to Florida. There's no point getting her all worked up, in case he never makes it. Anyway, I'm not even sure she'd want to see him.

Back at the house, Mom goes inside to start dinner while I head for the garage. There I open the pillowcase, remove the four snakes I caught, and lock them in one of the larger aquarium tanks. Then I rummage through a bunch of cardboard boxes until I find what I'm looking for.

My slingshot.

One of the first things I did after returning from Montana was ride my bike to the dentist's office and show her the tooth my father delivered by drone.

"Well, it's definitely a human molar, and definitely from a child," she said, "but I can't say if it came from your mouth or somebody else's."

"What about a DNA test?"

"We don't do that sort of thing here, Billy. The question doesn't come up very often."

I've been home a week and still haven't told Mom or Belinda about the tooth. Don't worry—I'm not keeping it under my pillow or anything. I hid it in the plastic case that holds the dental retainer I almost never wear.

But let's say the tooth was really mine. Is that supposed to prove Dad cares about me? Just because he saved a dingy little chomper all these years?

He'll have to do better than that.

One morning I'm working at the supermarket when I spot Chin, the kid who got jumped by the lacrosse player at school. He's waiting in the checkout line with a man who looks identical to him, only older. He calls the man Pop.

Chin looks totally recovered from the beatdown. The bruise above his eye has healed, and the bandage over his ear is gone. I try not to look at him or his dad while I'm bagging their groceries: a gallon of low-fat milk, a package of free-range chicken breasts, a head of romaine lettuce, two pints of Häagen-Dazs (vanilla and chocolate), half a dozen tomatoes, a can of black beans, a bunch of carrots. . . .

But Chin recognizes me, and now it gets awkward. If either of us says something, then Chin will have to explain to his father who I am and how we met. What happened in the school hallway that day is probably something he doesn't want to talk about—and I'd rather not be part of that conversation.

Finally we make eye contact.

He nods. I nod. That's it.

Chin and his dad walk out of the store with their grocery bags.

I'm feeling that I handled the situation pretty smoothly until I look at the checkout counter and see I forgot to bag one small item: dental floss.

Waxed, with spearmint flavoring.

I can't believe I missed it. Seriously.

The cashier hands me the little box of floss saying, "Go take it to those customers. Hurry up now. They paid for it."

So I jog to the parking lot and hunt down Chin and his father, who are arranging their groceries in the trunk of a small sedan. I step up and say, "Sorry, I forgot to bag this."

My tone is painfully polite. Chin studies me, standing there in my goofy green Publix apron. I'm not sure what he's thinking. His dad takes the dental floss and tries to tip me a dollar, but I shake my head saying, "No, sir, that's not necessary."

I turn around and propel myself back toward the entrance of the supermarket.

"Hey, thanks!" a voice calls out. A kid's voice.

It's Chin, not his dad.

I don't look back. "You're welcome," I say over my shoulder.

Mom swings by to pick me up after I get off from work. On the way I home I ask, out of the blue, if it was she or Dad who used to do the tooth-fairy thing when Belinda and I were little.

"It was always me," she says. "You didn't lose your first baby tooth until you were five and a half years old. Dennis was already gone by then, Billy."

"Oh."

"Gone on his great Wild West adventure."

"Right."

"What made you think to ask?"

"No reason," I say.

Back at the house, I walk straight to my bathroom, pluck the little yellow molar out of my retainer case, and flush it down the toilet.

I'm still in a crappy mood later, when Dawson shows up. Belinda invited him for dinner. She makes a point of holding his hand, a reminder to Mom: *See how much I care about him? Please don't make us move again.*

I feel like telling my sister her romance act is unnecessary. Mom hasn't said a word about moving, because the bald eagles are still happily sharing their nest on the Indian River. We faithfully check on them every Sunday morning. Basically it's our version of church.

"Dawson wants to go with us to see the birds next time," Belinda says.

Mom, who's broiling pork chops, says that would be fine.

"Bring some binoculars," I suggest.

"Dude, I've got something so much better," says Dawson. "My dad's camera. Just the lens cost ten grand!"

"Wow. Is it made from diamonds?" I ask with a straight face.

"It's a five-hundred-millimeter telephoto."

"So, that's what—twenty bucks per millimeter?"

Belinda says, "Knock it off, Billy."

Look, I know camera equipment is expensive. I just can't stand listening to people brag. Dawson is so dim that he doesn't even get that I'm roasting him.

Mom asks if his father is a professional photographer.

"Oh no, he's a venture capitalist," Dawson replies. "His specialty is funding start-up tech companies. You know, the Googles of the future!"

Now I'm ready to lose it, so I slip outside to practice with my slingshot. Our next-door neighbor has a tall palm tree that's full of green coconuts. I'm shooting copper BBs that bounce harmlessly off the thick husks. My aim is pretty good.

Of course, the coconuts are just hanging there on stems. It's not like trying to hit a moving target.

Dawson ambles out the front door and asks what I'm doing, as if it isn't obvious. He eyes the slingshot and says, "Hey, dude, let me try!"

This might turn out badly, but I can't come up with a reason to say no. I guess I don't want to hurt the guy's feelings.

"You ever used a slingshot before?" I ask.

"Are you kiddin'? My cousin's got one that's solid titanium. It's like shooting a twenty-two!"

"Well, this one is plain old oak."

"Here, Billy, observe . . . and learn."

Dawson snatches the Y-shaped piece of wood from my hand and grabs some BBs from the jar. His first shot somehow misses the entire tree. I hear the little copper ball plop into our neighbor's swimming pool. Dawson's second try pings off the trunk of the palm. His next shot lands at his feet because his fingers tangle in the rubber bands.

Finally he manages to nick one of the larger coconuts. Then he hits two more in a row.

"Now I'm officially bored," he declares, and turns to take aim at a calico cat that's been watching us from the cherry bushes.

I can't say what happens next, but it happens fast. Dawson ends up flat on the ground with my knees on his chest. He seems to be having trouble speaking.

The cat scampers off as I twist the slingshot out of Dawson's hand and fling it aside. I don't do this in a particularly gentle way.

Although he's bigger than I am, Dawson can't shake me off. His face goes red, and he splutters furiously. After he throws a wild punch, I pin his arms saying, "If you don't shut up, Belinda's gonna hear you. I'm guessing you don't want her to see this, right? Her boyfriend getting thumped by her little brother?"

Dawson quits thrashing and catches his breath. His face returns to its normal color, though I wouldn't say he looks calm.

"Why would you want to shoot somebody's pet cat?" I ask. "Where's the sport in that? You're pathetic."

He opens his mouth to reply, but no sound comes out. He's staring past me, over my shoulder, at something in the air above us.

It's not a bird, either. I can hear those little propellers humming.

Dawson cranes his sweaty neck to get a better look.

"What's that thing doin'?" he wheezes.

I climb off of him and pick up my slingshot.

"Go inside now," I say.

Then I grab a handful of BBs.

EIGHT

"Dad, is that you?" I ask the gray quadcopter.

Dumb question. Who else would be spying on our house?

"Dinner's ready," my mother calls from inside. She doesn't see what I'm seeing.

"Be right there, Mom."

After loading a BB into the pouch, I raise the slingshot and draw back the heavy-duty rubber bands. To counter the light crosswind, I aim a little left of dead center. The first BB sails too high. Instantly the drone begins to elevate.

I reload and shoot again. This time there's the sharp crack of metal on plastic. Something flies off the top of the quadcopter and flutters like a leaf to the ground.

It's part of a prop blade.

Down comes the drone, twirling in a sickly spiral. It crash-lands in the middle of our yard, shredding grass. I pounce on the crippled aircraft and carry it into the garage, yanking the door down behind me.

At the dinner table, Dawson won't look me in the eye. He's afraid I'm going to tell Belinda he tried to shoot the cat.

She and Mom are doing most of the talking, as usual. This evening's subject is the end of good manners in modern civilization. Belinda had a bad experience at T.J. Maxx today, a customer who flamed her for taking too long to count out his change.

Mom definitely overcooked the pork chops, but I'm not saying a word. This is why knives were invented.

"There was a cat in the yard," I say innocently. "Cute little calico."

Across the table, Dawson goes pale. His fork stops halfway to his lips.

Mom says, "Oh, that must be Mrs. Gomez's."

I nod. "What's its name again?"

"Muffin."

"She's supposed to be an inside kitty," my sister says. "But she probably snuck out the back door again."

Dawson finally gets the bite of pork chop to his mouth. He chews grimly, staring down at his plate.

I'm not letting him off the hook.

"How long ago was it that Mr. Gomez passed away?" I ask my mother.

"Right after Christmas."

"Seems like yesterday. That was really sad."

"Just tragic," Mom agrees.

"Heart attack," Belinda informs Dawson. "He gave little Muffin to Mrs. Gomez as a present on their last wedding anniversary. Can you pass the mashed potatoes?"

Dawson looks like he wants to shrivel up and crawl under the table. In other words, he looks like a person who almost shot a heartbroken widow's beloved pet. My sister would dump him in a nanosecond if she knew what he'd done, so he desperately hopes I won't say another word about it.

And I probably won't, if he starts behaving like a respectable member of the human species.

"Save room for dessert," Mom says. "I made a Key lime pie."

Belinda and I are clearing the dishes when somebody knocks at the front door. My heart starts racing because I assume the visitor is Dennis Dickens, my elusive father, arriving to retrieve his expensive quadcopter.

Mom takes one step toward the door, but I get there first.

The man standing on the front step isn't my dad. It's a much younger guy with no shirt, tanned arms, and stringy sun-bleached hair. Two sandy surfboards are strapped to the roof of his rainbow-colored van.

"Yo," the young guy says. "You see a drone come down around here?" Using his salt-crusted hands, he indicates the size of the missing craft.

From behind I hear Mom asking who it is.

"One of the neighbors," I say, and slip outside to speak to the surfer dude.

Everyone calls him Limpy. I've seen his beach van around town.

Limpy tells me he was practicing with his quadcopter when the signal "went all sketch" and the aircraft drifted out of control.

I take the broken prop blade out of my pocket and drop it in his hand.

He looks at it and says, "Not good."

I open the garage to show him the drone. "It crashed in our yard," I say.

"Bummer." He lifts the quadcopter and starts trudging to his van. I notice he doesn't have a limp, so I'm wondering how he got his nickname.

"Later, dude," he says.

Now it's decision time, one of those moral crossroads that Mom talks about. Since Limpy has no clue what actually happened to his drone, it would be easy for me to let him think it was just a mechanical glitch.

Except I feel lousy about what I did, so I hurry after him saying, "Hey, wait up! I'm really sorry, but I shot down your drone with a slingshot. I want to pay for the repairs."

A different look comes over his face, though it's not anger. It's curiosity.

"How come you shot it?" he asks.

"'Cause I thought it belonged to someone else. Long story, man. But I want to give you some money to get it fixed."

Limpy shrugs. "No worries, dude. One a these suckers buzzed my house, I'd probably plug it, too."

He smiles and sets the aircraft in the back of the van. "You must be really pro with that slingshot."

"Let me pay for the damage. Please?"

"No way. A new prop can't cost that much. We're cool."

He climbs into his van, which smells like sunblock and stale sweat. On the passenger seat is a crumpled tank top and three empty beer cans.

"You okay to drive?" I say.

Limpy chuckles and hitches his eyebrows. "Dude. Seriously?"

Like I don't know a thing about the grown-up life.

I ask if he uses the quadcopter to make surfing videos. He pauses to think about it before answering, "Yeah. For sure."

He drives away in a fairly straight line. I'm nagged by the feeling that he should have been unhappy—even angry—about what I did to his drone. His chill reaction seems weird.

Walking back to the front door, I step over the divot where the drone came down hard. Lying in the grass is something I hadn't noticed before, a small bright piece of plastic. The shape is thin and rectangular. As soon as I pick it up, I know exactly what I'm looking at. The factory label says "64g."

It's an SD card, a memory chip for electronic devices. Cell phones use SD cards. Cameras use SD cards.

So do drones.

I pocket the card and hurry inside to help finish with the dishes, but they're already done. Mom's on the phone, while Belinda and Dawson are watching some lame reality show where five supermodels who hate each other are stranded on a Pacific island with no spa. I head directly to my room and lock the door.

While waiting for my laptop to boot, I realize that

I didn't see something inside Limpy's van that logically should have been there—the remote-control unit for the runaway quadcopter.

I insert the SD card into my laptop, and find two videos in the file. The most recent is four minutes and twenty seconds long, from takeoff to crash. At the start of the video I recognize the launch point as a nearby city park, and at the end I recognize the kid aiming his slingshot up at the quadcopter. I'm a little surprised by the cold look on my face.

The second video on the SD card is longer, the time stamp showing that it was recorded yesterday morning. From the rising drone you can see a busy public boat ramp on the Indian River Lagoon. I've been there before. Judging from the angle of the sunlight, the craft takes a southern flight path, swooping above sailboats and Jet Skis and fishing skiffs. Eventually it slows to a hover above a stand of Australian pines on a shoreline that also looks familiar.

Slowly the drone spins in place, the camera sweeping the trees.

And there it is, in a half-dead pine—the nest.

And over there, high in a different tree, is one of Mom's two cherished eagles. Its snow-white head cocks upward, suspiciously eyeing the noisy little invader.

The other bird is busy pecking apart a dead mullet on another branch.

With a cry, the first baldy takes flight. The sudden tilt of the video frame indicates the drone has banked sharply, trying to race away. You catch a glimpse of a flapping shadow in hot pursuit, but the quadcopter is too speedy—the bird can't catch up.

I wonder if it was hungry, or just pissed off.

On the return flight to the boat ramp, the drone dips and weaves like a crazed fruit bat. The camera keeps recording, so I pay close attention to the landing:

There's a man on the ground holding the remote control. As the aircraft descends, the man's image in the frame grows larger and larger—and he looks less and less like Limpy the surfer.

I pluck the SD card from my computer and bolt out of the house so fast that Mom doesn't have time to ask where I'm going.

One time I saw a guy run over a snake on purpose. It was a pretty little king snake, totally harmless, crossing Strathman Lane early one Saturday morning. There was no car traffic, just me on foot with a fishing rod.

I was hurrying to move the snake off the road when some jerk on a bright yellow motorcycle swerved across the center line and drove over it. Then he slowed down, glanced back to make sure he'd struck his target, and sped off. He wasn't wearing a helmet, so I got a quick look at his scraggly, smirking face.

Because of its long, winding nervous system, a snake that gets badly injured takes a long time to die. It's not a pleasant way to go. I set this one in the bushes and waited until it stopped moving. Then I covered the shiny black-and-gold body with handfuls of dirt—not much of a funeral, but I was in a rush.

It was a short jog home, where I jumped on my bike and started riding up and down every street in my neighborhood, then the next neighborhood over, and so on. Eventually I found the yellow motorcycle. It was parked at a one-story house that needed new shingles and a paint job. The shaggy driver was lounging out front, drinking a Mountain Dew and gabbing on a cell phone. He paid no attention as I rode by.

What happened later isn't important. The snake killer's motorcycle mysteriously ended up at the bottom of a canal is what I heard. When he went to the police station, they saw that he had like seventeen unpaid traffic tickets, so now he pedals around town on a bicycle like mine.

The point of the story is that patience is important when you're hunting for something, whether it's a snake or a motorcycle or a rainbow-colored beach van.

It turns out that Limpy lives only eight streets from my house. There's plenty of daylight left when I spot his van under an oak tree next to an apartment building. The second door I knock on belongs to Limpy, who's surprised to see me.

"Whassup, dude?" he says, in a voice just shy of friendly.

"Here, I found this."

I hold up the little SD card. Limpy squints, totally puzzled.

"It must've popped out of your drone," I say, "when it crashed."

"It did? Oh, wow."

"You know what it is, right?"

Limpy purses his lips. "Yeah, for sure. Absolutely . . . it's a . . . you know . . . one a those thingies. . . ."

Quickly I slip past him, into the apartment. "Okay, where is he?"

Limpy wheels around. "Whoa, dude. Where's who?"

"The man who owns the drone."

"I don't know what you're talkin' about—"

"The man who paid you to come get it from my front yard," I say.

Limpy sniffs, looks down at his sandy bare feet, then back up at me.

"Listen, dude—"

"No, *you* listen." I waggle the SD card in front of him. "This is not a 'thingy.' It's a miniature data board for storing photos and video. Anybody who's into drones would know that. Speaking of which, where is it? Your quadcopter, Limpy."

"My what?"

"Oh, come on." I motion around the inside of the apartment, which is basically a minefield of surfboards, skimboards, skateboards, Styrofoam fast-food cartons, and mounds of reeking laundry.

Yet no drone.

"Dude, just get the hell outta here," says Limpy, and he's large enough to make me.

"Not until you tell me where he is."

"Hey, do I look like some kinda rat?"

Actually, Limpy *does* sort of resemble a 160-pound rodent. It sounds mean, but the truth is the truth. I don't have a problem with surfers, they're fine. A kid in my sister's class is crazy good on a short board. He gets all A's and B's, and he's going to the University of California in San Diego.

Limpy, I'm guessing, wasn't much of a student.

I smile at him and say: "The license tag on your van expired eight months ago. You're lucky some cop hasn't noticed."

He grabs his head. "Dude, why are you bustin' my butt? What are you, like, thirteen? Who do you think you freakin' are?"

"Just a law-abiding citizen," I reply, "trying to find his father."

Limpy's expression gets cloudy as his brain struggles to fit all this information together.

"How much did he pay you?" I ask. "Don't worry—you don't have to give the money back."

"Twenty bucks," he mumbles.

"How'd you meet him?"

"I was parkin' at that IHOP round the corner, okay, and he pulled up beside me and asked do I want to make some easy cash. He was in a mega-hurry. Said his RC drone went down and could I go pick it up for him."

"Didn't it seem weird that he wouldn't go get it himself?"

"People *are* weird, dude. I don't judge."

I describe what my father looks like, and Limpy says it

sounds like the same guy. I'm working real hard to stay cool. "Was he driving a red Chevy king cab?"

Limpy nods. "Covered with dust. I mean, it was *dog* dirty."

A subject on which Limpy is an expert.

"Did you take the drone back to the IHOP?" I ask.

"Naw, some motel down Highway One. He paid me the twenty, and I drove home. Well, not *straight* home. I stopped to pick up . . . groceries."

Limpy's so-called groceries are on the kitchen table: a tube of Pringles and a twelve-pack of beer.

"Which motel?" I ask.

"I don't remember the name."

"Then take me there."

"*Whaaaat?*" Limpy whines. "Gimme a break, man."

"I'll put my bike in the back of your van, and you can drop me off. Let's go."

Limpy folds his ropey brown arms. "So, this guy's really your dad?"

"Yep."

"But then how come he's spyin' on you? That's messed up, dude."

"It sure is," I say.

NINE

The sun goes down. I'm sitting on my bike in front of the Purple Pelican Motel. There's no sign of a Chevy king cab with Montana license plates.

I've got the phone to my ear waiting for Summer Chasing-Hawks to pick up on the other end. She doesn't. I've already texted her like nine times and gotten no reply.

My next call is to Little Thunder-Sky.

"Hello there, Billy Big Stick," she says.

"I've been trying to reach Summer, but—"

"She's hiking up Mill Creek. There's no cell signal on the mountain."

"It's about my dad," I say to Lil. "Is he in Florida?"

"That would be news to me."

"The note he dropped to me on the river said he'd be coming here, but it didn't say when. I didn't tell you about it because I figured it was just him . . . you know . . . trying to make me feel better."

Lil says she hasn't spoken to my father in days. "Said he's off on another mission, but as usual, he didn't say where."

I tell her about the mystery quadcopter, Limpy, and the dusty red truck.

"Him and that drone," Lil sighs wearily. "Why can't he just walk up and say hi like a regular person?"

"Sorry. Gotta go." I hop off my bike and duck behind a bus-stop bench.

A big red pickup has wheeled into the motel parking lot. A slender man steps down from the driver's side holding a white bag. It's too dark to see his face.

I try to shout "Dad!" but only a raw croak comes out. Pathetic.

The man enters one of the ground-floor rooms. When the lights come on, the blinds snap shut.

My phone vibrates. It's Mom calling, but I don't answer.

Instead, I text her, with shaky fingers: "I'm chillin at Dex's."

"Don't b 2 late," she texts back.

"K."

True confession: I don't know anybody named Dex. In fact, I don't know anybody who knows anybody named Dex. A more experienced liar would have come up with a normal-sounding fake friend.

I lock my bike to the bench and sneak over to the red pickup. It's got Montana license tags, new rear tires, and a gritty coat of dust. However, one of the fenders has a dime-sized puncture that I don't remember seeing when we came upon Dad's truck in the Tom Miner Basin. The hole might explain the gunshot that the Forest Service officer was on his way to investigate when he saw me hitchhiking.

Traffic is heavy tonight, and I'm worried that the passing headlights will reveal me crouching like a burglar by the motel. I ease into the shadows to plan my next move, and it turns out I'm not alone. Two heavyset dudes in T-shirts are leaning against the wall sharing a bottle of booze.

"Gimme your money," one of them says casually.

"Are you kidding?"

"Right now," says the other one, gulping from the bottle.

I can't see their expressions, but they sound fairly serious.

"I don't have any money," I say, which is the truth. My fists are clenched, but my whole body is shaking.

The first guy grabs the front of my shirt. He smells like cigarettes and rotten fruit. "Empty your pockets or we kick your ass."

"Yo, I don't think so."

I'm almost sure this is not me speaking.

The dude lets go of my shirt and takes a step back. I truly cannot move a muscle.

"I'll put botha you dumb suckahs down," says the unseen owner of the voice, which I now recognize.

The two muggers slink away, cussing. A hand settles on my shoulder.

"You awright, Snake Boy?"

"I'm good. Thanks, Jammer."

When he steps from the shadow, I see a straight blade in his right hand. He snaps it shut. "Ain't no rattlesnake," he says with a hard smile, "but I can sure make it bite."

"You saved me a trip to the hospital."

"Go on home, bro. This ain't no place for you to be hangin'."

Jammer slides away slow and easy, like he owns the street.

I watch until he disappears around a corner. Maybe he felt like he owed me a favor, but all I did was let him borrow my phone the day his car broke down. That's nothing compared to what he just did for me.

After taking a slow deep breath, I approach the door to the motel room, knock three times, and wait. Nothing happens.

I knock again, louder this time.

"Dad, it's me! Open up."

No sounds of movement on the other side. Did he fall asleep? Or is he hunkered down, waiting for me to go away?

Knock, knock, knock.

I'm not giving up, Dennis. Deal with it.

Knock, knock, knock, knock, knock, knock, knock, KNOCK, KNOCK, KNOCK!!!

He'd have to be in a coma not to hear me.

I back off and press myself against the wall, half expecting to see the two muggers returning with backup. I'm wondering if I'll have time to dial 911 before they punch my lights out.

Several minutes later, the motel room door cracks open. A head pokes out briefly, then disappears. After a while the man emerges and strides toward the red truck.

I step forward yelling, "Hey, you. Wait!"

And what does he do? My own flesh and blood? He runs. Unbelievable.

"Are you nuts?" I shout after him.

He glances back but he doesn't stop. It's pitiful, really,

because he's not very fast. I catch up quickly and tackle him from behind.

So this is quite a father-and-son reunion—the two of us rolling around on the sidewalk along U.S. Highway 1.

Once I get him pinned, I say, "*What* is your problem, Dad?"

He's panting like an old dog. "Billy Dickens, is that you? Let me up, son."

"You gonna chill, or not?"

"We better get out of here before somebody calls the cops. We look like two drunks wrestlin' in the road."

"No, the wrestling part is over," I say. "This is the part where you say you're sorry for running away from your own kid."

"You scared me, Billy. I swear I didn't know it was you."

I won't let him up until I'm sure he's too tired to take off again.

"Did you come alone?" he asks.

"No, Dad, I brought SEAL Team Six."

I pull him to his feet and we go back to his motel room. In the light he looks just like he did in the photographs at Summer and Lil's house—except tonight he's wearing a wrinkled black business suit, black shoes, a white button-down shirt, and a crooked black-checked necktie.

"Are you going to a funeral?" I ask.

"Actually, I was on my way to see you," he says, "and your sister. I'm real nervous, to be honest. That's why I did the flyover with the quadcopter—I didn't want to show up at the front door and find out your mom's got a jealous boyfriend, or whatever."

Dad's damp hair is mussed from our scuffle. His cheeks are flushed and shiny with sweat. I point to the drone, parked on the floor. "Am I the first person to shoot at that thing?"

"No, but you're the first one to hit it." He's still breathing hard. "Good thing all you had was a slingshot."

"Who put that bullet hole in your truck?"

Dad chuckles sourly. "It's what they call an occupational hazard."

"And your occupation is . . . ?"

"Geez, your mom never told me you play football."

"I don't."

"Then where'd you learn to tackle like that?" He's rubbing his left side. "I think you busted some ribs."

There's definitely something familiar about his voice. Is it possible my brain remembers it from all those years ago, before he left us?

"Why didn't you answer the stupid door? I knocked like a hundred times."

"I was in the shower." He holds out his right hand. "Good to see you, son."

We shake. I nod stiffly. "Good to see you, too. In person, I mean."

I should probably be angrier than I feel, but I admit

there's a huge sense of relief to be done with the first face-to-face moment, as crazy as it was. At least no punches were thrown.

A white paper bag from McDonald's sits open on top of the TV set. The whole room smells like fries. In one corner is a large black duffel, zipped tight.

When I sit down on the edge of the bed, the flimsy mattress sags. My father remains standing. He smooths his hair and brushes the smudges from the knees of his pants.

"I was going to the house to apologize," he says.

"For everything? Wow."

"Do you think your mom and sister will want to see me?"

"Is that really why you came to Florida?"

"Full disclosure? I'm also here on business."

Now we're getting somewhere.

A big-ass cockroach emerges from the closet and crawls halfway across the floor before Dad says, "Your call, Billy."

I motion to the door. He opens it. Together we watch the shiny brown fugitive scurry into the night. My father shuts the door and grins.

"Most guys would've stomped that thing," he says.

"I didn't want to mess up this lovely slime-green carpet. Why wouldn't you come out of the woods and talk to me in Montana?"

"It wasn't safe. I was working."

"So, tell me about this top-secret job. Lil said you do surveillance missions for the government?"

I do semi-snarky air quotes when I say the word *missions*.

My father's brow creases and his lower jaw grinds. I hardly know the man, but it's clear he can't decide how much of the truth to tell me.

"Is it the CIA? FBI?" I ask. "The NSA?"

"Let's go outside, Billy."

"Are you gonna run again? Because, no offense, you're not exactly Usain Bolt."

"No, son, I'm done running," he says.

Belinda and I have one living set of grandparents—Mom's father and mother. They live in Portland, Oregon, on the other side of the country, which means we see them only at Christmas. That's the time of year when Florida gets invaded by jillions of grandfathers and grandmothers desperate to escape winter.

Grandpa Dan is retired from Boeing in Seattle, where he worked on an assembly line building jet airplanes, mostly 737s. Grandma Jackie taught elementary school for thirty years. In addition to my mom, they had four other daughters, so now there are at least a dozen other grandkids scattered all over the place—my cousins. Honestly, I can't even name them all. Belinda and I have met only a few, and they seemed fairly normal. It's possible we'll never get to know the rest, because Mom's not real tight with her sisters. Besides, we move around so often that they've probably lost track of us.

On the other side of the family there are no cousins or aunts or uncles, because Dad was an only child. Mom said it was a brutal time for him when his mother and father passed away. How could it not be? Dad's father had one sister—Sophie was her name—who made sure he was able to finish college. He might have mentioned her when we were little, but I can't remember.

"Aunt Sophie," says my father, "was an odd character, though very kind to me. She lived all alone on a little island in the Bahamas."

"That's cool. What did her house look like?"

"I've got no idea, Billy. She never invited me to visit. In fact, I never met the lady in person."

We're standing on top of the drawbridge that crosses the Indian River Lagoon. A breeze ripples the water, and I can see the red and green lights of the channel markers winking all the way up to Vero Beach. A power line strung parallel to the causeway is lined with birds—gray doves, I think—dozing shoulder to shoulder. There must be a hundred of them.

I ask Dad if he and his rich aunt ever spoke on the phone.

"Just twice. The first time was the day after my parents died. The second time was the day after I graduated from college—she called to congratulate me. She asked what I intended to do with my brand-new bachelor's degree in wildlife ecology and conservation. I made up something that sounded righteous and noble, but I had no grand plan, obviously. Your mom found that out the hard way."

We're in a narrow pedestrian lane used mostly by fishermen. Wearing a black suit at nighttime makes Dad almost invisible to drivers, but luckily there's not much traffic. Since we've been here, the drawbridge has gone up only once, for a northbound sailboat.

Below us a pod of bottle-nosed dolphins plays in the waves. I hear them breathing through their blowholes. It sounds like soft valves on a steam engine.

"This would be an excellent place to launch the drone," Dad says.

I'm not sure how Aunt Sophie is connected to his secret missions, but I'm trying to stay patient and polite. Mom keeps texting, asking why the heck I haven't come home.

"Speaking of drones," I say, "did the government train you how to fly that thing?"

"I taught myself. It's easy, really."

"But they paid for it, right? The CIA? Or whoever."

He shakes his head. "No, Billy. Aunt Sophie paid for it."

"But you made it sound like she's dead."

"Oh, she is."

"This isn't funny, Dad." I start walking down the bridge, back toward the mainland. My father hustles after me.

"Wait, son, listen," he's saying. "Not long after I moved to Montana—"

"After you bailed on Mom and us. Right? Don't forget *that* part."

"All right, yes. After I went to Montana, I got a phone

call from some lawyer in Nassau. He told me Aunt Sophie had passed away and left everything to me and her pet parrot. I couldn't believe it."

Now I'm walking faster. Apparently my father thinks I'm a total fool.

"Please slow down, Billy! These church shoes are killing my feet."

"What was the parrot's name? Make it a good one, Dad."

"She called it Hubert, after the prime minister at the time."

"Sure. Of course she did," I say.

"I know it sounds crazy, but it's true. She and the prime minister were friends. Wait up!"

"So, how much did rich Aunt Sophie leave you and 'Hubert' the parrot?"

"Enough," Dad says.

"Enough for what?"

"To take care of you, your sister, and your mom. And Lil and Summer, too."

"Okay, but why do you need the money if you're flying spy quadcopters for the U.S. government? I'm sure the pay's pretty sweet."

He grabs one of my arms and hangs on until I stop walking. We've almost reached the bottom of the bridge.

"Son, I don't work for the government," he says. "I work for myself."

"Doing *what?*"

"Lil doesn't know. Neither does your mom."

"The truth, please. Why are you sneaking around with that drone?"

"I'll tell you," he says, "but first you've got to make me a promise. It's a big one."

"All right, Dad, but there's something I need in return."

TEN

"Where's your gun?"

It sounds like I'm talking with a gangster.

"In a safe place. Relax," says my father.

"You left a box of ammo on the seat of your truck at Tom Miner."

"That's Montana, Billy, not Florida."

We're riding through town in the red pickup. My bike is in the cargo bed.

I give him the SD memory card that fell out of his quadcopter. "You'll need this for future ops."

He slips the card into the breast pocket of his suit.

"I flushed that baby tooth you gave me," I say. "Whose was it, anyway?"

"Yours, Billy. Who else's would it be? I asked your mom to send me one. This was a couple years after I moved out."

"Dad, you didn't just 'move out.' You bailed out."

When he says he's sorry, I hear real pain. It makes me feel bad about getting rid of that dumb little molar.

"There's no excuse," he says, "for how I've acted, for not calling you all these years. I just didn't think I could handle it—the sound of your voice, and your sister's. I was afraid I'd fall apart on the phone and make things even worse. It was me being a coward, Billy, nothing more complicated than that. As time went by, the fear turned to shame."

I'm not sure what he wants me to say. He's right: there's no excuse.

"Sending that check every month—does that make you feel better?"

My father chuckles bitterly. "Like I was a better person, you mean? I've probably talked myself into thinking that. But I don't send the money just because I feel guilty. I feel *responsible*, too. There's a difference, son. You understand?"

Part of me likes it when he calls me "son," and part of me gets a little ticked off.

"The thing about the inheritance from Aunt Sophie—" Dad goes on, "it took away one of my worst worries. Because then I knew that, no matter what was going on in your mom's life, you guys would always have a roof over your head and some cash in the bank."

When we get to the house, he parks in the driveway behind Mom's car. We just sit there, and sit there, and sit there some more, while the engine idles. Finally I reach over to turn off the ignition.

"It's gonna be okay," I say. "She wants to see you. She sounded fine when I called."

His hands are still welded to the steering wheel. "I did a radius search using the GPS of this address as a base. That's how I found her latest eagle nest."

"I watched the video on the SD card."

"The male bird chased after my drone! You see that?"

"Yeah, it was sick. Hey, Dad?"

"What?"

"Are you ready to go inside?"

"Give me another minute," he says.

Mom's face is at the kitchen window. It breaks my heart to see that she's put on some makeup.

My father straightens his tie. He coughs a couple of times to clear his throat.

"Let's go," I say. "You hang out with grizzlies and wolves, and you're not afraid of *them*."

"They're more predictable, Billy."

I walk around to his side of the truck and open the door. When I reach for his arm, he pulls away, saying, "Easy now. I seriously think you busted some ribs."

In slow motion he descends from the pickup and follows me up the walkway. The front door swings open, and there stands my mother, framed in the light.

"Hi, Chrissie," Dad says.

"Hello, Dennis. Why are you dressed like an undertaker?"

"Fair enough," he says with a sheepish grin.

My sister is hopelessly addicted to social media—SnapFace, InstaTwit, MeTube, whatever. Sometimes I hide her phone as a test. Her average freak-out time is between three and four minutes. After that, she starts dashing around the house like an insane person, flipping over sofa cushions, yanking out drawers, and groping blindly under the furniture. "Where's my phone? *Where's my #&*! phone?*"

Truly, it's entertaining to see.

One night, while Belinda was in one of her online trances, I caught her staring at a photograph of a pot roast.

"Now you're scaring me," I said.

"Brittany's cousin posted what she cooked for dinner. I'm just 'liking' it, that's all. Mind your own business!"

"Let me get this straight. Some person snaps a photo of a greasy slab of meat and shares it with the world. Then the world is expected to respond."

Belinda frowns. "It's rude not to 'like' somebody else's picture."

"But what if you're a vegetarian and don't approve of beef? That's called an ethical dilemma, right? Maybe your response could be a picture of an artichoke."

"Just shut *up*, Billy."

Belinda also posts random photos of food—and photos of her clothes and her shoes and, for variety, Muffin, the neighbor's cat. I watch her taking these pictures, but I never see them because I avoid social media. It's a choice, not a judgment.

There are two types of people—those who want to be noticed, and those who don't. I'm not saying one is better than the other. I'm just saying I'd rather be totally off the radar. Clearly my father feels the same way.

Yet here's Belinda, tracking him with her cell phone the moment he enters the house. She's doing a video. He's trying hard not to look miserable.

"Hi, sweetie." He manages a smile. "Wow, you're all grown up."

"No kidding," she says.

I tell her to knock it off.

"Why? This is a major family moment. Someday we'll all cherish the memory. *Not.*"

Mom steps between my father and my sister, blocking her camera angle. Belinda lowers her phone.

Dad says, "You've got every right to be mad." He seems thinner, almost shrunken, in that depressing black suit.

My mother steers him to the couch and positions herself right beside him. "Belinda, could you please get us some coffee? Your father takes his with cream, no sugar."

Dad smiles gratefully. Mom and Belinda are locked in an icy stare-off, which Mom wins. My sister groans and stalks to the kitchen. I'm hoping she doesn't come back and dump the coffee in Dad's lap.

"So, what've you been up to, Dennis?" my mother asks. "Billy tells me you're married to a Native American."

You're thinking: *Could this possibly be* more *awkward?* Answer: Nope.

"She's from the Crow Nation."

"I love her name. 'Little Thunder-Sky.' Where'd you two get married?"

"Everyone calls her Lil. We didn't have, like, a court-house wedding."

"So it was a traditional tribal ceremony?"

"Uh, no, it was . . . private." Dad must be writhing on the inside. "Just me, Lil, and her daughter. We went camp-ing in the Crazy Mountains."

"That's what they're really called? No way!"

"Yup, the Crazies." He laughs drily. "Perfect, huh?"

I'm actually on the verge of feeling sorry for him.

Belinda returns with the coffee. She hands one cup to Mom and one to Dad. I can't stand the stuff. Mom claims it tastes better when you're older.

"Please stay," Dad calls to my sister, who's already half-way to her bedroom, "until I've said what I came to say."

Belinda sullenly returns and plants herself in a chair across from the sofa. "This should be priceless," she mutters.

Mom shoots her a glance that says: *Back off and give the man a chance.*

After a deep grim sigh, my father begins his apology speech. It's not terrible. He stumbles through some of it, probably because he's nervous. He repeats the "no excuses" line several times, which makes me believe he doesn't have a script memorized in his head; I think he means what he's saying.

Mom doesn't take her eyes off him. At one point she wipes something that might be a tear from her cheek. Still,

I'm not sure what she's feeling. Is it sorrow, or pity, or both? Dad doesn't paint a very flattering portrait of himself as a younger man—impulsive, restless, unreliable.

"I loved you kids, and I loved your mother," he says, "but it got to feel like I couldn't breathe. I had to leave. At least I *thought* I had to leave. So I did."

Belinda, who's been fake-staring at her fingernails the whole time, looks up and asks, "So why show up now?"

"I wouldn't have dreamed of coming all this way and bothering you, but after seeing Billy out in Montana—"

"No, it was your drone that saw me," I cut in. Mom and Belinda heard the whole story.

"The point is," says Dad, "knowing Billy had traveled so far to see me, I thought it was time to grow up and reintroduce myself to three people I've never stopped caring about. I was hoping all of you might be open to at least . . . listening. Which you have, and I'm thankful."

My sister rolls her eyes, one of her go-to snarky moves.

"Dad's actually here on business," I add pointedly. "That's the main reason."

"Not the main reason," he insists, "a *co*-reason."

Mom says, "Let's hear more about your work, Dennis. What can you tell us?"

"Not much, unfortunately. It's classified."

"So, you're a drone spy."

"Even if he is," I cut in, "he wouldn't be allowed to admit it."

Dad says, "Billy's right."

This is the promise I made to him—that I'd back up his story, even though I know the truth. It won't be a permanent commitment if he doesn't honor his end of the bargain.

"When you lived with us, you couldn't even hold down a job in a shoe store," says Belinda, sarcastic again. "Now you want us to believe you're a secret agent for the U.S. government?"

Dad smiles weakly. "It turned out I was actually good at something. Who knew, right?"

Mom says, "Belinda, Billy . . . could you guys please . . ." She motions down the hallway toward the bedrooms. "Your father and I would like a few minutes alone to talk."

I'm pretty sure that's the *last* thing my father would like, but this time he'll get no help from me.

Belinda follows me into my room, shuts the door, and sits on the floor. "So, what do you think?"

"He's trying," I say.

"Yeah, but what's his game? His angle?" Her legs are crossed, and her toes are wiggling. "Obviously he wants something."

"Maybe all he wants is forgiveness," I say, "or the *possibility* of forgiveness."

"Oh, that's a good one, Billy. That's rich."

"Look, he's got money, a nice house, a whole other family. Why would he risk messing up his new life unless his conscience was bothering him?"

"Wait—you're saying he's got a conscience?"

"I think he does, sure." I also think he's still got a few loose bolts rattling around inside his head.

"Know what scares me?" Belinda is serious now. No more snark. She's got my mother's sea-blue eyes, super-intense.

She says, "I'm scared Mom still has a thing for him."

"She doesn't," I say, which is what I want to believe.

"Did you check out that Katy Perry lipstick?"

"Come on, it's not that bad. And just because she wants to look nice doesn't mean she's in love with him."

"But what if she is, Billy?"

"Then we help her get past it."

"Because it's over, right?"

"So over," I say.

There's a light knock on the door, followed by Mom's voice: "Billy, your dad wants to see your snake collection."

My sister rolls her eyes. "Know what? You two nature freaks deserve each other."

Dad is waiting in the garage. I take the lid off the glass tank that holds the yellow rat snakes, which are actually pumpkin-colored. They've got thin dark stripes all the way to the tips of their tails.

"Can I hold one, Billy?"

"Better not. They're biters," I say.

"I'll be careful."

With hot-tempered snakes, the key is how you handle them. Most people try to grab them behind the head, which triggers a bite reflex. One trick I use is to slip both hands beneath the snake's body and lift up so slowly that it doesn't get alarmed. Rat snakes are climbers, so they're used to being above the ground. They'll stay pretty chill if they think they're up on a tree branch somewhere.

Again, this kind of information would be worthless to a normal person.

I pick up the five-footer and carefully place it in my father's hands.

"Now, don't squeeze," I warn, but it's too late.

He squeezes. The snake whips around, chomps him on the chin, and resets for another strike.

With a wince, Dad says, "Oops, my bad."

"Just stay super-still, okay?"

After a few moments, the rat snake lowers its head and starts peering around.

"Check it out, son—he's chillin' now."

"It's a she," I say.

My father proceeds to do an excellent imitation of a tree. The snake is definitely calmer, having wrapped around his right forearm. It's not strong enough to cut off the circulation, the way a python or a boa constrictor might do.

"See, Billy? Look how peaceful she is."

Dad is trying so hard to be still that he's actually speaking without moving his jaw muscles. Meanwhile, his chin shines with a U-shaped pattern of bleeding pin-sized holes. It looks like he's got a red goatee. I probably should've let him hold the king snake instead; that one doesn't bite.

"You're dripping blood on your suit," I say.

"Good. Now I've got an excuse to throw it away."

"You've never done this before? That's hard to believe, all the time you spend out in the wild."

Dad says he avoids snakes. "It's not a full-on phobia," he adds. "I just walk the other way when I see one. Live and let live, right? Also, Montana's full of rattlers."

"I saw a beauty," I tell him, "sunning right next to your truck."

"They den high up in rock cliffs all winter. When the weather gets warms, they swarm down to the valleys and do a number on the gophers." He is basically eye to eye with the rat snake. The fork of its glistening tongue feathers in and out of its mouth.

"What if your mother says no?" Dad asks.

"She won't," I say.

He's talking about our deal—the promise he made to me in return for keeping his secret. We've lowered our voices, so Mom and Belinda can't hear us.

"Billy, I've gotta leave tomorrow. First light."

"I'll be ready."

Gingerly I uncoil the snake from his arm and return it to the glass tank. Dad takes out a handkerchief and dabs the blood from his chin.

"What were you and Mom talking about in there? Old times?"

"That's personal, son."

"So, you still care about her."

"How could I not? My eagle girl," Dad says fondly. "One of these days she'll find the right guy, I know she will."

"Belinda's worried that Mom still loves you. I told her no way."

"Your mother and I talked about the way things ended between us, and we also talked about what's happened since then, the way I let you kids slip out of my life. She was kinder about it than I deserved, but, no, I'm definitely not the secret love of her life."

The relief I'm feeling is difficult to hide, but I try.

"So," Dad says, "did you come up with a good cover story for the trip?"

I tell him what I plan to tell Mom. He's not convinced she'll buy it. He stands back while I unfasten the lids from the other glass tanks.

"Is your sister still pissed at me?" he asks.

"Oh yes."

"And I totally get that. But, who knows, maybe someday . . ."

"Maybe," I say.

Quickly I bag up all the snakes. They don't mind sharing the same pillowcase.

Dad offers to give me a ride. I stick my head in the door to tell Mom we won't be gone long. "Can't this wait until tomorrow?" she asks.

"Not really."

Nobody else is driving on Grapefruit Road this time of

night. I show Dad where to park. He angles his pickup so the headlights illuminate a path into the scrub and the trees, where I let the snakes go. Dad seems impressed that the release operation ends without me getting chomped even once.

On the way back to town, I ask him what to bring on our "mission."

"Long pants, bug juice, sunblock, Band-Aids, a sleeping bag—oh, and binoculars," he says. "I've got all the food and water we'll need."

"Don't forget your gun."

"We don't mention the gun," Dad tells me sternly. "The gun is strictly for emergencies."

"But he's a bad guy, right?"

I'm talking about the man we'll be chasing, the one my father followed all the way across the country, from Montana to Florida. The same man who flattened Dad's tires and shot a hole in his truck trying to scare him off.

"Yeah," says Dad, "he definitely qualifies as a bad guy."

ELEVEN

Summer and Lil were relieved to learn Dad was all right, but they were curious about his sudden reappearance in Florida. We were communicating by text, which made it easier for me to avoid giving a full explanation.

"Guilt trip" is what I typed. "He wanted to see me and Belinda."

Their return texts sounded doubtful. Maybe they're worried that he won't return to Montana, that he's decided to move back here with us. I can't tell them the main reason he came. Silence is part of the deal.

Now it's crunch time—trying to convince Mom to let me leave with Dad for a few days. My story sounded way better when I rehearsed it in my bedroom.

"A camping trip?" She raises an eyebrow. "What kind of camping trip?"

"You know. Guy thing."

That's the best I can do. Pretty shaky, but I'm on my own. My father is talking with Belinda in her bedroom, trying to dent that iron shell of resentment.

"Was this 'guy thing' your idea or his?" Mom asks.

"Mine, totally."

That's true. It's also technically true that Dad and I will be "camping."

"Where, Billy?"

"Down in the Everglades." Also true.

"And what about your summer job?"

I'm ready for that one.

"I checked with Mr. Voss at Publix. He's fine with me taking a few days off. I told him it was a family vacation."

My mother frowns. We're in the kitchen, where she's cleaning the filter of the coffee machine. She says, "I don't have a wonderful feeling about this, Billy—you guys charging off into the swamp together. There are better ways to bond."

"I'll have my phone with me, Mom."

"Great," she says. "And if you don't answer, I'll assume it's ringing in the belly of an alligator."

I put my arms around her. "I promise not to get eaten. If I do, you can ground me for the rest of the summer."

"That's not funny, Billy. I don't think you should go!"

So I rattle off some statistics about how rare gator attacks are—lots more people die from bee stings, for example. My mother isn't swayed. When Dad comes out of Belinda's room, Mom cross-examines him for twenty minutes. Like me, he doesn't actually lie about the plans for our trip. He just leaves out a few key details.

Listening to their back-and-forth discussion, I notice something interesting: even though my father has been gone for years, living far away from what you'd call our "family dynamic," he still knows exactly what to say to Mom, and how to say it.

Not only does she give me permission to go along with him, but now she's offering to help me pack. Amazing.

So, props to smooth-talking Dad.

The amateur man-hunter.

I wish I could play the guitar. Mom once offered to pay for lessons, but I said no thanks. I haven't got enough patience to sit down and strum chords for hours after school. I need to be outside in the woods or on the water, even when it's pouring rain. Otherwise, I'll go cray-cray, as my sister would say.

If only somebody would invent a super-fast way to learn a musical instrument—some type of overnight audio hypnosis, where you could wake up in the morning and magically start playing like Eric Clapton.

The reason I'm thinking about this? We're in the truck, an hour before sunrise, and a Clapton song called "Get Ready" is blasting on the speakers. Dad's got a sweet playlist, I admit. Oldies but goodies. It's way better than being trapped in a moving vehicle with Belinda, which means nonstop Taylor Swift. Not even Taylor Swift's *mother* listens to as much Taylor Swift as my sister does.

Dad says, "If we have time, I'll teach you how to fly the drone."

"Did you replace that broken propeller?"

"I replaced all of them," he reports, "to maximize performance. You'll see."

We're passing through a town called Okeechobee, on

the north side of the famous lake. The outskirts feature vast sod farms that supply new grass for lawns and golf courses. The fields are so bright green that they look spray-painted.

My father asks if Mom got up early to make me breakfast.

"She tried. I sent her back to bed and ate a bowl of cereal."

"What was her state of mind, Billy?"

"I think she's a little worried about this trip."

"Are you?"

"Not at all," I say, untruthfully. "Tell me his name—the guy we're chasing."

"You mean the guy we're *tracking*."

"What's the difference?"

"Baxter." Dad spells it. "Lincoln Chumley Baxter."

"So he's crazy rich."

"How'd you guess?"

"Because regular people don't name their kids 'Lincoln Chumley' anything."

Dad laughs. "Even better: it's Lincoln Chumley Baxter *IV*. His family owns a couple of skyscrapers in San Francisco. He's never worked a day in his life. All he does is—"

"Where's the g-word?"

"Stop asking, Billy."

"Is it loaded? Because *that* would make me nervous."

A sod truck is ahead of us, its flatbed stacked high with freshly cut squares of grass. The back draft from the load smells like wet fertilizer. Mom would have rocketed past the truck miles ago, but Dad hangs back, taking it easy.

I'm still trying to deal with the fact it's just me and him

cruising along on a sunny summer morning, listening to tunes, like we do this together all this time.

Like this is how I grew up.

Like he never went away.

"Why did Baxter come to Florida?" I ask.

"Same reason he was in Montana. To kill something."

"So he's a poacher."

"Not just an ordinary poacher, Billy. He doesn't do it for food, or to make money. He does it purely for his ego, some lame notion of glory."

"What was he hunting in the Tom Miner Basin?"

"He wanted a big grizzly. He didn't get one."

"Thanks to you, right? That's why there's a bullet hole in your fender."

My father shrugs. "Mr. Baxter wasn't a happy camper. Literally."

Not long ago the government removed the Yellowstone grizzly from its list of threatened species, claiming there are now enough bears that they don't need to be legally protected anymore. Dad says some western states will soon start selling licenses to hunt the grizzlies, like in the old days.

In other words, we saved an animal from extinction just so we could start killing it again. How messed up is that?

According to my father, a bunch of lawsuits have been filed in protest, trying to block the bear hunts. So, until the courts make a decision, it's still a crime in Montana to shoot a griz, except in self-defense.

A few rich outlaws do it anyway, paying big bucks for their sick thrills.

I ask Dad why he didn't call wildlife officers when Lincoln Baxter was stalking grizzlies at Tom Miner.

"They couldn't make a case against him until he actually killed a bear, and I didn't want a bear to get killed. So I dealt with Baxter my own way—wherever he went, I went there, too, like a shadow. Eventually he got mad and gave up."

"So now he comes all the way to Florida to shoot what?" I ask. Then it dawns on me. "Oh no, not one of *those*."

Dad's hands curl into fists on the steering wheel. "Like I said, he's a bad guy."

We stop at a fast-food joint outside of LaBelle and order cheeseburgers with fries. I'm drinking regular Coke, he's drinking Diet. I didn't get much sleep last night because I was worried we'd run out of stuff to talk about, living such far-apart lives, but it's just the opposite. Dad's got as many questions for me as I've got for him.

"How are your grades in school, Billy?"

"They're all right."

"Play any sports?"

"I don't fit well on teams."

"That's okay. Some people are joiners, some people aren't."

"Besides," I add, "we don't live anywhere long enough for me to get too involved with school."

"Or friends?"

"There's no point. Not when you know you'll be moving again in a year or two." I realize it sounds like complaining, so I tell Dad I'm not. "Belinda's the one who's totally over the eagle-nest thing. That's the only reason she got a boyfriend, to guilt Mom into staying here until she goes to college."

"What's the boyfriend like?"

"Hopeless," I say.

"Same thing's been said about me, I'm sure." Dad gets up to refill his soda. When he comes back to the table, I ask about the day he met Lil and Summer, on the Crow reservation.

"Did you crash your drone into their trailer on purpose?"

"You mean just so I could meet Lil?" he says. "I wish that were true, 'cause it would make a better story. But the reality is I'm not that clever. It was a windy afternoon, too windy for flying, and the quadcopter got away from me. Luckily, it fell where it did, and the rest is history."

"Why haven't you told Lil and Summer about your inheritance from Aunt Sophie?" I've never had a problem being blunt. "Why do you let them think you're some sort of government agent? Just because the lie is cooler than the truth?"

He rocks his chair back, more surprised than angry.

"Well, being a 'secret agent' definitely sounds cooler than being the lucky nephew of some rich old lady. But that's not why I haven't told Lil my real situation. See, she'd never,

ever let me go out tracking poachers the way I do. She'd say it was crazy dangerous."

"Would she be right?" I ask.

My father looks at his wristwatch. "We're losing time, Billy. Let's get back on the road."

Lincoln Baxter's got a room at the Lonesome Rooster Motel in Immokalee, about twenty-five miles away. How Dad happens to know the poacher's exact whereabouts is a mystery. He refuses to reveal the source of his "intel," which he claims is rock-solid. I notice he's driving faster now.

We pass a crested caracara perched on a telephone pole. It's the first one I've ever seen in the wild. They've got vivid orange faces and a bluish tip on their hooked beaks. Some people call them Mexican eagles. They're so fierce that a single bird can scare a whole flock of buzzards away from a road kill. Dad says caracaras are common in this part of Florida. I'd like to go back for a closer look, but we're in a major hurry.

Or so I thought.

I fall asleep for a while, but when I wake up we're not in the sleepy old farm town of Immokalee. We're in a parking lot at a busy airport.

"Fort Myers," my father says.

"Change of plans?"

"Wait here. I'll be right back."

Dad hops out and heads for the terminal building. He's wearing a gray T-shirt, faded jeans, thick-soled trail shoes, and a Patagonia cap. The black church suit made him look much older, and not nearly so fit.

I step out to stretch my legs. The phone chimes—another text from Mom. That makes seven today. I text her back: "All good. Call u later."

Now the phone starts ringing. I press the answer key without looking at the caller ID.

"Mom, please relax. Everything's just fine."

"Wrong Mom, Billy, but it's nice to hear your voice."

"Lil?"

"You guys at the airport yet?"

"Uh . . . we just got here. How'd you know?" I lean against the shot-up fender of Dad's Chevy. "Tell me what's going on."

"Promise you'll check in every day. Otherwise I'll be worried to death. I don't need to remind you that communication isn't your dad's strong suit."

"Yeah, sure, but—"

"This wasn't my idea, by the way."

"*What* wasn't your idea?"

"I'm fishing with clients on the river now. The cell signal might drop when we float through this canyon. . . ."

A big jet takes off with a roar, drowning Lil's words. By the time I can hear anything again, the phone line is dead.

I'm wondering how much she knows about the "camping" trip, and why Dad detoured to the Fort Myers airport.

Did he get a tip that Baxter's flight was landing this afternoon?

The heat rippling up from the pavement is brutal, and my shirt is soaked with sweat. I set out toward the terminal in search of Dennis Dickens. A refreshing rush of cool air hits me when I walk through the doors into the bustle of passengers waiting around the luggage carousels. Then somebody shouts:

"Yo! Billy Big Stick!"

And here comes Summer Chasing-Hawks, pulling a small plaid suitcase on rollers. My father trails a few steps behind, not looking overjoyed. When he sees me, he shrugs and raises his hands.

"Big surprise, right?" Summer chirps as she gives me a hug.

I pretend to be glad to see her, but the truth is I'm confused and not all that thrilled. It was supposed to be just me and Dad on this trip.

"She called late last night," he murmurs sideways to me. "I couldn't say no."

"Okay. Wow." I grab the handle of Summer's travel bag, and we all head for the exit.

"Faster, Billy," she says. "The clock's tickin'."

Once we're in the truck, she puts on a pair of hot-pink, heart-shaped sunglasses she bought at the Atlanta airport during a layover between flights. She says she wants to look like a true Florida tourist. I tell her she looks like a true Florida dork.

"Lighten up, Billy. The shades are a joke."

But she doesn't take them off, even after we stop at a barbecue joint. Dad and I aren't hungry but Summer says she's starving after a long day on airplanes. "Three crummy bags of pretzels is all I ate," she reports. The restaurant is crowded, so we keep the chatter light.

Back in the pickup, I'm riding shotgun and Summer's in the rear seat. She taps Dad on the shoulder, saying: "Billy Big Stick doesn't understand why I'm here. Should I fill him in?"

"Please do," says Dad.

Finally she whips off the goofy sunglasses. "I always wanted to see the Sunshine State, so I decided to take a page from your playbook, Billy. I borrowed my mom's Visa card and bought myself a plane ticket. She was mega–ticked off, but I told her Dennis said it was okay. He didn't really have a choice. Blackmail is a harsh word, but that's basically what I did."

My father doesn't flinch. He steers straight ahead, eyes fixed on the horizon.

"See, I know all about Aunt Sophie," Summer says. "A while back, when Dennis was away on one of his trips, a registered letter from a lawyer came to our house. It looked important, so I opened it. The very first sentence said Hubert the parrot was dead. I thought it was some kind of spy code. What a name for a bird!

"But it wasn't a coded message. The letter said that from

now on Dennis gets a hundred percent of all the payments from something called the Sophia Dickens Trust. So what I did, I called the lawyer's office in Nassau and pretended to be your dad's 'executive assistant.' We had a real interesting talk. Aunt Sophie left half her fortune to Hubert, and the other half to her only nephew. So when Hubert died and flew off to parrot heaven, his share of the inheritance went to you-know-who."

"Not that I needed more money," my father cuts in. "My aunt had been incredibly generous."

I don't say anything, because I've already figured out what happened next.

"When Dennis got home from his trip," Summer continues, "we took a walk to the river and I told him what I'd learned. I was pretty mad, 'cause I thought he'd made up the part about being a government agent just so he could sneak around on my mom. Then he told me he was actually spying on wild-animal poachers—which is super-ballsy but also semi-nuts. Mom would go ballistic if she knew, so I never said a word. But when I called Dennis last night and told him I was coming to Florida, he said no way, it's too risky. So I had to play hardball, Billy."

"Meaning you threatened to tell Lil the truth about Dad's drone trips?"

My stepsister's response is a half-mischievous smile. "Did I cross the line, brother?"

She's asking the wrong person.

"So, what does Lil think you're doing here?" I ask.

"Camping with you guys." She grins. "Experiencing the Sunshine State!"

Dad steps on the brakes. I expect him to turn around and snap at Summer, but that's not the reason he stopped. He points to a yellow sign posted on the shoulder of the road. It features the black silhouette of a large sleek cat.

"Panther," Dad says. "That's what Baxter came here to shoot."

Summer asks, "Aren't they the same thing as the mountain lions out west?"

"Different subspecies," I explain. "Ours are almost extinct."

"Which is why Baxter wants to kill one," my father adds, "before they're all gone."

Summer hisses, "What a jackass," or possibly a stronger word. "Okay, Dennis, tell us the secret-hero plan. You've got one, right?"

"Not yet," he sighs. "See, usually I work alone."

TWELVE

The Crow Indians have faced many fierce enemies, including the Blackfoot, Cheyenne, Lakota, and other competing tribes. If nobody had ever bothered them, the Crow might have stayed in Ohio, of all places, where they grew crops. Their descendants ended up on horseback in Wyoming and Montana, roaming the plains and river valleys in pursuit of the great buffalo herds.

Then the white men arrived and slaughtered almost all the buffalo. Many Crow died from smallpox, brought by the waves of strange settlers. Tribal leaders tried to maintain peace with the U.S. government, even as their lands were being taken away. Now, after more than a hundred and fifty years on a reservation, the tribe is struggling to save some of its sacred customs.

I got this from an online search about the Crow culture. That's also how I recognize the earrings that Summer Chasing-Hawks is wearing. They're made from fossil seashells. It's an ancient tribal craft.

She says, "They belonged to my great-grandmother. She lived to be ninety-nine years old. I guess that's a good thing."

I'm getting used to the idea of Summer joining the Everglades mission. She keeps the mood light, which is helpful.

We're staying at a motel called the Diamond Checkers.

The room has only two beds, so I laid out my sleeping bag on the floor. My father walked down to the Lonesome Rooster to see if the poacher's SUV was in the parking lot. It wasn't. Dad says Baxter drives a jet-black Range Rover with a joke bumper sticker that says TROPHY HUSBAND.

"How can you be sure he's here?" I ask.

"Reliable informant." Dad is stretched out on one of the beds. His eyes are closed. "There aren't many Range Rovers in this town. We'll find him."

"This is the same informant who helped you in Montana?"

"Correct," says Dad, rolling over to face the wall.

Summer and I turn off the lights, go outside, and sit on the tailgate of the pickup. The heat makes the damp air feel heavier. In the distant sky is a tower of violet clouds that will soon bloom into a thunderstorm. I hear the piping cries of an osprey, which means we're near water.

"I think I like Florida," Summer says.

"Wait till you see the concrete parts."

"You know what I can't get over? How totally flat it is."

"Makes it easy for the bulldozers," I say. "Tell me the real reason you decided to come on this trip. It wasn't just because you wanted to see a palm tree."

She shrugs one shoulder. "I was pretty sure Dennis would visit you and your mom and your sister while he was here."

"And you were afraid he wouldn't come back to Montana?"

"No!" Her brown eyes flare. "Not afraid—concerned is all. Just a little."

So I was right. "Summer, there's no way he'd ever leave you and Lil. You're his family now."

"So were you guys, once upon a time—and he left *you,* didn't he?"

"A lot's happened since then. Dad's changed."

I'm surprised to hear myself defending him. I hope I'm not wrong.

Summer smiles. "You got a girlfriend, Billy Big Stick?"

"Nope."

She slaps a mosquito on my arm, leaving a small smear of blood. "Aren't you going to ask if I've got a boyfriend?"

"I wasn't planning to."

"His name is Davey. He's a full-blooded Crow, and he's older than me. It's not like we're serious, or *doing* anything. All the girls like him, so I expect to be dumped. Maybe I'll dump him first. What do you think?"

I think I need to escape this conversation.

"I'm thirsty," I say, pointing to the 7-Eleven down the street. "You want something to drink?"

Summer gets the hint. "Sounds good."

Inside the store we seem to be the only ones speaking English. All the other customers are migrant farm workers, sun-beaten and sweaty. Their faces are dusty and their hands are worn from picking row crops all day. It's rough, hot work. Dad said the spring harvest is mostly over, but some fields still have new tomatoes and sweet corn.

Summer and I order blue-raspberry Slurpees. I ask her what kind of gun Dad carries on his surveillance trips.

"Twelve-gauge side by side," she replies.

"Good choice," I say, like I actually understand what she's talking about.

Outside the 7-Eleven we sit on the curb to finish our Slurpees. Three short-haired hounds are watching us from the front seat of a gray kennel truck, the same kind used by Animal Control, only this one has no lettering on the side. The driver's window is open halfway, so I walk across the parking lot to check out the dogs.

They look like triplets, lean and long-legged. The saddled patterns on their coats are practically identical—brown, black, and white. When I reach in to pet their snouts, they wiggle their butts and whine excitedly.

A man walking out of the store yells: "Don't touch them dogs!"

I step back from the truck.

"They'll bite your fingers off, boy."

I find that very hard to believe.

The man has a cigarette in his mouth and a bag of groceries in one arm. A six-pack of beer swings in his free hand. His eyes are hidden behind mirrored sunglasses. The pale hat on his head is a Stetson-style, though his rubber-soled boots are made for hiking, not horseback riding.

"What are their names?" I ask the man.

"Mandy, Candy, and Andy."

"Oh, come on."

"You best stand clear," he says, with zero trace of a smile.

The dogs quiet down the moment he gets in the truck. He speeds away without waving, or even a nod.

Summer walks up and says, "What's *his* problem?"

"He didn't want me petting those vicious hellhounds."

"I thought Texans were friendly."

"Anyone can buy a cowboy hat."

"I wasn't talkin' about the hat," she says. "I was talkin' about the license plate."

"What made you look?"

"It's a Montana thing. We always check out the tags on cars and trucks to see where the tourists are coming from. One July, I counted twenty-four different states, and even Guam. That's the only bad part about living in a beautiful place, right? The summer stampede."

"In Florida it's all year round," I say.

The dark clouds have arrived, and it's starting to sprinkle. We hear thunder breaking not far away.

Summer says, "You never told me what to do about Davey, my boyfriend."

Just when I thought I'd dodged this subject.

"Can he cast a fly rod?" I ask.

"I doubt it."

"Then you should definitely dump him."

She looks surprised. "Seriously, Billy?"

"No, *not* seriously. But that's what you get for asking someone like me about relationships."

Back at the motel, my father is sitting on the bed,

watching TV and waiting on a phone call from his informant. I tell him about the guy who owned the matching dogs with rhyming names.

"He was one grumpy-ass Texan," says Summer. "Last of the Marlboro men."

Dad bolts upright and swings his bare feet to the floor. "What'd he look like? How do you know where he's from?"

She explains about the license plate. "The dude was about the same height as you, only older and all leathery, like a legit cowboy."

"What about the dogs?" Dad asks. Now he's tying on his shoes. "Were they black and brown and white? Kinda skinny?"

"Yeah, with big ears," I say, "and a thin tail that curves upward."

"Walker hounds!" He points at my phone. "Google a picture of a Walker! See if it's the same breed."

Summer and I scroll through the photos online. There's no question it was the same kind of dog we saw in the Texan's kennel truck. Dad tucks in his shirt, snatches up his keys.

"One more thing," he says. "Those hounds—did they bark? This is important. Did you hear any barking?"

Summer and I both shake our heads.

"Damn," Dad grunts, and practically runs out the door. We're right on his heels.

Something else I picked up from the internet:

Lincoln Chumley Baxter IV was born thirty-two years

144

ago in San Francisco. He's the son of Lincoln Chumley Baxter III, the grandson of Lincoln Chumley Baxter II, and the great-grandson of Lincoln Chumley Baxter I. (If he ever has a boy of his own, Lincoln Chumley Baxter IV will undoubtedly name the poor kid Lincoln Chumley Baxter V.)

At least on paper, Baxter the poacher has a day job. He is listed as a "vice president" of the Royal Alcatraz Development Corp., which is owned by his father and two uncles. The company builds office towers and high-rise condos in Northern California.

Dad says Baxter the poacher has no regular contact with the family business. They basically pay him not to show up. The photograph on his LinkHead page is of a tanned man with a smug, wormy smile, a bent nose, and silly blond-tipped hair. He describes himself as a "prominent corporate executive, generous philanthropist, experienced pilot, 6.0 tennis player, and international sportsman."

It's the same profile that he posted on a site called BraveWhiteHunter.com, where Summer found his name next to a different photo: Baxter wearing a bush hat and a leather vest, cradling a rifle while posing on top of a dead Alaskan moose.

"Macho man," Summer snorts when she shows me the picture.

From the driver's seat Dad says, "Here's somebody else you need to google: Axel Burnside."

"Is that the Texan?" I ask.

"He spells it A-x-e-l."

The name pops up immediately: Axel Burnside of Waco, Texas. It's the same guy we saw outside the 7-Eleven. Wikipedia says he's a famous trainer of hunting dogs, and not just any old hunting dogs. He specializes in Walker hounds that track mountain lions and other wild cats. His reputation reaches all the way to Central and South America, where wealthy landowners hire him for jaguar hunts in the rain forests.

I had no idea they used dog packs. "Not exactly a fair fight, is it?"

"Duh" is Summer's response.

Dad says Walkers are fast, and they can run for miles. "They'll chase an animal until it's totally exhausted. All that's left for the hunter is to walk up, aim his gun, and—*bam!*—point-blank. That's the ball game."

"What's so special about Burnside's dogs?" I ask.

"He trains 'em not to bark, Billy. They track silently, so the cat doesn't hear 'em coming till it's too late. Once it goes up a tree, the dogs start howlin' like maniacs. That's how they let the hunter know where they're at."

Summer says, "So you think Baxter hired Burnside to help him find a panther."

"There's no other reason for Baxter and those dogs to be in the same town at the same time."

We drove all over searching for Burnside's truck. Now we're parked in a steady rain across the street from the Lonesome Rooster Motel, where Baxter is supposedly staying.

Dad's secret informant finally called up with a few details about tomorrow's hunt.

I'm reading what's been posted about Axel Burnside on the internet. It sounds like the man has all the legit business he can handle.

"Why risk everything for an outlaw job like this?" I say. "He could wind up in prison."

Dad thinks it's no mystery. "Baxter probably offered him so much money, he couldn't turn it down. Cash talks, and big cash talks even louder."

An hour passes with no sign of the poacher or the dog trainer. Dad's got the air-conditioning blasting and the radio tuned to a "deep rock" station. The music is fine with me, but Summer acts like she's being tortured. Finally she plugs in her earbuds and retreats to her own private playlist, disappearing behind those tacky three-dollar sunglasses.

Dad says Baxter doesn't use hounds when he's hunting grizzlies in Montana.

"He tried once. The dogs never came back, and he had to pay their owner twelve grand. So now he just leaves a dead deer in the meadows where the bears like to feed."

"Is that what happened at Tom Miner?"

"Yeah, and it almost worked," Dad says. "But some concerned citizen buzzed the bear with a drone, and it ran away before Baxter could take a shot. Turns out grizzlies aren't fond of low-flying objects."

Picturing that scene makes me grin. "I bet Baxter was mad."

"Extremely."

"So mad," Summer says, "he slashed the tires on the drone pilot's truck?"

"And put a bullet in the fender," I add.

My father smiles ruefully. I ask him if the bear he frightened off was a female with two cubs.

"How'd you know?"

"Because I saw her, too. At first I wasn't sure if she was real, but I am now."

Dad switches on the windshield wipers for a few flaps, to clear our view of the motel across the street. Fat raindrops thump the roof of the truck.

The song on the radio is called "Mr. Tambourine Man." I've heard it before, on one of Mom's stations. She likes to sing along with the music, no matter what's playing. It's sort of annoying, even though she has an okay voice.

You want to sing, my sister always tells her, *go to a karaoke bar.*

Mom knows all the Taylor Swift songs, so there are times when I've got to restrain myself from leaping out of the car window. I don't complain like Belinda, though, because if singing makes Mom happy, it's worth putting up with.

After observing my father all day, I can totally picture him and Mom getting together when they were young. Both of them are free spirits—by that, I mean they sail with no anchor—but they care about the same sorts of things. Mom's got her eagles, Dad's got his bears and panthers. Their hearts are on the same page.

Not that I wish they were still married, because I can also see why it didn't work. My father was the one who packed up and left, but my mother's just as restless in her own way. Maybe one day she'll find someone who can steady her the way Lil steadies Dad.

I've been waiting for a quiet moment to ask what happened to his parents, so I do.

"Car accident," he says. His voice is a raw whisper.

"How come you never talked to Mom about it?"

"Back then I never talked to anyone about it. I should have, but I didn't." He turns to check on Summer in the back seat. She's got her eyes shut, rocking out to her tunes.

"There was a turtle in the road," he says.

"A what?"

"The woman driving behind them said they swerved to miss a turtle in the road. This was at, like, seventy miles an hour on the turnpike. My father lost control and the car veered into a canal."

The sadness on his face is crushing. All I can say is, "Dad, that's terrible. I'm really, really sorry."

"A turtle! It was even in the police report."

He's not crying, but that's what I feel like doing.

"Your grandpa and grandma—what a pair of characters they were, Billy. I wish you could've known 'em."

"Me too." It comes out as a dry squeak. I feel like a monster for bringing up such a painful subject.

Dad reaches over and pats my arm. "It's all right, son. I think about them every day. I *need* to. You understand?"

A nod is all I've got left.

What saves me from turning into a total bawling mess is the sight of a jet-black Range Rover, screeching into the parking lot of the Lonesome Rooster. Trailing close behind is the gray kennel truck.

My father straightens in his seat and flicks on the windshield wipers again.

A bent-nosed man who can only be Lincoln Chumley Baxter IV steps out of the Range Rover wearing full storm-weather camo gear and mouthing a fat brown cigar. Axel Burnside emerges from the kennel truck shielding his cowboy hat with a folded newspaper.

In the beating rainstorm, the dog trainer and the poacher stand toe to toe. The conversation doesn't look warm and friendly. My father has a trace of a smile as he studies the unhappy pair. Summer sits forward to watch.

"What do you think they're arguing about?" I ask Dad.

"I've got no idea," he says, "but it's a glorious way to get this party started."

THIRTEEN

Nobody knows the exact number of panthers that are left in Florida, but biologists say it's less than three hundred. The surviving cats are skittish and solitary animals that try to stay away from humans, which isn't easy in a state where more than a thousand new humans arrive every single day.

A few years ago, scientists imported some Texas cougars to mate with the remaining panthers in the hope their kittens would grow up stronger and tougher. The problem is they've basically run out of territory to roam. Most of the old scrub woods and prairies are now concrete—subdivisions and strip malls—while the last of the wide-open spaces are crosshatched by highways. Lots of young panthers get killed by cars.

Yet, despite the constant crush of civilization, the animals are rarely seen. They travel after dark across farms and cattle ranches to hunt wild hogs, deer, or, occasionally, calves. While some landowners don't mind the big cats hanging around, others feel just the opposite. Dad suspects an unsympathetic rancher complained to somebody about a visiting panther. That person then tipped off Lincoln Chumley Baxter IV, who reached out to Axel Burnside and his legendary barkless hounds.

The argument between the poacher and the dog man

outside the Lonesome Rooster had ended with each man stomping through the puddles to a different room.

"I bet they were fighting about money," Summer said as she climbed into bed.

Dad was doubtful. "Baxter's so rich he can afford to double or triple whatever Burnside charges for a hunt."

"Then what else could it be?" I ask.

"Let's get some rest." He turned off the lights and tugged the blanket up to his chin.

By midnight he and Summer were snoring like walruses. I was still awake on the floor, trading texts with my mother, who wanted to know why we were "camping" at a roadside motel. I told her it was too rainy to pitch a tent.

She said Belinda might split up with Dawson, not exactly heartbreaking news. It would save me the trouble of telling my sister that the blockhead she was dating tried to take out the neighbor's cat with a slingshot. Mom said another boy from school had asked Belinda for a date, and she was deciding whether or not to "like" him. He was an AP student heading for Yale. I said anybody with an IQ higher than a doorknob's would be an improvement over Dawson.

Afterward, I dimmed the phone, tucked it under my pillow, and closed my eyes. At three in the morning Dad's alarm chimed, rousing me from an awful dream: I was trapped inside a car that was sinking in a lake. Turtles with glowing yellow eyes were swimming all around, peering through the windshield.

Now I'm fumbling around, trying to roll up my sleeping bag. I can't seem to line up the corners.

"We'll stop for coffee," my father says.

Summer looks as groggy as I am, but Dad's totally wired and ready to go. He says we need to be hiding "on location" before Baxter and Burnside arrive with the hounds. Last night at dinner he'd ordered three medium-rare hamburgers to go. His plan is to use the drone to air-drop the meat patties, distracting the dogs from the panther's scent. The odds of this plan succeeding are about one in a trillion, based on what I've read about Walker hounds. Once they catch an animal's scent, nothing short of an earthquake can break their concentration.

Dad insists it's worth a try. The bag of burgers goes in the red pickup with the rest of our gear, including the quadcopter, which I still don't know how to fly. Because of all the rain, I never got my pilot lesson.

The damp streets are empty, and the traffic signals are blinking yellow. We're the only customers at the 7-Eleven. Dad and Summer beeline for the coffee machine while I grab a bottle of tea. It's so cold inside the store that the front window is fogged. The clerk is actually wearing a ski sweater.

"How far is the place we're going?" I ask my father.

"Nine point four miles. When we get there, we might have a gate issue."

"I can pick a lock," Summer volunteers. When I give her a look, she says, "What—you don't believe me?"

Dad buys a box of cinnamon rolls, and we all agree not to peek at the expiration date. That's how hungry we are.

The door of the 7-Eleven opens with an electronic *cheep*, and in walks Axel Burnside. He doesn't seem to recognize me, probably because today I'm wearing a hoodie. Standing at the register, he asks the clerk for a carton of cigarettes. Dad, Summer, and I slip outside to the parking lot, where we can hear the dogs scrabbling inside the vented aluminum kennels on Burnside's truck.

"Let's get outta here," Dad says, and we scramble into his pickup.

Summer buckles up quickly. Not me.

Sometimes an idea pops into my head, the opposite of common sense, but I just can't let it be. The moment my father turns the ignition key, I hear myself blurting, "Hold on, I forgot something."

"No, Billy, don't go back in there—"

Too late. I'm fairly sure Dad won't follow me, because he can't afford to let Burnside see his face. He needs to stay undercover.

Inside the 7-Eleven, the dog man taps a scarred, deformed finger on the counter while the store clerk reloads the coffee machine. I pull down my hoodie and say, "Hey, remember me? How's Candy, Andy, and Mandy?"

His response is a granite stare, although he looked meaner yesterday behind those mirrored sunglasses. His eyes are light green and not particularly badass.

"Why aren't you home in bed at this hour, boy?" he asks.

"I'm here to do you a favor."

He laughs gruffly, showing a top row of stained teeth. "*You* gonna do *me* a favor? Such as what?"

"Such as keeping your butt out of jail," I say.

The clerk glances up from the coffee machine. Burnside grabs my arm and steers me to the rear of the store, the aisle with all the chips and dips.

"Take it easy," I say. "They've got security cameras everywhere."

He releases my arm. "Talk, boy."

My hands are a little shaky, so I shove them in my pockets.

"I know who you are and why you're here," I tell him. "This isn't Texas, okay? And you're not hunting regular mountain lions. Did you even bother to look up the law on endangered species? 'Cause if you get caught with a dead Florida panther, they'll put you in handcuffs—and confiscate those expensive hounds for evidence."

I'm not certain if that last part is true, but I'm definitely making Axel Burnside uncomfortable, which is the whole point.

"Just who are you, boy?"

"I'm nobody."

The clerk calls out: "Dude, your coffee's gettin' cold."

"Let's you and me go out front," says the dog man.

"They got cameras there, too."

"I'm aware of that."

I go outside to wait while Axel Burnside pays for his

coffee. My father looks like he's ready to vault out of the pickup and charge across the parking lot, but I give him a low wave that says: *Relax, I got this.* He and Summer slide low in their seats so they won't be seen.

The first thing Burnside does when he leaves the store is fire up a cigarette. He blows the smoke over one shoulder, props an elbow on the kennel truck, and orders the excited dogs inside to settle down.

"Personally, I don't see much sport in what you do," I say, "but you've got a reputation in the big-game world as a straight operator."

"And you know that how?"

I hold up my cell phone. "By reading everything I could find about you. Blogs, newspaper stories, magazine articles. They say you're such a big deal, there's a waiting list of people who want to go hunting with you and those dogs. But, see, I wonder what would happen to your business if you went out and killed an animal on the endangered list."

The dog man studies his coffee. "You mean, what would happen if word got out?"

"Oh, word would get out," I say. "Count on that."

His pale gaze narrows. "You got some guts, boy."

"Mr. Burnside, I've never laid eyes on a wild Florida panther but I would like to, someday. So I've got a big problem with what you're doing."

He sets the coffee cup on the fender of the truck, pulls a scuffed leather wallet out of his jacket, and hands it to me. "Count the cash in there. Go on."

"But I don't want any money! That's not why I'm here."

"Just count it up, boy."

Three twenties, two tens, and a one-dollar bill.

"Eighty-one bucks," I say, placing the bills back in the wallet, and the wallet back in his hand.

"Know how much I had on me yesterday? Twenty *thousand* and eighty-one dollars. Are you listenin'?" Burnside takes a sneering drag off the cigarette. "Rich fella from California, he calls up and says he and his college fraternity brothers are doin' a big coon hunt. They're all makin' bets on first and biggest, and he wants *me* to be his personal guide. When I tell him my usual fee, which ain't cheap, he says, 'No problem, pardner.' So I drive my three Walkers all the way from San Antonio, and when I get here, he drops this fat stack of cash on the table. I count it all out and say, 'Mister, this is way too much. Nobody in their right mind would ever pay that kinda money to track a damn raccoon.' And he says, 'That's not what we're gonna hunt.' Then, when he tells me what it is he really wants to shoot, well, I can't repeat the words that came outta my mouth. This was at a Cracker Barrel, too."

"We saw you guys arguing outside the motel."

"Yeah, that was shortly after," Burnside says.

"After what?"

"After I threw the man's cash in his face." He picks up his coffee and opens the truck door. "I got a long drive home," he says.

"I'm sorry, Mr. Burnside. I didn't know—"

"Whatever you might think of me, boy, I don't break the law."

I ask about the scar on his twisted finger.

"Snakebite. It was either me or Andy, so I took the hit. He's dumber than the other two dogs put together, comes to rattlers."

"Diamondback?"

"A six-footer, thick as my arm. You know your snakes, huh?"

"Can I ask one more thing, Mr. Burnside?"

"Make it quick."

"How do you train those hounds not to bark?"

"Trade secret," he answers with a raspy chuckle. "Love, patience, and lots of bacon treats."

Sometimes you can be dead wrong about a person. Once the embarrassment of your mistake passes, it's actually a good feeling—being surprised in a positive way by human behavior. Not everyone lives by a code of honor, but the dog man does. He said no to a *major* pile of money.

I wait until the kennel truck's taillights are out of sight before running to my father's pickup. When I tell Dad what Axel Burnside said, he gives a joyful whoop and says, "The hunt's off! Let's hit the road!"

Summer starts rocking out, doing jazz hands in the back seat. I grab the dog-bait hamburgers Dad bought last night, dash back into the 7-Eleven, and motor straight for the microwave.

That's our breakfast, and those day-old burgers taste fantastic. The cinnamon buns we're saving for later.

The town of Immokalee is in the rearview mirror when Dad's phone starts ringing. He presses the answer button and crows: "I've got some amazing news!"

Pause.

"What? Say that again."

Another pause, heavier than the first.

"Are you serious? But *how?*"

Dad pulls his foot off the gas pedal.

"Tell me where he is!" he shouts at the phone.

Now he's turning the truck in a steep one-eighty, tires yelping on the pavement. I spin around to look at Summer, who offers a bleak shake of her head.

Dad tosses the phone in my lap and slams the heel of his fist against the dashboard.

"Was that your informant?" Summer asks.

"Correct."

"So what's wrong, Dennis?"

"The panther hunt is still on. That's what's wrong." His tone is oddly flat, showing no trace of the anger he must be feeling.

It can't be easy facing the fact you've got a fool for a son.

I tell him how sorry I am. "The dog man lied to me! He said he was driving straight back to Texas. He stood there lying to my face, and I believed every stupid word."

"Burnside wasn't lying. He's gone," Dad says, still with

that dull metal voice. "Lincoln Baxter's doing the hunt all by himself. He's on his way to the ranch right now."

The speedometer says sixty-six, which is twenty-one miles per hour over the speed limit. Getting stopped by police is the last thing we need, but there's not much I could say that would make my father slow down.

Summer asks how Baxter can find a panther if he's not using the hunting dogs.

Dad says: "Same way he does it with grizzlies, I guess."

"Except big cats don't show themselves the way bears do."

"If they're hungry enough, they might."

Summer sniffs. "I predict he won't even get a shot!"

"Can we take that chance? No."

My father ends the discussion by cranking up the radio. After a few miles he relaxes his death grip on the steering wheel, and the speedometer needle begins to drop. When it hits forty-five, I turn down the music. Dad doesn't object.

"Don't you think it's weird," I ask, "that your informant— whoever he is—would know exactly what the poacher's doing at four in the morning?"

"I wouldn't say that's weird."

"Then he must be tailing him, like we are."

"No, Billy, my informant is *not* sneaking around, following Lincoln Baxter."

"Then how does he know so much?" Summer demands.

"Because my informant isn't a he," says Dad. "She's a she."

Now I get the picture. It's a love story gone wrong.

FOURTEEN

I've never had an official girlfriend. There were friends who happened to be girls, but we never got to "relationship" status.

The one I liked most, I guess, was Anna Lee. This was when we lived in Key Largo. She was a star volleyball player, even though she stood barely five feet tall. I forget where we met, or how the subject of unusual hobbies came up. But on the afternoons she didn't have volleyball practice, we'd ride our bikes up County Road 905 to hunt for snakes. We were scouting old junk piles, which are major reptile magnets because of all the mice and rats.

Anna Lee had no fear. I'd flip over a board or a scrap of sheet metal, and she'd grab anything she saw—even black racers and coachwhips, which bite like maniacs. I've never met any person with faster moves than Anna Lee. She wouldn't wear gloves, either, even in the upland hammocks, where scorpions were an issue. Poisonous centipedes, too. Anna Lee wasn't scared of anything.

I wish I could remember her last name. Goldman, Goldstein, Goulding? I could probably find her somewhere online, but then what?

Exactly. She's there, and I'm . . . wherever.

Lincoln Chumley Baxter IV married a girlfriend of his

named Daisy Marlowe. The ceremony took place at one of the many Baxter family estates. Daisy loved the outdoors, though not for the same reasons as Lincoln. He bought her a fancy Italian shotgun and she got pretty good at blasting clay pigeons out of the air, but she had no desire to shoot real birds or anything else that was alive.

Daisy Marlowe Baxter wasn't aware her husband was a big-game poacher until my father told her. Then she became his secret informant.

According to Dad, their one and only meeting took place after he followed her to a fancy "spa and wellness resort" in a place called Monterey. Daisy Baxter was lying on a massage table under a tall white tent overlooking the Pacific Ocean. Her face, arms, and legs were plastered with green "healing" clay that smelled suspiciously like Play-Doh, and her eyes were covered with slices of cucumber.

That's the reason she didn't see my father scaling the wall of the resort. She was startled to hear a strange voice saying: "Mrs. Baxter, there's something you ought to know about Lincoln, something that might test your affections."

A security guard tried to hustle Dad off the property, but Daisy Baxter sat up, flicked the cucumbers off her eyelids, and said she wanted to hear what this odd, soft-spoken trespasser had to say.

Dad recalled being uneasy because Mrs. Baxter wore only a towel. He politely aimed his gaze elsewhere while he explained that a hunter friend of his had been approached by Lincoln Baxter about guiding him to a Yellowstone grizzly bear.

Daisy Baxter became very upset. "I suspected Linc was up to something shady, but I had no idea it was this bad! How can I help?"

"Convince him to stop. Tell him how wrong it is, and not just because it's illegal. He'll listen to you."

"Are you kidding?" Mrs. Baxter replied. "He'll look me dead in the eye and claim he doesn't know what I'm talking about. I've questioned him before about these 'special' hunts, and he swears they're legit. Except he never posts any pictures, which is strange."

That's my father's memory of the first conversation with his "informant." It might not be word for word, but it's probably pretty close.

The bottom line is that Daisy Baxter agreed to contact Dad whenever Lincoln went on one of his suspicious trips. She checks in often with her husband—like she did a few minutes ago—and the next call she makes is to my father. She even bought an app called *Spouse-Finder*, which can locate Baxter within a radius of two hundred yards, using the GPS signal in his phone.

In exchange for her supplying all that key information, Dad made one promise to Daisy: he would never personally do anything to harm her husband.

"Does that include getting him tossed in jail?" Summer asks.

"Oh, Mrs. Baxter's got no problem with that," Dad says. "She thinks the experience might straighten him out, though I doubt it. He's got plenty of money for bail and slick lawyers."

We're approaching the ranch on a long unpaved road. Dad's no longer in touch with Mrs. Baxter because the cell service quit, but a fresh set of tire tracks is visible on the packed gravel ahead. Dad switches off the headlights so nobody will see us coming. He drives extra slowly, watching for stray cattle—and a black Range Rover.

A bank of wispy fog makes it feel like we're bouncing through the clouds. Summer and I are wide awake now.

"What would happen," I ask my father, "if Baxter found out his wife was secretly helping you monkey-wrench these hunts? Would he hurt her?"

"She's got a black belt, Billy. We're talkin' tae kwon do. Daisy Baxter's not afraid of Lincoln."

"Would he leave her if he knew the truth?"

"A better question," Summer pipes from the back seat, "is why *she* doesn't leave *him?*"

Dad says he's obviously no expert on marriage. "Some are more complicated than others. That's one of the few things I know for sure."

The gate to the ranch property is made of wire fencing and aluminum crossbars. A NO TRESPASSING sign is screwed to one of the wood posts, and a NO HUNTING sign is nailed to the other.

We could easily climb over, but Dad doesn't want to

leave his truck parked on the dirt road, where ranch workers would notice it. They'd call a towing company and then come looking for us.

Hanging from the gate latch is a heavy-duty brass padlock. Summer tries to pick it open with a bent paper clip. The lock won't surrender, and I can hear her cussing under her breath.

"My turn," Dad says impatiently, pulling out a pair of bolt cutters.

After he steers the truck through the entrance, I shut the gate behind us and hang the broken lock back on the latch. A few miles down the ranch road, we finally nose out of the fog. Dad coaxes the pickup into a thick stand of palmettos, the fronds screaking against the paint.

He turns off the engine, and we sit to listen. The mockingbirds are waking, and cows bray in the distance. A soft violet glow in the sky means the sun will be rising soon. Hungry mosquitoes pour into the cab of the truck.

"Vicious little vampires," my father growls.

We jump out and spray each other's clothes with bug juice. Summer and I sort the hiking gear while Dad prepares the spy quadcopter—he wants it airborne at daybreak.

Lincoln Chumley Baxter IV is nearby, stalking a panther.

"I wonder where," Summer says.

The answer comes with the crack of a gunshot echoing across the misty scrub.

My father looks up from the drone and says, "Oh no."

* * *

One time, before Belinda or I was born, Dad surprised Mom with a trip to see wild flamingos, her second-favorite bird on the planet. They drove through Everglades National Park to a place actually called Flamingo, on the shore of Florida Bay. In a rented boat they went searching for a famous flock that lived near the tidal flats, not far from the ranger station.

But that day the flamingos weren't there, not even one. My mother took lots of cool pictures of blue herons, white pelicans, cormorants, and even a pair of roseate spoonbills. She had a fantastic trip, but Dad was bummed because he couldn't find the only birds he'd promised to show her.

A few years later, waiting at a dentist's office, he saw a magazine article about a place in the Bahamas where flamingos can be found any time of the year, guaranteed. Right away he started planning another expedition.

Mom pointed out that they now had two small children, and that an island vacation wasn't cheap. Dad said no problem, and charged the plane tickets to their credit card. Then he took Belinda and me to the courthouse to get U.S. passports, which we used exactly once—for that Bahamas trip.

I'd like to say I remember it, but maybe looking through Mom's photo album makes me *think* I remember. After all, I was only two and a half.

Even so, I carry in my mind a crystal vision of those flamingos—rows and rows of them wading with slow jointed strides across the shallows. With bowed heads, they stir their down-curved bills through the clear water, sifting for tiny brine shrimp and baby crabs.

As our motorboat approaches, the birds all stop feeding and turn toward the sound of the engine. One starts to flap away and more follow, rising in soft puffs of color—some have blood-orange feathers, some are hot pink, and the younger ones look pale, almost milky. The front edges of their wings are as black as asphalt, matching the tips of their bills.

The flamingos rise in clusters before melting together into a single V-shaped squadron. They aren't exactly sleek. Their heads seem too heavy for those long thin necks, and their legs dangle behind them like loose ropes. Yet flying as a single wave, they make an unforgettable sight, a swipe of creamy rose paint on a bright blue canvas.

I see my mother in the bow of the boat, aiming her camera at the soaring birds. My father sits beside her, his hands steadying her shoulders. There's no picture in Mom's photo album of the two of them like that, but I swear I remember the moment. Belinda won't admit she remembers, too. She'll say only that after Dad set me on her lap, I kept waving and waving at the flamingos until they disappeared beyond the mangroves.

Sometimes, when the memory of that morning gets hazy, I take out my passport just to look at the ink stamp that says "Bahamas Immigration." The passport is expired now, but I'll probably hang on to it. Belinda says that island trip was the last real family thing we did together. Mom never figured out how my father paid off the credit-card bill, but my guess is Aunt Sophie helped.

What made me think about the wild flamingos is the red-topped sandhill crane that's studying us now as we creep through the Everglades scrub. Sandhills are my mother's third-favorite bird. Like bald eagles and flamingos, they usually choose a mate for life. This one is out walking all by itself.

Summer whispers, "We've got sandhills in Montana, too."

It's weird to see a girl carrying a shotgun, but then again I've never seen *anybody* carrying a shotgun. Dad assures me that Summer knows how to shoot.

"And it's got nothing to do with being a Crow," she adds, throwing me a sharp look. "The key is good eyes and steady hands."

"I'll take your word for it," I say.

Guns make me nervous. So do gunshots. When most people hear one, the natural impulse is to go the other way. We're doing just the opposite, sneaking toward the shooter as quickly as we can. The unspoken fear is that we're too late, that the shot we heard was Lincoln Chumley Baxter IV killing one of the last panthers in Florida.

My father is carrying the quadcopter. I've got the hatchet, bug spray, binoculars, water bottles, and a few protein bars that we dug out of the console in the truck.

The lonesome sandhill crane croaks loudly as we trudge past. Normally I'd stop and text a photo to Mom, but we're in a major hurry.

Summer and I are still eagerly waiting to hear Dad's master plan.

"It's flexible," he tells us.

"So it's not really a plan," I say. "It's more of a floating concept."

"Keep your voice down, Billy."

We're following a game trail so narrow that we're forced to move single file. Summer goes first because she's the one with the gun. When Dad asks her if the safety switch is on, she sighs: "Of course. *Duh*."

We're all jittery, breathing fast. When a spooked rabbit darts between Dad and me, I jump like two feet in the air.

Finally we enter a small clearing, and Dad motions for me to pass him the binoculars.

"You see something?"

"Stay low, please. Both of you."

Summer and I drop to the ground. My father raises the binoculars and clearly dials in on something.

"What is it?" Summer asks.

"Baxter's Range Rover. He tried to cover it with palmetto branches, but I see the sun glinting off the chrome grille."

"But do you see *him*?" I ask.

"Not yet."

"So it's drone time."

"Correct." Dad hands me the binoculars. "You're kneeling in an ant pile, son."

There's nothing like firebolts of pain to take a person's

mind off a sketchy situation. These particular ants—the nasty red variety—have scaled my hiking shoes and sneaked under the cuffs of the pants I foolishly thought would protect me. Now the little ghouls are biting my legs. I roll on the ground kicking and clawing at myself, trying not to yell. Summer has intelligently scooted out of the way. By the time I finish neutralizing the nibbling insects, the quadcopter is in the air.

You're probably thinking: *What kind of father would take two kids into a wilderness to chase down a heavily armed poacher?*

Don't forget—this wasn't Dad's idea. Summer and I each asked to go with him, and we made it difficult for him to say no. We've both got a secret he wants us to keep.

The drone is circling high above the Range Rover. We see what the aircraft's camera sees. The live image is displayed on Dad's smart phone, clipped to the remote-control box.

When the poacher eventually comes into view, he's a speck in the swamp. Dad lowers the quadcopter for a closer view.

Lincoln Chumley Baxter IV is garbed all in camo, no surprise. He moves through the glades like someone who's not supposed to be there, carrying a long black object that can only be a rifle. A large, limp animal is slung around his neck. The animal's fur is tan.

My stomach twists into a hot knot as I think about the gunshot we heard.

"He did it!" I blurt angrily. "We're too late, Dad."

"No, son, we're not."

"What are you talking about? Just look!"

"That's not a panther he killed," says Summer. "It's a deer."

Suddenly the poacher crouches and looks upward, as if he hears something. Dad toggles the quadcopter's controls, sending it higher and eastward, where it can't be seen by a person squinting into the glare of a rising sun.

Once again Baxter appears bug-sized on the video. However, he has resumed moving, apparently satisfied that he's alone on the hunt.

"So he shot the deer for bait," I say to Dad.

"Without Burnside's dogs, that's all he can do."

"How do we stop him?" Summer asks. "It's time to make, like, a real plan."

"If the panther shows up, we buzz him with the drone and spook him off before Baxter can take a shot," Dad says, "just like I did with the grizzly at Tom Miner."

Summer is skeptical. "But we could be waiting on that cat for hours. What happens when the drone's batteries run out?"

I thought of the same thing, but my father reacts like it's a silly question. "Ever heard of a power pack? I brought four of 'em. No, *five*."

"Hey, Dad," I say.

"What?"

"Where's the bad guy?"

"Uh-oh."

The three of us are hunched shoulder to shoulder over

the remote-control unit. Lincoln Baxter is no longer visible on the quadcopter's camera feed.

"Where'd he go? What happened?" Summer says with a groan.

Dad looks slightly sick to his stomach. "He didn't go anywhere. It's the drone that's moving away."

"All by itself?"

"They do this sometimes," he mumbles, frantically working the joysticks.

"Do *what* sometimes?" I ask.

"It's called a 'flyaway.' They just, you know . . . fly away."

Summer and I glance at each other wondering the same thing: *How far away is "away"?*

The remote begins beeping rapidly, probably not a good sign. Summer asks Dad if the drone will return on its own.

"It's not a dog," he says.

"So, how are we going to find it?"

"Don't worry, there's a built-in GPS tracker."

"I hope it works underwater," I say.

The quadcopter is plummeting toward what is obviously a pond. The brown and black objects we see dotting the shoreline are thirsty cows.

Desperately my father claws at the control levers, which has no effect. Summer and I watch helplessly as the aircraft's video shows the shimmering body of water looming larger by the second. The queasy descent ends with a splash—then Dad's phone beeps faintly and goes black.

He sets down the remote. The flight is over.

"If a drone hits the water," he explains gloomily, "it's dead as a doornail. The electronics drown instantly."

Summer lowers her head. "So we're done? Just like that?"

Having lost our eye in the sky, it will be almost impossible to spy on the poacher without drawing his attention—and possibly a warning shot.

"We should probably get out of here," I tell Dad.

"Hold on, Billy, I've got a Plan B."

"It can't be great," Summer grumbles.

And it's not great. In fact, it's more like a Plan B-minus.

But we take a vote. None of us is ready to give up the mission.

FIFTEEN

I don't know who called the sheriff.

Maybe nobody did. Maybe the deputy was being truthful when he told us he was on routine patrol and heard all the racket.

Like I said, it wasn't a great plan to begin with. Make lots of noise, basically—enough to scare the panther. The cats are frightened of people, and they'll bolt from any sign of human activity. And we all wanted that one to run away.

It was a big tawny male. Summer was the first to notice the tracks, but I was the one who spotted the animal moving in the direction of the poacher.

Who, Dad whispered, was likely perched in a tree overlooking the carcass of the deer he'd shot earlier.

Laying eyes on the panther was lucky, unexpected—and unreal. At first I thought that it must be a mirage, that subconsciously I'd made myself imagine it. It was the same feeling I got after seeing the grizzly in Montana.

But, just like the bear, the panther was no illusion. Dad and Summer caught a glimpse, too. With swift taut strides it crossed a clearing, its ropey black-tipped tail seeming longer than the cat itself.

That would have been an ideal time to launch the drone,

except the drone was at the bottom of a cattle pond. That's why we needed another way to scare the panther, meaning Plan B-minus.

Dad was firing his gun into the air, Summer was beating a heavy stick on the trunk of a dead pine, and I was honking the horn of the Range Rover that Lincoln Chumley Baxter IV had neglected to lock. The keys were in the ignition and a smelly half-smoked cigar sat in the cup holder. On the passenger seat was a yellow scrap of paper. A name and phone number had been written on it.

The instant Dad started shooting, I mashed both hands on the horn and held it down. It was loud. So was the gun. So was Summer's tree-whacking.

The woods got very noisy, very fast. Every living creature within a mile probably heard the ruckus. The panther, which was much closer than a mile, undoubtedly ran away. Fear will cause even the hungriest wild animal to lose its appetite.

My father had brought a dozen shotgun shells. They didn't last long. As soon as he finished firing, we sprinted to his truck and made a teeth-rattling race for the ranch gate.

Which was blocked by a police car.

The sheriff's deputy stood there twirling the broken padlock on his finger.

"You're trespassing," he said, "with a firearm."

My father told him about the poacher who was stalking a panther.

"He killed a deer, too, and they're out of season. The man's name is Lincoln Baxter and he drives a black Range Rover. I can show you where he is!"

The deputy said, "Deer hunters use rifles. What I heard was a shotgun."

My father pointed to his, in the bed of the truck. "It's right there, Officer."

"Sir, what were you shooting at?"

"Nothing," I interrupted. "He was firing in the air."

"To spook the cat," Summer added.

The deputy checked Dad's gun to make sure it was empty. After writing down our names and dates of birth, he told us to get back in the pickup.

An hour later, we're still here. The deputy took my father's keys to prevent him from driving off, which I'm pretty sure he wouldn't have done. But with no car keys, we can't turn on the engine, which means no air-conditioning. It's too hot outside to roll up the windows, so the mosquitoes are enjoying a hearty breakfast of human blood. Ours.

"Sorry, guys," Dad says.

Summer asks if we're going to jail.

"Not you two," he replies. "Me? Possibly."

The deputy is on his phone. Soon a jacked-up swamp truck with humongous mud tires appears. The driver is a chunky young man with red hair and a red mustache. He wears a trucker cap, worn jeans, and dirty boots. The deputy brings him over to have a look at us.

"This fella works on the ranch," the deputy says to Dad. "Tell him what you told me."

My father repeats the account of the poacher and the panther.

The ranch hand responds with a blank expression. "I just come from down that way and didn't see nobody. No non-authorized vehicles, neither."

"I know exactly where the hunter is. I can take you," Dad insists.

"Ain't nobody else out there," the ranch hand says flatly. He turns to the deputy. "The boss man wants these jokers off the property."

"Does he intend to press charges?"

"Not unless they went and kilt somethin'."

"Well, they killed his padlock." The deputy shows the battered remains to the ranch hand.

My father flips open his wallet. "Will fifty bucks take care of that?"

"Make it a hunnert," says the ranch hand, "to cover my time and unconvenience."

Not actually a real word. I keep my mouth shut as Dad gives the man two fifty-dollar bills.

Summer is boiling. "Rip-off," she fake-coughs under her breath.

I lean out the truck window and say, "Hey, are you Rusty?"

The ranch hand whirls in surprise. "Who tole you that, kid?"

"I got your name from the same man you say isn't out here hunting panthers."

Rusty's cheeks turn almost as red as his hair. He stomps back to his four-wheeler and roars away.

"I'm not sure what's going on," the deputy says to us, "but the smartest thing you folks can do is follow me out of here."

Dad says, "Ready when you are, Officer."

The cinnamon buns were stale and gummy. We were too hungry to care.

"How'd you know that man's name?" my father asks.

"It was on a piece of paper in Baxter's SUV. Soon as the guy rolled up, I figured it had to be him. With that hair, right?"

Summer says, "So, rude Mr. Ranch Hand was in on the whole thing."

My father is sure that was Baxter's inside connection. "The ranch owner probably doesn't know anything about this. That's why Rusty didn't want the deputy to press charges. He couldn't risk us telling a judge what we saw. If it got out that he was in business with a poacher, he'd get fired in two seconds."

Dad says there's a web network of outlaw hunters who travel the world stalking rare and endangered species. They put out the word that they're willing to pay big bucks to shoot certain animals—a grizzly in Montana, for example, or a black rhinoceros in South Africa—and usually somebody's greedy enough to make the arrangements.

Rusty probably heard through the grapevine that some rich dude was looking to bag a Florida panther. The ranch hand figured it would be an easy side hustle, a quick way to pocket some cash.

"He was seriously freaked that Billy knew his name," says Summer.

"Another glorious moment," Dad chuckles, flicking a cinnamon crumb from his chin. "I bet poor Rusty had to go change his underwear."

All that really matters is that Lincoln Chumley Baxter IV never got a chance to kill that cat. By now the panther is probably all the way to Glades County, and still running hard. Baxter must be spooked, too, knowing he was followed to the ranch.

Even though our mission went the opposite of smooth, it turned out okay. The only casualty was the drowned drone.

"And blisters," says Summer, holding up her palms. She'd whaled on that dead pine tree with all her might.

Too bad we couldn't see Lincoln Baxter's reaction when all the banging, honking, and gunfire started. No doubt he phoned Rusty in a panic. It turned into a real bad day for both of them.

As instructed, we follow the deputy's car back to Immokalee, where he leaves us at a service station. Dad walks away from the gas pumps to make a phone call—probably to Baxter's wife.

Summer and I use the break to be responsible kids and check in with our moms. Mine is busy on an Uber pickup, and she can't talk long. I tell her we saw a wild panther, which she agrees is amazing luck.

Lil is guiding two anglers down the Madison River, so she also only has time for a quick hello. Summer tells her the Everglades is crazy beautiful but the bugs are beastly. When she hears about the panther, Lil wants to know if it was bigger or smaller than a Montana mountain lion.

"Big enough," Summer laughs.

When she gets off the phone, I decide to ask about her dad. She hasn't mentioned him once.

"Because he doesn't exist," she says.

"Everybody's got a father."

"Biologically, that's true. But as for participating—you know, being a functioning member of the family unit—my dad has less than zero presence. He's a Lakota, not that it makes a difference. He lives far away from here."

"What does he do?"

"Stares at the walls, I guess. He's in prison, Billy."

"God, I'm sorry."

"*God*, don't be!" Summer manages a smile. "He's right where he belongs."

I've said too much already. But you know how some people have a talent for changing the subject? Not me.

"Why'd he get locked up?" I ask.

"He beat up my mom."

"In front of you?"

"Same as always," she says. "Only this time, they had to carry him off on a stretcher. I honestly don't remember hittin' him, but he definitely ended up bloody on the ground. The cops showed me what was left of the snow shovel. I went a little bonkers, they said."

"How old were you?"

"Eight. The shovel was practically bigger than me. Mom and I, we never talk about the drunken ass. We don't even speak his name. The man does *not* exist for us anymore."

"What man?" I say.

"Thank you."

I look out the window at Dennis Dickens, pacing around the parking lot, still talking on his cell. He's far from a perfect father, but I don't believe he'd harm a soul. It's hard to think of what Summer and Lil experienced, trapped under the same roof with someone who just explodes like a land mine.

"Your dad's in his own flaky world," Summer is saying, "but it's not a scary world, okay? Mom and I would vote for flaky over scary any day."

"Still, all those years and not a phone call—I mean, come on. Belinda might never forgive him."

"I'd be pissed, too, Billy. In some ways, Dennis is a kick-ass dude, chasin' these hard-core poachers all by himself. For that he should get mad respect, right? But in other ways, he's a big dopey chicken, too scared to call you and your sister.

But, hey, at least he's here now. My old man? I hope I never lay eyes on him again. That's a cold true fact."

Summer's view throws a different light on my situation, I admit. It's a reminder there are fathers way worse than mine.

After he gets off the phone, Dad confirms he was speaking to Daisy Baxter. She said her husband seemed extremely agitated when he called her earlier. He wouldn't tell her what he'd been doing or what happened, but she correctly concluded that the poaching expedition had fallen apart. According to my father, Mrs. Baxter was elated to learn the panther got away.

Her husband's rotten luck apparently didn't end in the woods this morning. On the road, heading south from Immokalee, we noticed a black Range Rover flying by in the opposite direction—tailgated by a jacked-up mud truck driven by a scowling red-haired man. My guess is that Rusty the ranch hand wants Lincoln Chumley Baxter IV to explain how Rusty's name fell into enemy hands.

If I were Baxter, I wouldn't take my foot off the accelerator.

Dad was heading toward the cross-state highway they call Alligator Alley, the quickest route back to the east coast, but Summer and I talked him into staying one more night. There's a campground on Chokoloskee Island, across the causeway from Everglades City, the fishing village where Mom had settled for a while with me and Belinda.

Last summer, this part of south Florida got smashed by a monster hurricane named Irma. Everything was underwater for days. I'm wondering what happened to our old neighborhood, so I give Dad driving directions.

Somehow, the houses on our block are still standing. The one we lived in is a small yellow wood-frame with a screen porch. You can see a brown water line running five feet high along the outside walls, but otherwise the place looks pretty good. Amazingly, the hurricane didn't knock down the giant royal poinciana tree in the yard.

Dad is smiling as he looks over the place. "I totally see why your mother picked this house," he says.

The new owners have a bay boat on a trailer in the driveway and two candy-striped paddleboards propped against a side wall. The mailbox is painted to look like a strawberry grouper with its jaws open. I text a picture to Mom.

At the campground we're eagerly greeted by clouds of saltwater mosquitoes, so we set up our tent at world-record speed. While waiting for a bag of ice at the marina, I notice two bald eagles flying in a clockwise circle over the bay. From a distance most adult eagles look alike, but I'm wondering if these are the same birds Mom took us to watch when we lived here, the same pair whose nest got trashed by the funnel cloud. I kept telling her they'd come back, but she wouldn't believe me.

Even though many of the buildings in Everglades City have been fixed up since Irma, I wasn't expecting to see much wildlife. The eagles are a nice surprise. I'm definitely going to tell Mom they're the same ones.

It's too buggy to cook outdoors, so we go to a restaurant

I remember near the stone-crab docks on the Barron River. The place looks brand-new. Photos on the wall show the wreckage of the kitchen and splintered docks after the hurricane.

We take a table by the water. Dad says he and Summer will start the long drive home to Montana tomorrow, after dropping me off in Fort Pierce.

"You've got to go back so soon?" I ask.

"I promised Lil," says Dad. "I've been away a lot lately. Too much."

And I get that.

"Billy, you think Belinda would like Montana?"

"I don't know. All depends."

Summer cackles. "It's humanly impossible *not* to like Montana."

"Belinda's got the boyfriend thing going on," I say.

"Me too. But if I had to choose between Davey and the Rocky Mountains, Davey's history."

Dad says, "Just for a visit, I was hoping—before she goes off to college. Your mother might want to come along, too. Lil won't mind."

It's like he's trying to bring all the people in his life together with one big move. That might be a tough fit.

"I'll ask Mom," I promise. "And Belinda, too."

We order fish tacos, slaw, corn on the cob, and a pitcher of iced tea. While we're waiting, an osprey swoops down and plucks a shiny mullet from the river. It occurs to me that the same kind of bird is doing the same kind of thing to some poor trout, two thousand miles away on the Yellowstone River.

After dinner, Dad says he wants to witness my snake-grabbing skills in person. Summer's down for a night drive through the Everglades, too. I tell them about a prime reptile zone along a dirt road in the Big Cypress Swamp. By the time we arrive, it's already dark. Usually this is when the action starts.

My father switches on his high-beam headlights and brakes the truck to a crawl. Traveling snakes often stretch to their full length, but sometimes they rest in the shape of an S. Other times they just coil up. They're not always easy to spot from a moving vehicle, but all three of us have sharp eyes—especially Summer, it turns out.

On the first pass our catch is two garter snakes, a four-foot king snake, a corn snake, and a little ringneck spied by Summer moments before the truck almost flattened it. Summer and Dad get out to observe each of the captures. One of the garter snakes nicks a knuckle when it snaps at me, but that doesn't count as a legit bite.

We didn't bring a pillowcase, so I release every snake after we take a few pictures. Dad gets a cool shot of Summer with the black-and-orange ringneck curled around one of her pinkies, like an exotic piece of jewelry. He texts the photo to Lil, while Summer texts it to Davey the boyfriend.

On the return drive we don't see any more snakes, although there's other critter activity. At one point Dad stops the pickup to let a mother raccoon lead her three babies across the road. Later we roll up on a fat old opossum that won't budge; it just blinks at the headlights and bares its pointy teeth, a standard opossum bluff. Dad casually lifts the snarling grouch by its pale hairless tail and moves it into the woods. Personally, I'd rather deal with an angry snake any day.

The campground is silent and dark by the time we return to Chokoloskee. Unfortunately, the mosquitoes aren't asleep. We dash for the tent and zip ourselves inside. There's not much room to move around. Snug is a polite way to describe it—father, son, and stepdaughter packed together like sardines. For some reason it was easier to talk in the car. Now that the panther mission is over, I'm not sure what kind of conversation to start, if any.

By the glow of a battery-powered lantern, Summer and I each tap out goodnight-mom texts. Dad's listening to a voice message on his phone.

"#@%&!" we hear him mutter.

What now? I'm wondering.

He tosses the phone into his duffel. "That was my, uh, informant."

Summer sighs. "You can say her name. We know who she is."

"Lincoln Baxter isn't driving straight home to California, like I thought."

"Then where's he going?" I ask.

"He told his wife he's got some 'unfinished business' in Montana. To me, that sounds like another grizzly hunt."

Summer elbows me in the ribs. We're both thinking the same queasy thought.

"What if his 'unfinished business' isn't a bear," I say to my father. "What if it's you?"

SIXTEEN

Mom liked the picture of our old house in Everglades City.

"I knew it was sturdy!" she said.

"I saw your eagles, too."

"The same ones, Billy? They came back?"

"Just like I told you they would. And they made it through the hurricane just fine."

"Well, that's awesome."

Here's the roster at lunch: me, Mom, Belinda, Summer Chasing-Hawks, and Dad.

Summer and Belinda are seated next to each other, a little awkward because they've got almost nothing in common—and completely opposite opinions of my father. Meanwhile, Mom and Dad are directly across the table from each other. She looks at him more often than he looks at her. There wasn't much he could reveal about our so-called camping trip, so that strand of conversation lasted about two minutes. Now it's mostly small talk, and Belinda acts like she'd rather be at the dentist. When Dad congratulates her on the Cornell scholarship, she pretends it's no big deal.

He says, "You should come out to Montana before college starts. Your mother, too. Billy said he mentioned it to you."

I did. Belinda's reaction was chilly.

She makes a bored face. "Right, there's *so* much to do out there."

"We can float the river. Hike in the mountains," says Dad. "Do you like to ride horses? Come on, I'll take care of the plane tickets."

Mom looks interested. Belinda grunts.

Trying to be upbeat, Summer starts chattering about the golden eagles, how huge and graceful they are. Mom gets pretty excited, as expected, and fires off a bunch of questions about the birds. What's their wingspan? Do they mate for life? Do their nests blow away in a blizzard?

My sister just glowers at the half-eaten burrito on her plate.

I'm not saying much because my mouth is crammed with food. The long ride home from Chokoloskee made me hungry as a horse. Along the way, Dad stopped at an electronics shop in Fort Lauderdale to buy a new quadcopter. He picked a super-expensive model, but it's still not waterproof.

Mom is very curious about the Crow Indians, so Summer gives a brief history of the tribe, the reservation, and her family. At last, Belinda seems to be paying attention.

Dad and I go outside to assemble his new drone. This one is black. He downloads the control app onto his phone and mine, promising a future flying lesson.

"Out west would be the easiest place to teach you," he says.

"You'll be too busy for that, with Baxter hot on your tail."

"Billy, how would he ever find me?"

"He slashed the tires on your truck, so he must have seen the license plates."

"So what? Only cops can trace a private tag."

"Can't you find another poacher to spy on?"

"Baxter's number one on my list."

"Then go after number two," I suggest.

"Number two is temporarily out of action. He fell out of a tree."

"Dad—"

"After shooting himself in the foot."

"Dad, you need to be more careful."

"I'm always careful."

For a test flight, he sends his new drone cruising across the Indian River to peek at Mom's bald eagles. The high-res camera finds one of them sitting on a limb overlooking a small bay. The other bird is probably in the air scouting for fish—or for an osprey clutching a fish. Baldies are master thieves.

Dad guides the quadcopter back to our neighborhood and smoothly lands it in the backyard. As soon as we enter the house, Mom announces:

"It's a done deal, guys. We're flying to Montana next week!"

I'm not sure who's more stunned, me or my father.

"Next week?" he says.

I can tell what he's thinking. He'd rather have us visit after Lincoln Baxter is out of the picture, safely back in California.

Apparently, while Dad and I were outside with the drone, Lil called Summer, and my mother asked to speak with her.

"What a cool lady!" Mom says. "I told her about your invitation, Dennis, and guess what? She knows a motel where we can stay for twenty percent off. There's even a Laundromat."

Belinda is nowhere in sight. She's probably fuming in her room.

Dad says, "Honestly, I was thinking more of August. It's one of my favorite months—"

"August is gonna be way too crazy around here. So much shopping for Belinda's college wardrobe—she owns basically no winter clothes. Not even a hat! No, Dennis, I think now would be the perfect time for us to come."

"What about your gig with Uber?" he asks.

"Oh, they're super-flexible."

"But don't the kids have summer jobs?"

Mom says, "Don't worry, we'll get all that stuff worked out."

My father caves. This was, after all, his idea.

"Chrissie, you're gonna love it out there," he says.

"I know! I am *totally* psyched to see my first golden eagle."

Summer glances up from a bowl of ice cream and smiles at me. I'm glad to be going back next week. The sooner the better, especially with Lincoln Baxter unaccounted for.

"Let's hit the road," Dad says to Summer. "It's a long drive home."

* * *

There's always a waiting list for part-time jobs at Publix. Mr. Voss says that he'll have to fill my position but that I can reapply at the store when we get back to town. It's pretty much what I expected, and truthfully I'm not heartbroken. I'll miss the extra money, but not the social demands of bagging groceries.

On my way out of the store, I spot Chin and his father again. I try to slip by with just a wave, but Chin sidesteps quickly, blocking my escape.

"'Sup?" I say.

"I've got something for you."

"Uh . . . okay."

"Can we go outside?" he asks.

I accompany them through the busy parking lot to one of the striped safety lanes where people drop off their shopping carts. Privacy isn't as crucial as avoiding bad drivers. Chin's dad hangs a few steps back, arms at his side. From the way he's looking at me, I know that he knows what happened in the D-5 hallway, that I'm the one who saved his son from the loser lacrosse player. It's ancient history to me, though obviously not to Chin and his family.

The kid says, "I was afraid you didn't work here anymore. We haven't seen you in a couple days."

"I went camping with my father in the Everglades."

"Sweet," Chin says. "We're going to Yosemite in July. Dad rented an RV."

"Sweet."

"Here. Hope you can use this."

A handmade pocketknife is what the kid gives me. A coiled rattlesnake is carved into the polished wood handle. Etched on the other side are the letters *B.A.D.*

My initials. Billy Audubon Dickens.

This blows me away. I open the knife and use my thumbnail to test the impossibly fine edge of the blade. It feels sharp enough to split a hair.

"This is crazy," I say to Chin. "It's not like you owed me anything."

He's grinning because he sees how much I like the gift. "The reason I had them put your initials on it," he says, "is so you couldn't give it back."

I've got to laugh. "Thanks, dude."

Carefully, *very* carefully, I fold the blade closed.

Chin's father says, "Billy, you did a brave thing."

Nope. I did the only thing a person like me could possibly do, wired the way I am. No way could I stand there watching a small kid get pounded by a big kid. Not an option. That isn't bravery, it's just reflex.

Pedaling my bike down the street, I feel the weight of the knife in my pocket. It isn't as large as the one Jammer carries, but it's heavy enough for me.

When I get home, my sister announces that Dawson broke up with her. "You happy now?" she says. "All because of this stupid trip out west. Dawson says he can't do long-distance relationships, even for a week."

"I thought you were going to dump him, anyway."

"So what if I was?"

"You should be celebrating," I say. "He's a creep. He tried to shoot Mrs. Gomez's cat with my slingshot."

"Muffin? You liar! Dawson wouldn't hurt a flea." But Belinda knows I'd never make up something like that.

"I predict you'll get over him," I say, "by lunchtime."

She stomps to her room and halfheartedly slams the door.

Dad and Summer are making good time. She texted me from somewhere in Alabama. Mom is working an Uber job, driving an elderly person to a doctor's appointment. I'm okay with her taking riders like that.

Something's been bothering me ever since we got back from Immokalee. I dial the phone number I'd memorized from the scrap of paper in the Range Rover. He answers on the second ring.

"Good morning, Rusty," I say, pleasant but firm.

"Who the $#@! is this?"

My name isn't showing up on his caller ID because I blocked it, using *67. I remind him that we met on the ranch road two days ago, in the presence of a sheriff's deputy.

"How'd you get my number?" he demands angrily.

"Same way I got your name. Your buddy Mr. Baxter ought to be more careful. By the way, did you ever catch up with him?"

"None a your business," Rusty snaps. "What the hell do you want?"

"Take it easy. This is just a courtesy call."

"Huh?"

"A courtesy call. To warn you," I say, "about what's going to happen if you try to set up another panther kill."

"I got no idea what you're talkin' about." Rusty's indignant tone is fake and shaky. He's worried.

"If you ever do something like that again," I say, "whether it's for Baxter or any other low-life poacher, I'm gonna call your boss and get you fired. After that, I'm gonna call the game wardens and get you arrested. Whatever money you have in the bank, you'll be spending all of it on lawyers—and even then you'll probably end up in jail for a couple years. But, listen, there's another path. A smarter way to go."

"Like what? Be a rat snitch?"

"No, it's real simple," I tell him. "All you've got to do is make sure nothing bad happens to any of the panthers on that ranch. From now on, Rusty, you be their guardian angel. Chase off anyone who tries to mess with 'em, or call the law. Can you handle that? I know you can."

Rusty simmers on the other end of the line. Then: "Why should I listen to anything you say? Yer just a dumb kid. Anyway, who's ever gonna know if one a those cats gets shot, way out in the middle a nowheres?"

Here's where I'm prepared to do a little exaggerating. Okay, *major* exaggerating.

"Rusty, we've got a network of secret informants and a whole fleet of high-altitude drones. If one of those panthers gets even an itty-bitty hangnail, we'll know about it."

I can sense the ranch hand doesn't like the idea of being spied on.

He says, "Is this, like, blackmail or somethin'?"

"It's not blackmail if you're being made to do something honest."

He chuckles glumly. "I don't see where I got much of a choice."

"It sounds like your heart's not in this," I say. "Just forget I even called. You go ahead and take your chances—"

"Now, hold on! I'll do it."

What happened at the ranch shook up Rusty pretty badly. He didn't know it, but he was ready for a phone call like this. Deep down, he's probably relieved.

"One more favor," I say. "If Lincoln Baxter calls you back—"

"That ain't happenin', kid. I'm the last voice on earth that man wants to hear."

My mom and dad share the same view on the whole religion thing, which is simple: everybody gets to make up their own mind.

Is there a God? What's his deal? Or *her* deal?

I'm not sure what I believe. But the more I see, the more I wonder if God is taking a hands-off approach to the human race. How else can you explain so much bad behavior? I think it's very possible God got totally disgusted with us and said, "I'm done here. You poor dumb mortals are on your own."

Working at a grocery store, you meet lots of nice folks

and see many acts of kindness. But you also witness scenes that make you wonder if our species is evolving in the wrong direction—backward, into the ancient slime we crawled from millions of years ago, when we were just innocent little fish growing legs.

I remember a Saturday morning when two women got into a shrieking fistfight in the produce section. Each of them weighed like ninety-two pounds, and both were old enough to be somebody's grandmother. In fact, they probably *were* somebody's grandmother.

The women had been chugging toward the same rack of ripe melons when their shopping carts collided. They argued, cussed, squawked, and then started to scuffle. Mr. Voss went on the PA system and told me to hurry to Produce right away. By the time I got there, the old ladies were clobbering each other with cantaloupes.

I separated the women and steered the loudest one to a neutral aisle. The melon she clutched was cracked and leaking like an egg. A policeman who showed up could hardly keep from laughing.

Because this happened on Christmas Eve, okay? Supposedly the holiest, most peaceful time of the year.

I realize a melon fight between two old crones is just one small stupid incident, but it's still a lousy advertisement for the human race. Can you imagine God looking down and beaming with pride? No way.

Meanwhile, check out the daily stream of bad news, if you can deal with it—terrorist bombings, massacres, loony dictators, crooked politicians, hackers, scammers, bigots spewing hate all over the internet. . . .

Sometimes it's hard to feel much hope for the planet.

My personal remedy—Belinda calls it my "disappearing act"—is to go places where I hear bugs buzzing instead of cars speeding down a highway. Places where birds outnumber tourists.

Solitary escape isn't easy in Florida, because it's so insanely overcrowded. Depressing true fact: twenty million people live here.

That's nineteen million more people than live in the entire state of Montana, which is actually *twice* as big.

No wonder I can't wait to go back.

SEVENTEEN

The landing in Bozeman was bumpy, though Mom didn't seem to notice. She couldn't stop talking about all the huge mountains out the window. Even my sister was impressed.

Now, two days later, everyone's doing fine. I wouldn't call it a miracle, but I'd been expecting some tension.

At first Belinda was crazed because of the lame Wi-Fi reception, but she's adjusting. Instead of checking her social media every three or four minutes, she now waits like half an hour—sometimes even longer. This is major progress.

The first night, my father took us to the Rib & Chop House in Livingston. Lil sat on one side of him and Mom was on the other. Dad edged his chair back so that the two of them could speak past him, directly to each other, which they did. All during dinner he kept smiling—proud of himself, I guess. It's a busy joint, so I couldn't pick up everything Mom and Lil were saying, but I got the impression they were trading battle stories about raising teenagers in the modern world.

Meanwhile, Belinda and Summer got into a deep conversation about boys—how impossible they are and so *not* worth the trouble. That left no one at the table to talk with me, which was fine. I was glad to be back in Montana, and there wasn't much else to say.

The second day was a long, lazy Yellowstone float. Dad borrowed a friend's raft and we followed Lil's drift boat downriver from the put-in at Carters Bridge. Summer rode with us, while Belinda and Mom went with Lil. Dad showed he was pretty good with the oars, though not as strong as Lil, which he's the first to admit.

It was a clear bright morning, breezy enough to keep us cool. An hour into the trip, we heard Mom's voice rise excitedly ahead of us.

"Jackpot," my father said with a wink.

We could see Mom standing in the bow of Lil's drift boat, aiming her iPhone up toward a rock wall where a golden eagle posed motionless on a pale ledge.

Mom was too far to get a good photo, but she eagerly clicked away, her shouts skipping across the open water. She was truly overjoyed to see that bird. It never spooked, or even flared its wings. Dad said they get accustomed to the sight of humans, especially in the summer.

That night, Lil fixed a huge dinner—salad, corn, and spaghetti served with meatballs made from real ranch bison. I demolished two monster helpings. Mom was still hyped from the river trip and even Belinda was in a decent mood, probably because some dude dressed like a rodeo cowboy had stopped to flirt with her in the parking lot of the Albertsons.

I rolled with the chill family vibe, thinking that maybe my father was right after all, that it actually was a great idea bringing Mom and Belinda out here to connect with his universe.

But now, right this moment . . . not so sure.

I'm standing outside the hardware store on Main Street. My father is inside buying water bottles and extra bear spray for a hike to the Pine Creek Falls with Mom and my sister. The reason I'm on the sidewalk is that I've been trying to get a phone signal so I can reach Lil, who's floating the Yellowstone this morning with a couple of trout fishermen. Dad wants me to ask her how much fencing she needs for their backyard garden, which is getting raided by hungry deer.

Finally my phone screen shows three bars. I should be dialing Lil yet instead I'm staring at a dirty black Range Rover parked down the street. There's a sticker on the rear bumper, but I'm too far away to read what it says.

The vehicle stands out among the local pickup trucks and tourist rental cars not only because it's too fancy for a small western town but also because of its unusual condition. The Range Rover is cratered with dents from one end to the other. Plastic garbage bags have been duct-taped across the window openings where glass used to be. The SUV looks like it was attacked by a person swinging a crowbar or a baseball bat.

A person who wanted to make a point, and whose name might be Rusty.

That would explain why the ranch hand assured me that Lincoln Baxter would never call him about another panther hunt. He must've caught up with the poacher during that road chase through Immokalee.

I hurry inside the hardware store to tell my father, who's

waiting in line to pay. By the time we walk out, the Range Rover is gone.

"What if it's Baxter? What if he's looking for you?" I ask.

"Billy, the guy has no clue who I am or where I live. If he's here, it's because he came to shoot a grizzly. He might be heading back to Tom Miner, or maybe down to Jackson Hole—if that was even his car you saw, which I doubt."

Still, Dad agrees to snoop around, just in case. Riding in the pickup, we cover all of downtown Livingston in about six minutes, and that's moving slowly. There's no sign of the damaged Rover, so we head back to the house and pack for Pine Creek.

I'd assumed Summer was coming along, but she's staying home to finish chapter whatever in an online American history class. When I pop my head into her room, I see Sparky, a.k.a. Satan, curled up at the foot of the bed. The mangy old cat is snoozing on the windowsill. "Have fun on the hike," Summer says. "It'll be good for those scrawny Florida legs."

Pine Creek is a dream trip for my mother, though Belinda keeps complaining that her feet hurt. After reaching the waterfall, we sit on the smooth slanted crown of a boulder to eat lunch—ham-and-cheese sandwiches and apples. Mom loves watching the mist rise from the cascade. She says somebody should bottle it as skin moisturizer. The forest shade smells rich and piney, and the tourists are behaving. Some of the locals brought along their dogs, so Mom made lots of new friends on the trail.

On the trek down the mountainside we step around a fresh pile of berry-filled poop that Dad says came from a black bear, not a grizzly. I trust him to know the difference. Belinda says a bear's a bear, and suddenly her feet don't hurt anymore; she's moving faster than all of us. On purpose I hang back, because Mom and Dad are walking and talking side by side and I don't want to be an eavesdropper. From the soft tone of their voices, I know the conversation isn't an argument, but I can also tell it's personal.

The ride back to town seems quieter than the ride out. My mother and sister are still getting used to thin air, and the hike tired them out. I ask Dad to drop me on Park Street so I can check out Dan Bailey's, a famous fly-fishing shop.

Dad says, "Could you grab some feathers? Lil's tying some new flies." He tells me what to buy—something called a *rooster cape*—and gives me a twenty-dollar bill.

I spend almost no time in Bailey's shop, because it's not really why I wanted to get out of the truck. The true reason is that I'd spotted the bashed-up Range Rover parked on a side street.

Approaching the car, I try to act casual, but as soon as I see the TROPHY HUSBAND bumper sticker, I'm ready to jump out of my skin. A pair of dirty feet extends from the only window not covered by a garbage bag. The feet are medium-sized and attached to a person sprawled in the back seat.

I keep on strolling to the end of the block, turn around, and go back. To the dirty feet I say: "Excuse me?"

The feet don't move. From where I stand I can't see the features of the person they belong to.

"Yo!" I call out.

"What? Go away," croaks a groggy male voice.

"Are you okay?"

"So now it's a federal crime to take a nap?"

"I was worried you might be sick." Somehow I make these words sound totally sincere.

The dirty feet withdraw from the window, and a long-unshaven face appears. The man's mussed hair is gray at the temples, one of his top teeth is missing, and his nose is as straight as a pencil.

"You're not even him," I say.

"Not who?"

"A friend of my father's drives one of these SUVs—same color, same model."

The man squints at me doubtfully. "So happens I just bought this thing yesterday, junior. Nine hundred bucks, 'as is.' Every dollar I had to my name but, hey, it's a flippin' Rover! We're talking like eighty thousand bucks, brand-new. All it needs is a little bodywork."

I'm thinking: A little? *More like a whole new body.*

"Once it's all fixed up, I can resell 'er for like fifty, sixty grand," he declares. "Then I'm set for life!"

"Uh. Okay." I'm not an expert on the resale market for rebuilt luxury vehicles, but the barefoot man sounds way too optimistic. "The person who sold you the car—he was real tan and had a crooked nose, right?"

The stranger scowls. "I don't pay attention to noses. But, yeah, the dude was tan. A rich-guy tan, though, not a workin' man's tan. Also he had some serious Hollywood hair."

"The tips all dyed blond?"

"Yeah. What's up with *that?*"

"Lincoln Baxter's his name."

"Yeah, that's what it said on the paperwork," the stranger says. "When I see him park this thing, all dented to crap, I go over and ask did he drive off a cliff, or what? He says, 'You wanna buy it?' I say, 'Seriously?' And he says, 'How much cash you got, bro?' So I run 'n' get all the money from outta my sleepin' bag, and he signs over the title right there on Callender Street." The man yawns and swigs from a liter bottle of Mountain Dew. "What time izzit, anyway? Whoa, I forgot—there's a sweet clock with a second hand, right on the dash. Check it out."

I didn't feel the need to tell him I'd already sat in his SUV, or the circumstances.

"Did Mr. Baxter say what happened to this thing?"

"He said he drove through a hailstorm. Never saw it comin'."

"Epic fail," I say.

"Bad luck for him, good luck for me." The barefoot man's expression clouds as a new thought occurs to him. "Listen, junior, you tell your daddy's pal it's too late to change his mind on this deal. We ain't in Cally-fornia. This is Park County, Montana, where a handshake's a handshake."

"Don't worry," I say. "He doesn't want this car back."

*   *   *

Walking to Geyser Street, I pass a two-story brick house with a wooden toolshed off to one side. Small sleek birds with curved wings are swooping in and out beneath the overhang of the shed's pitched roof. On my first float down the Yellowstone, I saw the same kind of birds—Summer identified them as cliff swallows. She said they use their beaks to collect wet dirt and mold it into nests that stick to the walls of rock canyons, bridges, and buildings. The grown-up swallows zoom all over, snatching flies and mosquitos in midair, then carry them back to the baby birds inside the mud nests.

But that's only part of what's happening at the wooden shed beside the brick house. Black ravens are gathering along the edge of the roof. I count five of them, standing in a row.

They are surprisingly tall, larger than some Florida hawks, and their loud calls of *kraa-kraa-kraa* are nagging and obnoxious. They hop one-footed from side to side, cocking their blue-black heads as they study the swallows coming and going. The little birds know the deal. Occasionally they peel off and dive-bomb the tall noisy birds, trying to drive them away.

Of course the ravens aren't going anywhere. They're hungry, but they're patient. They can hear the baby swallows cheeping in their mud cribs.

This is nature, right? Harsh things happen.

Some people believe it's wrong to interfere in the wild cycle of life and death. I get that. Every living creature has a place in the food chain.

But it's impossible to just stand here with my hands in my pockets watching those five sneaky ravens, knowing what they've got in mind.

Just like it's impossible for my dad to look the other way and do nothing while an outlaw aims a gun at a bear or a panther. Except there's an important difference between a common raven and a poacher like Lincoln Baxter: one is part of the natural world, and one is a criminal intruder. The bird kills for food, while Baxter kills for entertainment.

Either way, it's nothing I really want to see.

So I snatch up a handful of rocks and make a long, high throw. They clatter on the roof of the shed, flushing the ravens. In a mad flurry of wings, the flock takes off, *kraa-kraa-kraa*-ing above the cottonwoods until it's out of sight.

The swallows go back to gobbling insects and tending the young in their mud nests. Ravens have wickedly sharp memories, so I'm sure they'll return to try again another day. By then maybe the baby birds will have sprouted enough feathers to fly away on their own. I hope so, because I can't hang around here to stand guard.

Nature always gets the last word.

That's not my line. I read it in a magazine article written by a rock climber. His point was that nature is as coldhearted as it is beautiful, and that forces beyond our understanding can deliver a random life-or-death surprise at any moment.

It might be a landslide, a flash flood, or a bolt of lightning on a cloudless morning.

Or if you're a baby swallow, a hungry raven.

I don't want my father to get surprised by Lincoln Baxter, so I plan to inform him that the poacher no longer owns that fancy Range Rover. The information isn't very useful, unfortunately, because I've got no clue what kind of vehicle Baxter is driving now. He might be in a Prius, a minivan, a Winnebago, a Ferrari, anything with wheels. Since Dad won't know what to look out for, Baxter should have an easy time following him—if that's actually his plan.

And assuming otherwise could be disastrous.

Dad keeps saying the poacher doesn't know who he is or where he lives, but there's a chance he's wrong. Just because Baxter isn't a cop doesn't mean he has no way to identify the owner of the Chevy king cab that trailed him to Tom Miner Basin. While he was slashing Dad's tires, he could've photographed the license numbers and texted them to somebody he knows in law enforcement—maybe one of his hunting buddies—who could sneak on the state computer . . . and boom!

And even though the pickup is registered in Lil's name, the poacher would then have a county, a city, and a home address. He could show up on Lil's doorstep one day when Dad isn't home.

I'm not saying that's what will happen, but we really have no idea how much Baxter knows or what he's doing here. My father can't afford to underestimate him.

Back at the house on Geyser, Dad is on his knees in the living room, adjusting the blades on his new quadcopter. I wave and step past on my way to Summer's bedroom, where I shut the door and say: "Lincoln Baxter's in town."

"Please don't tell me that, Billy."

"Well, it's true." I describe my encounter with the barefooted dude who purchased the poacher's SUV, and offer my license-plate theory about how Baxter ended up in Livingston.

Summer's response: "We need to tell my mom."

"Everything? She'll freak."

Then the door opens. It's Dad.

Summer and I freeze.

"Have you seen Belinda?" he asks.

"Uh, she's at the grocery store," Summer says, "with her mom."

She and I are as stiff as scarecrows. Dad gives us a narrow look. "What's wrong, guys?"

"We need to talk," I say. "All of us together."

"Okay, so let's talk. You go first."

"Not without Lil."

"No, Billy, now wait a minute—"

"Follow me," Summer snaps. "Both of you."

I'm only one step behind her. Dad's two steps behind me. Summer leads us downstairs to the basement, where classical music is playing.

Lil sits at a small table tying chicken feathers to a tiny fish hook clamped to a slim steel vise. She wears round rimless magnifying glasses. When she sees us, she puts down the tweezer-like tool she's using to wrap the wispy strands on the shank of the hook.

"What's the occasion?" she asks.

Summer glances anxiously at me.

Lil eyes us over the top of her glasses. "Did you all come down here because you're fans of Mozart, or because you've got something to tell me?"

I hand her the package I got at Dan Bailey's. She spreads the rooster cape on the table, saying, "That's a beauty, Billy. Thank you."

Summer nudges me from behind. My father gives a slight, stern shake of his head—not a warning so much as a plea.

Sorry, Dad, but the deal's off. I can't keep your secret anymore. The stakes are too high.

"It doesn't take three people to carry a bag of feathers down the stairs," Lil says, "so somebody please speak up."

Slowly I raise my hand, like we're in algebra class or something. Lil turns off the music. Now the basement is as quiet as, well, a basement.

"Dad doesn't really work for the government," I say.

His shoulders sag. Summer looks down at her shoelaces. It's possible I've actually stopped breathing.

Lil calmly takes off her glasses.

"Oh, Billy, I know that," she says. "I've known for a long time."

EIGHTEEN

She had discovered the truth on a frigid January day when Summer was at school, Dad was on a trip, and the river was full of ice. A person called the house identifying himself as a lawyer in the Bahamas. It was the same man Summer would later speak to about Hubert the parrot.

The lawyer told Lil he was updating some legal papers regarding the money from Dad's aunt Sophie, and he needed to double-check the mailing address in Montana.

Lil didn't know what he was talking about, so she asked, "And how *is* dear Aunt Sophie these days?"

"Uh, actually . . . she's deceased," the flustered lawyer replied. "Didn't Mr. Dickens tell you?"

By the end of the conversation, Lil knew far more than the lawyer should have told her. Yet she didn't say a word to Dad. Instead she decided to tail him on one of his "missions."

After leaving Summer with a relative in Billings, Little Thunder-Sky spent seventeen hours tracking my father through knee-deep snow in the Absaroka Mountains. He had no clue that somebody was spying on him while he was spying on a poacher, or that the somebody was his very own wife.

Hidden by a hillside boulder, Lil watched through

binoculars while Dad sent his quadcopter to dive-bomb a trophy bull elk, causing it to bound into the heavy timber moments before the poacher's bullet would have struck. Lil crept away and returned home, torn about how to deal with the situation. As risky as Dad's drone expeditions might be, she understood that protecting those animals was a passion, something that gave him a sense of duty.

There are worse hobbies a man could have, she thought.

"So I decided to let you keep thinking your secret was safe," Lil says to Dad, "but enough's enough."

He winces like he stepped on a rusty nail. "I am really, really, *really* sorry," he says. His face shows regret and also relief that he no longer needs to lie about his mystery missions.

Lil isn't mad, but she's far from happy. We've already told her about the panther expedition, and the possibility that Baxter came here to settle the score with Dad.

She says, "Dennis, I figured you were going to Florida just to see your kids, and I was cool with that. You should have done it a long time ago. But now I find out you took Summer and Billy along while you chased some armed psycho through the Everglades. Have you totally lost your mind?"

I jump in: "That wasn't all Dad's fault. We didn't give him a choice."

"Oh, he had a choice." Lil's cutting stare swings from Dad toward me and Summer. "He is a full-grown, functioning adult. It's his job to be in charge of himself."

My father says, "She's right. I took you two along because I was afraid you'd spill the beans if I didn't. But listen, Lil—you know I'd never put these kids in any danger. Baxter didn't know he was being followed, until we wanted him to know."

"And we never got close enough for him to see us," I add, Summer nodding at my side. We both feel guilty about our sneaky role in the Everglades trip.

Lil says, "None of us can be sure what this creep is capable of doing. It's time to call the sheriff."

Dad raises his hands in protest. "And tell him what? A man sold his beat-up SUV to some stranger on the street. That's not a crime. Being in the same town with *me* isn't a crime, either. We've got no proof Baxter came here for revenge. He hasn't made a single threat to me, or to any of you."

"He sliced your tires," Summer pipes up, "and shot a hole in your truck."

"Yeah, but we can't prove that was him," Dad says. "The sheriff's going to listen to our story and, basically, shrug."

He's right, and Lil knows it.

"Fine," she says, "but the kids and Christine need to leave right away, just in case."

"Now, hold on a second—"

Lil cuts him off. "No discussion, no debate. It's too risky for them to stay—even if there's only a one percent chance this guy's coming after you."

My father looks whipped. He's got no ammunition for an argument. "So, what am I supposed to tell Chrissie and Belinda?"

"I don't know, Dennis. Truth twisting is not *my* department." Lil sits forward, eyeing me and Summer. "We don't want to alarm Billy's mom and sister, so you two come up with a good creative excuse why we've got to cut short the family visit."

Summer says: "Grandma got real sick and we've got to drive up to the reservation?"

My suggestion: "The government called Dad for an emergency drone assignment in, like, Utah?"

Lil nods. "Sounds good. We'll use both those stories."

Dad stands there wilted and depressed. His only comment: "It sucks to do this."

On that we all agree.

This one kid, he got kicked out of school because he brought a BB pistol.

The gun wasn't loaded, but he still got expelled. That's the rule. They warn students at the start of every year: no weapons of any kind, period.

The kid was in two of my classes. Jervis was his name. He was a pretty good student, had never been in trouble before. They didn't tell us why he'd brought the pistol to school, but I found out the reason. Some fool was messing with him on the bus ride home, almost every afternoon.

The other kid's name was Tickmore.

For real. Timmy Tickmore.

He wasn't much bigger than Jervis, but he was loud and mean and dumber than a mud fence. You know the type. He didn't throw punches, but he specialized in using his elbows and knees. Sometimes he'd stomp on somebody's foot, and then laugh when he saw how much it hurt.

One afternoon, Tickmore elbowed Jervis in the back of the neck and told him he was going to do something bad to Jervis's little sister when she got old enough to ride the bus. Cut off all her hair or throw her books out the window, whatever.

When Jervis went home from school that day, he took the BB pistol from the garage and hid it in his book bag. It was a cheap target gun that could barely shoot a hole in a soda can, but it looked like a real nine-millimeter. Jervis's idea was to flash it at Timmy Tickmore, scaring him so much that he'd promise to leave Jervis's little sister alone. Obviously it was a terrible plan, something only a frightened and desperate person would try.

In addition to being frightened and desperate, Jervis was also unlucky. The same morning he brought the BB pistol to school there was a random locker search. You can guess what happened. After finding the gun, Officer Thickley called Jervis's parents to come get him, and that afternoon he was officially kicked out of school. He never rode the bus again, never saw Tickmore again—and never told the principal why he was carrying that stupid BB pistol.

But he told me. A week after the locker search, I saw him in the dairy aisle at the supermarket. When he recounted what had happened, he didn't sound bitter. He just sounded defeated.

That night, I locked the door to my room, opened my laptop, and typed a letter to the school. The letter said I needed to ride bus number 537 for one day because I'd be staying with an uncle on that pickup route while my mother was out of town for a funeral. Then I signed Mom's name to the letter—Christine Jane Dickens. I even put a double dot over the last *i*, the same way she does.

I know, I *know*. It was weaselly, dishonest, and totally wrong—though not as wrong as what Timmy Tickmore did to Jervis.

The letter I wrote to the school looked super-legit. I took it to the office, and with no hesitation, Mrs. Lipton gave me a yellow pass to get on the bus. She didn't call Mom to double-check, because she didn't want to bother her before the (nonexistent) funeral.

"Please tell her we're so sorry for her loss," Mrs. Lipton said sincerely.

"That's very kind of you," I replied.

Problem solved.

The next morning I woke up early, walked to Jervis's bus stop, and waited with the other kids for number 537. I knew from talking with Jervis that Tickmore boarded at one of the earlier stops and always took the bench seat in the back

216

of the bus. That's straight where I headed after handing my permission slip to the driver.

Tickmore was sitting with two kids who looked equally brainless.

"Could you guys scoot over?" I asked nicely.

"What?" cackled one of the nitwits.

"I need to sit next to Timmy."

"Yeah? How come?" snarled the second nitwit.

"Because I've got some key information for him. What they call a *game changer*."

Tickmore looked at me warily. "Aren't you the dude they call Snake Boy?"

Immediately Nitwit One slid over on the seat. I sat down between him and Tickmore. My backpack was on my lap.

"What you talkin' 'bout, you got 'information'?" Tickmore said, trying to sound like he wasn't interested. "I never seen you on this bus before."

"That's right. You've never seen me at 1728 Mango Lane, either."

That's where he and his family lived. It was easy to find the address. They were the only Tickmores in the city phone book.

"Timmy, what's the reptile situation in your neighborhood?" I asked.

He clenched up and began to squirm. I mean, physically squirm, like a slug on a hot sidewalk. He was extremely nervous, but he didn't want to look like a wimp in front of his friends.

"You must like pain," he said, working his face into a sneer. It was actually comical.

"Pretend I'm Jervis," I whispered to him. "Stomp on my feet. Slap me in the head. Hey, you can even jab me in the neck with your elbow. Go on, don't be scared."

Nitwit Two howled. "Dude, the Timminator's not scared of nuthin'!"

Tickmore's forehead got pink and sweaty. He started looking around the bus for other seating options. I didn't mind watching him tremble, the way he made other kids tremble.

Leaning sideways into him, I said, "Yo, check this out."

I lifted my backpack and shook it lightly from side to side, like a bag of popcorn. Tickmore and the two nitwits were mystified.

"Listen close, Timmy," I said.

Inside the backpack, something started to rattle. It was a sound made by only one creature in all of nature. Tickmore's phony sneer disappeared, and his eyes got wide.

"No sudden moves," I advised.

Even if he'd wanted to, Tickmore couldn't move a muscle. Fear bolted him to his seat. Every time the rattling stopped, I'd shake the backpack again.

By the time we arrived at school, Tickmore and I had reached an understanding. If I heard about him bothering anybody on that bus—or anybody in the halls, or anybody in the cafeteria, or anybody in the gym, or anybody *anywhere*—there would be serious snakes in his future.

As he bounded for the exit door, he was clutching his books low, in front of his pants. I assumed that he'd peed himself. Maybe I'm an awful person, but I still didn't feel sorry for him, not after what he did to Jervis.

You're probably thinking: *What kind of maniac gets on the school bus carrying a live rattlesnake?*

Not me, don't worry.

Hidden in a side pocket of my backpack was my cellphone, cued to a SlitherTube post of a real six-foot diamondback shaking the rattle on its tail. Every time I jostled the backpack, I'd slip a hand inside the zipper and tap the play button. Even with the volume only halfway up, the noise was impressive. Tickmore's nitwit peeps practically climbed over his shoulders in their rush to flee the bus.

The point of the story is that while honesty is a good thing, lying is occasionally necessary in order to protect people. I wrote a totally bogus letter and forged my mother's signature just to get on bus number 537, so I could deal with Timmy Tickmore. And though I never actually told him there was a real rattlesnake coiled inside my backpack, I definitely made him think there was.

So that's basically two lies, which is nothing to be proud of. On the other hand, nobody at my school has to worry about that creep anymore. He won't mess with any other kids the way he did with Jervis.

And now I've got a few more lies to tell if I want to make sure Mom and Belinda go straight home to Florida, safe from anything bad that might happen here.

"My pics of the golden didn't turn out so fabulous," my mother remarked, scrolling through the photo file on her phone. In the pictures, the distant eagle looks like a chunky brown post planted on the side of the cliff.

"But you saw one. That's all that matters," I told her.

She beamed. "And it was awesome, Billy. Better than awesome! Awesome *squared*."

Then came the hard part: "Mom, I've got some bad news."

I deliver the two phony stories—that Lil's mother is ill on the Crow reservation, and that my father is being called away on another government mission.

"We'll have to go home earlier than we planned," I said.

She was really disappointed, but she said she understood. "I hope it's nothing serious with Summer's grandma," she added.

"Me too. Dad's rebooking our flight to Florida."

"I'll tell your sister in a minute." Mom went back to studying her golden eagle photos. "You know what I'm wondering, Billy? Where was this bird's mate?"

"Probably back at the nest," I assured her, "feeding their little ones."

"Of course. That makes sense. I bet you're right."

The next morning it was still dark when Dad dropped us at the Bozeman airport. Mom gave him a proper peck on the cheek and that's all. She gets the whole Montana thing now, and seems honestly okay with Dad's new life—what she calls his "second act." Even Belinda offered a hug. Waving goodbye, he looked sad enough to be going to a real funeral. All that was missing was his grim black suit.

Now I'm sitting in seat 9C, wondering how much my ticket cost and—since the airline doesn't do refunds—how long it will take me to pay him back.

When Dad rebooked our flight, he couldn't get us three seats together, so Belinda is four rows behind me. She's still sulking because my mother wouldn't buy her a three-hundred-dollar pair of hand-stitched cowgirl boots. Mom is sitting five rows farther back, dozing with a book on her lap.

Meanwhile, my eyes are locked on the no-nonsense flight attendant holding the microphone at the front of the plane. He's been patiently telling passengers to please clear the aisles, buckle up, and get ready for takeoff.

He'll say it once more, right before he closes the cabin door. I know the drill because I went online and found a Delta Airlines flight attendant training manual.

So, the moment I hear the words over the intercom, I undo my lap belt and march up the aisle. The flight attendant thinks I'm going to the restroom. He tells me I have to wait in my seat until after the aircraft takes off and reaches cruising altitude.

I nod agreeably, slide past him, and dart out the cabin door.

"Stop, you can't get off now!" he calls after me.

"I left something at the gate!"

"But they won't let you reboard!"

Exactly.

Technically, what I told the flight attendant wasn't a lie. I really *did* leave my carry-on at the gate—accidentally on purpose.

The bag is still under the seat where I put it. As soon as I'm out of the terminal building, I text Mom with another fake story:

"I forgot my bag in the airport. They wouldn't let me back on the plane!! All OK now. I'll catch a flight home 2morrow. Call u later."

Either she is still asleep or she's already turned off her phone, because I don't get a response to my text. The cab ride to Livingston costs way more than the thirteen bucks in my wallet, so the driver parks in front of Dad's house to wait.

Summer has a toothbrush in her mouth when she comes to the door. "Whath inna whirl are *you* doon here?"

"Can I borrow some money for the taxi?"

The cash comes from Lil's cookie-jar stash, and the driver leaves happy. Summer doesn't fall for my story of how I missed the flight.

"You came back here because of Baxter, right? Well, guess what, Billy Big Stick. We were wrong, you and me."

"Wrong about what?"

"He's not stalking Dennis," she says.

"And you know this . . . how?"

"Your dad got a call from Mrs. Baxter this morning. She said her hubby came here to shoot a grizzly."

"Hold on—Baxter admitted that to his wife? That he's poaching?"

"Of course not. But he had her FedEx one of his big rifles to the Murray Hotel. He made up a story that it's broken and the best gunsmith is here in Livingston."

"Total bull," I say.

"Exactly. Dennis says it's strictly a bear gun, too. I called the hotel pretending to be Baxter's assistant, and they said the package was delivered this morning."

"Where's Dad now?"

"On his way down to Tom Miner," Summer says.

I don't like anything I'm hearing. Baxter didn't need to trace Dad's license tag to get his name, because he didn't need Dad's name. All he needed was a way to lay a trap.

"Summer, where's your mom?"

"On the river."

"Do you know how to drive?"

"Come on. I'm fourteen."

"That's not what I asked."

She realizes I'm serious. "Sure, Billy. I mean I'm not *supposed* to drive without a grown-up in the car, but I know how."

"Where can we get a vehicle?" I say. "Any vehicle."

"You think it's an ambush, don't you?"

"Maybe I'm wrong again. I *hope* I'm wrong. But what if Baxter figured out his wife was talking to Dad, and now he's using her to set Dad up?"

From Summer's expression I can tell she's had the same chilling thought.

Her eyes flicker, but her voice holds steady. "I've got a knucklehead cousin who lives over on M Street."

"What kind of knucklehead?" I ask.

"The kind that always leaves his keys in his car."

NINETEEN

The cousin owns a toad-gray Subaru with 199,009 miles on the odometer. I'm sure it came off the assembly line before Summer or I was born.

She says, "I learned to drive on a tractor, like half the kids in Montana."

"But you've also driven a car before, right?"

"More than you, I bet."

She's undoubtedly right. My entire road experience is one tense afternoon with my mom, going ten miles an hour back and forth in an empty church parking lot—not exactly good training for mountain highways.

As predicted, the keys to the Subaru are in the ignition. Summer says her cousin bartends at night and sleeps all day. She sticks a note in the mailbox saying she's "borrowing" the car.

"Hop in, Billy Big Stick."

"Please tell me the seat belts work."

Although Summer's tall enough to see over the steering wheel, she still looks too young to be in that seat. Her solution is a wide floppy hat and a pair of Lil's wrap-around shades. It turns out she's a pretty good driver.

We brought water, bear spray, snack bars, and the plastic whistle that Dad gave Summer to take on hikes. She offered to carry the binoculars, which means I've got extra space in my backpack. I plan to use it.

I say I need to pick up two things for our trip. Summer asks what. I tell her.

Her response: "Are you nuts?"

The first item we can find at the drugstore. The second will require some luck.

Later, heading south on Highway 89, I get a call from my mother freaking out at the Denver airport, where she and Belinda have a layover.

"I cannot believe you got off that plane! You are so permanently grounded!"

"That's fair."

"Don't you dare be sarcastic with me."

"I'm not, Mom. Whatever you decide to do is okay."

"Where's your father? Put him on the phone right this minute."

"You're gonna miss your connection," I say. "Text me when you and Belinda get home tonight. Bye."

After ending the call, I hear myself let out a sigh.

Summer laughs. "How long are you grounded for?"

"Only until I turn twenty-five. You want me to google directions to Tom Miner?"

"I know how to get there," she says. "Hey, I broke up with Davey on the phone last night. Want to know why?"

I'm thinking: *Not really.*

"He was getting bored with me, I could tell. And I was semi-bored with him."

"Summer, one thing you're definitely *not* is boring."

"It's all good. No pain."

The radio in her cousin's car is broken, so I can't turn up any music to end the boyfriend discussion. My only escape is changing the subject.

"Do you think you'll ever move back to the reservation?" I ask.

"Maybe after college," she says. "Why don't you look more surprised?"

"Because I'm not."

"I want to be a doctor. How about you?"

"No clue. I can't think that far ahead."

"Billy, I can totally see you as a veterinarian. A reptile veterinarian!"

"Right," I say. "Can't wait to run that one by Mom."

Midday traffic is steady on the main road through Paradise Valley—mostly tourists streaming to Yellowstone National Park. Summer is careful to drive below the speed limit, which means we're getting passed constantly by rental cars, minivans, trucks pulling drift boats, even a Winnebago.

But she's smart to go easy on the gas pedal. If we got stopped by the police, we'd never be able to BS our way out of this—two underage kids cruising along in a vehicle that doesn't belong to them. Summer has kept one eye on the rearview mirror ever since leaving the Livingston city limits.

She relaxes a little once we reach the turnoff to the Tom Miner Basin. Not many cops up here.

"I hope this is the right place, Billy."

"If Baxter's setting a trap for Dad, it makes sense to do it here. He knows the area from the last time."

"When Dennis buzzed that big old grizzly."

"The drone master himself," I say.

"Too bad we never got to see the video."

My father erased the file from the quadcopter's SD card. He was afraid someone who didn't know a poacher was on the scene might think he was dive-bombing the bear just for a sick thrill.

Summer slows down to show me a young elk browsing in the emerald-green alfalfa, hundreds of feet below us. The crop is being watered by the rancher's pump station, on the bank of a silvery creek.

I ask Summer if Lil knows that Dad went chasing after Lincoln Baxter.

She says, "He didn't have the you-know-whats to tell her. He waited until she left this morning before he took off."

Heading uphill toward the campground, we spot my father's red Chevy king cab. It's parked on the shoulder, not far from where we found it the last time. None of the tires are flat, and the fenders show no fresh bullet holes. Summer and I agree that's encouraging.

This bumpy dirt road would be Baxter's only way in or out, but we don't encounter any other vehicles until we pull into the campground. There's a chrome RV occupied by two friendly couples from Canada, a Honda sedan carrying college kids getting ready for a hike, and a rust-chewed Jeep Wagoneer that appears to be the permanent residence of a snowy-bearded geezer with four scrawny dogs, all yappers.

Summer does like a seven-point turn, motors back down the road, and parks behind Dad's pickup. She taps her knuckles on the steering wheel and says, "Where the heck is Baxter?"

"Maybe he's on horseback."

"Horses get hauled in by trailers, Billy. You see any trailers?"

"Then maybe he's not here. Maybe I *was* wrong. Maybe he was never coming."

I just now thought of this: "What if the real plan wasn't to ambush Dad? What if the real plan was to send him on a wild-goose chase?"

"But why would Baxter do that?" Summer asks.

"So he could sneak off somewhere else and shoot a bear, drone-free. See, he makes his wife think he's hunting up here again, knowing she'll rat him out to Dad and then Dad'll come looking for him—"

"Only meanwhile," Summer interjects, "Baxter is miles and miles away, over in the Tetons or the Beartooths, killing a grizzly."

"The ultimate revenge, right?"

"Another solid theory, Billy Big Stick. But so was the last one."

"I'll keep trying till I get it right."

* * *

One thing we forgot to pack was rain jackets. I don't know where the storm came from. In a matter of minutes the afternoon sky changed from sunny to dark, angry purple clouds spilling over the mountain ridges.

You're not supposed to stand near a tall tree during a lightning storm, but Summer and I find ourselves stuck in the middle of a towering forest. In a pounding downpour we crouch low on the trail, flinching whenever a lightning bolt strikes close by. The car is more than a mile away, so there's no sense making a run for it. We're already soaked to the skin.

This is my second serious Montana thunderstorm, and I'm not sure if I'm safer here in the woods than I was on that rock beside the river.

One time I got caught in weather like this with Mom and Belinda, down in Everglades City. It blew in on a Sunday morning while we were out in the neighbor's boat watching the bald eagle nest. The stupid outboard engine wouldn't start, so all three of us lay down in the bottom of the boat, pressing our cheeks against the aluminum hull. It seemed like the lightning and thunder went on for hours, but the worst of it probably lasted only ten minutes. Still, we had to keep bailing rainwater out of the skiff, Mom using her coffee mug while Belinda and I scooped the best we could with empty Gatorade bottles.

That was the first time I'd been close enough to experience the sound of the sky being ripped like a sheet, in that frozen split second right before lightning strikes. And I totally admit being scared out of my freaking mind, though I also remember wondering if the baldies were all right, hunkered in their ragged treetop nest. Then the rain quit, the wind died, and the clouds rolled away. We looked up and saw Mom's eagles circling overhead, scouting for baitfish, as if the storm was no big deal. A minor inconvenience.

But at this particular moment it's hard to stay patient and calm, because Summer and I smell smoke. A blinding spear of lightning struck a dead lodgepole pine not far down the trail, and the tree is smoldering in the rain. It probably won't catch fire, but I'd still rather be somewhere else. Summer isn't delighted about our situation, either. The temperature has dropped sharply, and we're getting cold.

She says, "Well, this truly sucks."

"What do bears do in weather like this?"

"Party, I guess. They're *bears*."

A drenched raccoon walks out of the woods, shakes itself like a weary dog, sniffs the smoky air, and ambles away.

"He wouldn't even look at us," I say.

"Because we're so p-p-pitiful, Billy."

Summer's teeth are chattering. I move closer to warm her up. All she's wearing is a soccer jersey, hiking shorts, and neon-green cross-trainers. She wrings her hair and knots it into a soggy ponytail.

"Maybe this is payback," she mumbles, "for me breaking up with Davey."

"Or for me lying to my mom."

"The list goes on," she says, and we both manage to laugh.

Soon the thunder stops and the rain slacks to a drizzle. We stand up, dripping and stiff-jointed. The dirt trail is now pure mud, and the tracks we'd been following are all gone.

They were impressions made by a man's hiking boots. I wear a size 10½, and my shoe fit easily inside one of the tracks. Summer said Dad's a size 12.

We decide to resume walking the same way the boot prints had been pointing—a logical plan until we come to a three-way fork in the trail.

"Now what?" I say to Summer.

"Don't look at *me*. Just 'cause I'm an Indian doesn't mean I'm good at this stuff."

We crawl around on our knees searching for a broken twig or any tiny clue that might reveal which of the paths my father chose.

"Major confession," says Summer as she combs the wet grass and pine needles. "I was actually glad to get off the rez, Billy. It can be a dark, sad place. Some of our people, they drink too much. And do bad drugs. You look in their eyes, it's like they just gave up. And some of 'em are kids my age!"

For her this is a brutal subject, and as usual, I'm not sure what to say.

"You want to stay part of this amazing culture," she goes on, "but you're afraid the bad stuff might drag you down so far you'll never climb out. Truth is I'm not sorry we moved away. I'm sorry for the reasons I feel that way—especially when somebody tells me and Mom how lucky we are to be here and not there."

"Summer, it's not like you totally disconnected from the tribe."

"Yeah, I know, we go back on weekends and hang with family. But that's not the same as *living* it, day and night. And sometimes—like right now—it's hard to feel like a real Native American. Not when a white boy knows more about tracking than I do."

"Hey, who found those panther prints in the Everglades? You!"

"That was dumb luck."

"No, it wasn't," I say.

I'm right, too, because moments later I hear her exclaim, "Billy, check this out!"

She's pointing to a bright blue, bean-sized beetle, lifeless in the muck on the middle of the three paths. The beetle did not die of natural causes—it's been squashed almost flat.

Summer says, "Something heavy landed on that little dude."

"Yeah, like a size-twelve foot."

Farther along we come across a broken branch, still green. Dangling from the sharp end is a thread of khaki fabric, confirming that a human has passed this way. We hurry on, trying to keep our voices low. A patch of blue above the treetops signals the storm is officially over, though the branches are still shedding raindrops.

The path leads us out of the woods to a wide rocky meadow that looks familiar to me. I'm almost certain it's the same place where Dad's drone dropped his first note, the same place I spotted that momma grizzly and her cubs.

Summer takes out the binoculars. Something in the distance caught her attention.

"Bad news, Billy," she says.

I grab the binoculars from her hands and have a look. At the far end of the meadow, a raft of large dark birds is circling. They are definitely not eagles.

"I wonder what they're looking at," Summer murmurs uneasily.

"Whatever it is," I say, "it's probably dead."

Because that's what buzzards hunt.

TWENTY

Deep in griz country, Summer and I don't want to draw attention by crossing the open fields. Instead, we take the longer route toward the buzzards by following the edge of the trees.

I start chanting: "Whoa, bear! Hey, bear! Don't eat me, bear!"

Summer pokes me in the back and says, "Knock it off."

"But you told me to make noise so we don't surprise 'em."

"Can you please come up with something not so lame?"

"Like what?"

"I don't know, Billy. Sing a song. That's what lots of hikers do."

"No way. I'd sound terrible."

Summer doesn't sound terrible. She has a really nice voice. I can't understand the words, but it doesn't matter.

She says it's a "push dance" song from Crow social gatherings. She only remembers the first part, which she sings over and over. The melody is high and piercing, but the vibe sort of fits our situation. There's no danger of startling a grizzly now—they will definitely hear us coming.

As we hurry along the timberline, the sun pops out and a warm breeze starts to blow. Classic Montana weather—one minute you're shivering, the next minute you're sweating.

As the meadow lights up, Summer and I notice something that wasn't visible in the first gray aftermath of the storm:

A large military-style tarpaulin, in prairie camo. The tarp has been pinned down to conceal something bulky beneath it.

Leaving the cover of the pines, we venture out for a closer look. In the distance the buzzards keep circling. Both Summer and I fear the same awful possibility, though neither of us dares to say it aloud.

Meanwhile the tarp is flapping like a ship's sail in the gusty wind. We start yanking out the stakes until one side billows upward, revealing a small red helicopter. It's a two-seater with folding rotors.

My latest theory was wrong, obviously. Lincoln Baxter didn't send my dad on a wild-goose chase. He's right here. He also didn't lie on his profile about being a pilot.

"This is not good," Summer says, folding her arms.

"I know, I know. Just give me a minute!"

"We gotta hurry, Billy."

I step into the chopper and take the pilot's seat. It's like sitting in a glass bubble. Randomly I start turning dials and flipping levers, anything to stall Baxter's escape. I've got something else that might work, too, the second item we picked up on the way to Tom Miner.

As I unzip my backpack, I notice Summer striding away, crossing the meadow.

Straight toward the circling buzzards.

I yell for her to come back, but she can't hear me. The cockpit glass is too thick. As soon as I hop out of the helicopter, she takes off running.

I'm faster. That's not a knock, just a fact.

Even though I tackle her as gently as possible, it's not exactly a soft landing. She cusses and kicks, but I'm not letting go until she settles down.

And I totally get why she's so frantic.

"It's not safe out here," I whisper into her ear. "We need to get back in those trees, like, *now*."

"No, but what if that's Dennis out there on the ground under those birds! He could be—"

"Stop, Summer. Don't even *think* it."

Once in a while I wonder about my dad's mother and father, the grandparents I never got to meet. And it sounds weird, but I try to imagine the phone call Dad got on the day they died. How do you deliver such horrible news? What words do you choose?

It was a car accident, Dennis. They swerved to miss a turtle.

Okay, that's not funny, I would have said, if it had been me. *Now what's the real reason you're calling?*

The truth is when you're young, it's impossible to think of your mom or dad dying all of a sudden. In fact, you try not to think about them dying ever.

Sometimes, though, reality grabs you by the throat. This

one kid at school, his mother has cancer. Right now she's doing okay, but whenever she goes for a doctor's appointment, this kid gets sick to his stomach the whole day, terrified they might find something bad. I mean, he's literally throwing up until she comes home.

He's a tough dude, by the way. Tougher than me, for sure.

Belinda and I are lucky because Mom's always been super-healthy. Still, I worry about other things—like her Uber job, driving around all alone with total strangers in the car. There are lots of jerks in this world, which isn't exactly front-page news. Sometimes Mom isn't as careful as she ought to be.

But I'd never worried about Dad that way, because he was gone from our lives so early. As they say: out of sight, out of mind. If he'd died back then, I'm not sure how sad I would have felt. It's hard to miss somebody you barely remember.

I'd miss him now, though.

Summer and I just found his gear—hat, sunglasses, backpack, bear spray, and drone. Most of the stuff is scattered down the slope of a small ravine. We see the satellite phone smashed to pieces at the base of an aspen tree. At the bottom of the ravine is a small creek where the barrel of Dad's submerged shotgun glints in the shallows.

I take out my plastic whistle thinking the high note will travel farther than a human voice. Our hope is that Dad's hiding somewhere nearby. Even if he can't signal back, at least he'll know we're out here searching for him. My mouth is dry as chalk, but somehow I get a few sharp bursts out of the whistle.

Summer clambers down the rain-slicked bank to retrieve the case holding the quadcopter. It seems to be undamaged. We kneel at the edge of the trees and use the binoculars to spy once more on the creepy fleet of buzzards.

This time we're close enough to see what's grabbed their attention. Two deer are lying on the ground, and I'm pretty sure they didn't drop dead from heart attacks. It looks like Lincoln Baxter is up to his old poacher tricks, baiting the bears.

"Why don't those birds land?" Summer says. "What are they afraid of?"

Good question. The buzzards should be down by now, devouring those carcasses before other forest scavengers arrive.

"Maybe they see something we can't see," I say.

If they do, it's probably not Lincoln Baxter. He would be well hidden somewhere, waiting and watching through the magnifying scope of his rifle.

"Hey, Billy."

"What?"

"Something moved! One of those deer!"

"Maybe it's still alive."

That might explain why the buzzards are waiting to land. They prefer their meals to be thoroughly expired.

Summer hands over the binoculars. "Check it out," she whispers hoarsely. "Only one of those things is a deer."

"Oh no."

The other body on the ground belongs to my father. Now I see his hiking boots.

"You're sure he moved?" I ask.

"Positive, Billy."

"A hundred percent sure? Because to me he looks . . . quiet."

"I'm a thousand percent sure. He moved."

"There's a rope around his ankles."

"I saw that," says Summer. "Which—why tie up a person who's dead?"

Excellent point.

So Dad's alive. That's the good news. The bad news is we can't run out there to help him without putting ourselves squarely in Baxter's view.

I snap open the case that holds the drone.

Summer says, "I thought you didn't know how to fly that thing."

"Now's a great time to learn."

"Time is the problem, Billy. We don't have any."

"The wind's dropping. This could actually work."

I set the quadcopter on the flattest piece of ground I can find. The four propellers attach easily. Then I program my phone to control the video camera—again, easier than I was expecting. Just click on the app Dad installed for me. After that, snap the phone into the cradle on the remote-control unit, and we're ready for lift-off.

Well, almost.

The remote has dual joysticks, one for "thrust" and one for "altitude." From watching Dad launch the drone, I remember him toggling both switches at the same time, though in opposing directions. That requires nimble coordination, and probably more than a few practice flights.

The first time I try it, the quadcopter rises to a measly altitude of three feet—maybe four—before suddenly streaking straight into the branches of a chokecherry tree. Luckily, there's no harm to the aircraft.

The twin joysticks would be easier to use if I were a hardcore gamer, but I'm not. I don't even own an Xbox. On my next attempt the drone goes higher but then loses power and spirals downward, bouncing on impact. This time one of the blades snaps. I scramble to replace it with a spare from the kit.

"So it's a crash course," Summer says. "Literally."

"You wanna try?"

"Just hurry up, Billy."

A few miraculous minutes later, the quadcopter is staying airborne. The camera works, too, feeding live flight video that we're watching on my phone.

"Now let's buzz those buzzards," I say.

They aren't as aggressive as eagles. Confronted by the speedy aircraft, the birds break formation and scatter high into the thermals.

I toggle back on the thrust, easing the drone into a

stationary position. It's a wobbly hover, though, so the view of the scene below is a bit unsteady: one extremely dead deer and one extremely uncomfortable Dennis Dickens.

A strip of gray tape covers Dad's mouth, and he's completely trussed with ropes. The knots binding his ankles and wrists are pegged to the ground with the same type of stakes that held down the helicopter's tarp.

Finally we know Lincoln Baxter's true plan. He never intended to kill my father himself. The grizzly that comes to eat the dead deer will do that. Then Baxter will kill the grizzly.

Summer and I feel sick and helpless. With no cell service for miles, our phones are useless. There's no way to call for help.

Dad wriggles against the ropes to let us know he sees the quadcopter.

"I want to go get him," Summer pleads, her voice cracking.

"Not yet."

Walking straight into Baxter's rifle sights would be crazy. Even if he didn't try to kill us, a warning shot could be deadly if it ricocheted the wrong way.

"You can't tell me what to do, Billy!"

"No, but I can chase you down and drag you back here," I said. "It's too dangerous out there, Summer. Let's try something else, okay?"

The drone's GPS isn't working, so I steer manually. I must be getting better—the aircraft returns to us as if it were on a wire, settling softly in the same spot it took off from. Inside the case is a small clawlike attachment—the same kind of device Dad used in this very meadow to deliver his first message to me.

After connecting the claw to the underside of the drone, I click on my phone app to enable the grab-and-release functions.

Summer says, "Fine. Now what?"

"This is what." I pull it from my pocket.

"Whoa." Summer's face lights up.

"A kid named Chin gave it to me."

"B.A.D. Is that you, Billy?"

"We'll see."

I untie one shoe, peel off my sock, and slide the heavy pocketknife inside. After hanging the sock on the mechanical claw, I launch the drone toward my father.

And, yes, I know his hands are tied. He'll figure it out. Mr. Government Spy.

When it stops, the quadcopter's altitude is twenty-three feet, slightly higher than a two-story house. Dad lies absolutely still, his eyes locked on the hovering drone.

I touch the button. The claw's talons open. The knife drops . . .

. . . and hits my father right between the legs.

"Ouch," says Summer.

The sock helped cushion the blow. I honestly think so.

Still, Dad's eyes are clenched tight, and the veins in his neck are bulging. It's probably a good thing there's no audio.

On the plus side, the impact caused Dad to jerk so violently that he yanked the top stake out of the dirt. His hands remain tied at the wrists, but at least he'll be able to grab the sock, shake out the knife, and open it.

And he'd better move fast.

I move the toggles to turn the drone around.

Summer and I are glued to the video feed. Our last screen glimpse of Dad shows him fumbling with the sock. I wonder if Lincoln Baxter is seeing the same thing through his rifle scope. With any luck, he's looking elsewhere, scanning the meadow and timber ridges in search of his long-awaited prize.

Which the quadcopter spies first.

The unmistakable image flashes on my phone, striking us cold with dread.

Summer cries, "Make the drone go back!"

Easier said than done, for a rookie pilot. An incredibly nervous rookie pilot.

The aircraft is sluggish to respond. Summer raises the binoculars.

"Can you see it?" I ask.

"You mean 'her.'"

"How far from Dad?"

"A hundred yards, max," Summer says. "Maybe less. No, definitely less."

This is what they call a worst-case scenario.

After what feels like an eternity, I finally coax the quadcopter into a stable position high above the grizzly, which is standing tall on two legs and sniffing the air.

It's got to be the same bear I thought I saw—and obviously did see—the first time I was here. Her two cubs stop wrestling in the goldenrods to peer up at the sky. They hear the high-pitched hum of the mini-spycraft.

On the camera the baby bears look like chocolate fur balls, while momma on her hind legs is a brawny, unhuggable tree trunk. Suddenly she drops to all fours and starts loping toward the poacher's target zone, double-baited with a lifeless deer and a roped-down human.

"You know what to do," Summer says. "Make it fast."

Using a puny little drone to scare a big-ass alpha predator requires precise flying skills and flawless reflexes. My father is pro at this, but he's currently not available to instruct me. Cautiously I thumb the thrust lever to begin the pursuit.

As quick-footed as grizzlies are, the quadcopter easily keeps pace. I drop the altitude until the drone is flying at eye level with the running bear. She's trying to figure out whether the airborne invader is just a noisy pest or a serious threat.

At once she slams on the brakes, her cubs crashing clumsily into her rear end. It's impossible to stop the drone that fast, so I fumble with the joysticks, trying to navigate a crash-free U-turn.

Summer reports that the big grizzly is very close to the

spot where Dad is tied down. "She's standing up again, Billy. Not a happy mom."

I struggle to keep the quadcopter positioned between my father and the bear family. The drone is fluttering like a dizzy duck, but eventually I get it stopped in exactly the right place—floating near enough to bother the momma grizzly, but far enough to avoid those ham-sized killer paws.

Even though I'm viewing her through a tiny camera lens, the expression in the bear's eyes makes the hair rise on my neck. She's deciding whether to attack or run away with the cubs.

Running away is what we want her to do—the faster and farther, the better.

For the moment it's a standoff between a mountainous beast and a pint-sized flying machine. Standing beside me, still watching through the binoculars, Summer asks, "Is that you beeping?"

"It's the remote control."

"What does that mean?"

"I'm not positive," I say, "but I think it means the battery's low."

"The battery in the drone? The one that makes it fly?"

"Okay, we need to stay chill."

Without a proper pilot lesson, I'm unaware of all the high-tech features on Dad's new quadcopter. Apparently it came with advanced software that automatically guides it back to the takeoff location when it needs recharging. This ultra-smart program is very convenient—unless the GPS doesn't work because there's no cell tower nearby, and an angry four-hundred-pound carnivore is standing between the aircraft and the spot where you want it to land.

"What's going on?" Summer says. "Does that crazy drone have a death wish?"

"It doesn't know where to go. No GPS signal!"

"Then *you* be the GPS, Billy. Steer it around the bear!"

Once again I grasp at the toggles, but there's no time to change the flight direction. The quadcopter is way too close to the grizzly, and the grizzly is way too quick.

Helplessly I watch the fateful collision on my phone. The final image is a ferocious flash of teeth. Then the screen goes blank.

"She got it!" Summer blurts. "One bite."

I snatch the binoculars to see for myself. The mother grizzly is gnawing on the mangled drone. With a snarl she spits out the pieces and rakes a claw through the pile of cracked plastic and shredded wires.

Summer exhales in despair. "She's not leaving, is she?"

"Nope."

"Billy?"

"I know, I know."

The bear and her cubs are still hungry, and they smell dinner.

Catered by Lincoln Chumley Baxter IV.

TWENTY-ONE

The animals march toward my captive father's location. All that Summer and I can do is try to spook them.

Frantically we clap, yell, even whoop, trying to make the scariest sounds two medium-sized humans can make. The grizzlies act the opposite of scared. They don't even bother to glance our way.

After chomping the noisy mutant bumblebee—or whatever she thought the drone was—the momma bear seems calm and confident as she leads her offspring to the wilderness version of a LongHorn Steakhouse.

If deer is the main course, Dad will be dessert.

Or the other way around.

It seems impossible that he hasn't gotten the pocketknife open by now, yet I still see him wriggling on the ground. For me and Summer to dash out there and distract the grizzlies would be a suicide mission. She's ready to try, but I won't let her. None of us, including my father, would get out of here alive.

Leaving Mom and Lil brokenhearted forever.

Despite the horror I'm feeling, I can't put down the binoculars. Tears are puddling in the eyecups.

The knife drop should have worked, I swear. It was the smart play . . . our *only* play.

"Whoa, bear," I whisper to myself.

Summer says, "Look, she's up again!"

Only a few strides from the deer carcass, the mother bear has halted and risen to her full height. Behind her, the cubs are standing, too.

So, finally, is Dad.

"They're staring at him," I say in a shaky voice.

"Obviously."

"What in the world is he doing?"

"I have no clue," says Summer.

Everybody who lives in Montana knows the drill if you cross paths with a wild grizzly: Take out your bear spray, just in case. Don't run. Stay as motionless as possible. Speak in a low, non-threatening tone. Avoid eye contact. Back away slowly.

Dad's can of bear spray is in the ravine, so scratch that off the list.

And he's definitely not standing still.

"Is that some kind of Crow dance?" I ask Summer.

"No," she says. "That's a crazy white guy trying not to get eaten."

Draped with dangling lengths of rope, Dad's arms are up-raised and swaying like palm trees in a breeze.

The mother bear seems totally puzzled. Who wouldn't be?

Summer says, "I get it now. He's trying to make himself look big."

I remember reading about an old hiker who always car-ries an umbrella when traveling through wild country. If he encounters a grizzly, the first thing he does is open the umbrella above his head. He says it gives him the shape of a much larger animal, and discourages the bear from charging.

The umbrella trick isn't often recommended by wilderness pros, but this must be Dad's version, using the ropes he cut off with Chin's knife. From here he looks like a tall, shaggy capital Y.

The momma grizzly has never faced such a peculiar creature, and she's not sure how to react.

A ringing gunshot makes her decision easy. She wheels around and gallops toward the woods, the cubs at her heels. A second shot follows, pinging off a rock.

Summer says, "Where did he go? I lost him!"

"Me too." Instead of watching the bears retreat, I should have been watching Dad.

"Look over there, Billy! More to the right. No, over *there!*"

"Where?" The binoculars are shaking in my hands. "How far?"

"Between us and that bare split pine, on the far side of the meadow."

"Now I see him!"

My father is moving away from the grizzlies and gunfire—though not as rapidly as he should.

"Could he possibly run any slower?" Summer groans.

"That's not running," I say. "That's limping."

And at the very instant Dad comes into perfect focus, he disappears into the high timber.

* * *

You're probably thinking: *Now would be a good time to go for help.*

The bears are long gone, and it should be easy for my father to locate a hiding place where Lincoln Baxter can't find him. The sensible thing for me and Summer to do is hurry back to the road, jump in her cousin's car, and race to the nearest ranch that has a working phone.

Except for one thing: Dad was limping, which means he's hurt. The question is how badly. Did he twist an ankle, which is no big deal, or did he get hit by one of the poacher's bullets?

This time, when Summer says we should go after him, I say, "You're right."

First we backtrack to the ravine and retrieve Dad's gear. I gather up his backpack, sunglasses, hat, and bear spray. Summer wades into the creek for the shotgun.

"Broken," she calls up to me.

"Then leave it."

Walking through the thick pines and underbrush is a slog, because there's no trail to follow. I blow the plastic whistle hoping Dad's close enough to hear.

Unfortunately for us, someone else is closer. We don't discover this until he steps in front of us and says, "Stop right there, both of you."

I've never had a real gun pointed at me before. Judging by Summer's expression, this is her first time, too.

"Who are you?" barks Lincoln Chumley Baxter IV.

He's got the full camo thing going on—gloves, a hood, even face paint. He looks furious and jumpy at the same time, gnawing an unlit cigar. Two more are visible in his vest pocket.

The rifle he's carrying is a big one, but I'm sure they all look big when they're aimed in your direction.

Summer and I respond with first names only.

"What the hell are you doing out here?" Baxter demands.

"Hiking" is my answer.

"Don't lie to me, *Billy*. Or whatever your real name is."

We've messed up his scheme, big-time. Now he doesn't know what to do with us.

"We came to find my father," I say.

"That guy you tried to feed to the bears," Summer adds fearlessly.

Baxter looks angry enough to shoot us right here and now. His bleached-white teeth are bared, giving him the appearance of a rabid poodle.

He doesn't pull the trigger, though. Some tiny corner of his tiny macho brain is telling him that poaching humans is way more serious than poaching grizzlies or panthers.

"Mrs. Baxter doesn't think much of your hobby," I say.

It's not that I'm trying to piss him off. I just want him to realize that we know his name, and that we've also got a pipeline to his wife. If anything bad happens to us, she'll know who did it.

When you're in the middle of negotiating, this is known as *leverage*.

"You've got no idea what you're talkin' about," Baxter says, without much steam.

Summer waggles a finger at him. "Please don't point your gun at us. I'm a Crow Indian, FYI."

Which is the perfect line, because it gives Baxter one more thing to worry about.

"Trust me," Summer says. "You don't want the whole Crow Nation mad at you."

She's guessing that his view of Native Americans comes from the movies. She wants him to think there's an arrow in his future.

And sure enough, he lowers the rifle.

"I wasn't gonna shoot anybody," he says, "unless they gave me no choice."

I tell him we don't have any weapons.

"How do I know you're not lying?"

"Right. We're gonna attack you with what—a stale granola bar?"

"If you don't believe us," says Summer, "check our backpacks."

We drop all three of them—mine, hers, and Dad's—on the ground. Baxter empties the contents and shrugs. "Fine. Whatever."

He stomps both of our cell phones and kicks them into the bushes.

One thing he does *not* do is order us to empty our pockets.

"So, your plan was to let the grizzly kill my dad," I say. "Then you'd shoot the bear, and tell the game wardens . . . what exactly?"

"That it was justified, of course," says Baxter. "It's completely legal to take a grizzly in self-defense. First the bear attacks your old man, then he charges after me. That was my story—and they would've believed it, too."

"But you shot a deer for bait, and it's not even hunting season. How were you gonna explain *that*?"

The poacher allows himself a smile. "There's not a single bullet in that deer. It got hit by a car on Highway Eighty-nine, and it was dead when I found it. Now, how it got all the way out here for the bears to eat—who knows?"

Summer cuts in: "We saw your helicopter, Mr. Baxter. Mystery solved."

There's something I need to ask the guy before all this ends.

"Why shoot a grizzly bear?" I say. "What's the point of killing an animal that's disappearing from the planet?"

"That's easy. It's the challenge—they're humongous and dangerous and, best of all, very rare." Baxter clearly has no shame. "There's barely seven hundred grizzlies left in all of Montana, Wyoming, and Idaho. Once it's legal to hunt 'em, they'll get smart and super-hard to find. That's why I'm out here now, before they catch on."

"You're serious, aren't you?"

"I am, boy. And you're too young to be judging me."

Summer clasps my arm but, hey, I'm not crazy enough to throw a punch at a person holding a loaded gun.

She says, "Mr. Baxter, the bear you shot at today had two cubs."

"They'd be fine on their own, honey. They're tough little *hombres*."

Summer tightens her grip. Now she's the one who looks like she wants to jump him.

"Besides," he adds, "I was only trying to save your old man's life—which I did, by the way."

"But you'd tied him to the ground!" I say.

"No, here's what really happened. I was sightseeing in my personal helicopter, minding my own business, when I spotted this dumb-ass hiker all by himself in griz country. Then I saw a huge bear start following him. So I landed the chopper, grabbed my gun, and fired two rounds to scare off that vicious beast. That's my new official story. And if you or your daddy says otherwise, I'll tell the game wardens he brought his drone out here to spy on the grizzlies, so he could shoot one himself. I'll even show 'em the creek where he 'dropped' his gun. And, guess what—it'll be my word against his."

"And ours, too," Summer bristles.

Baxter laughs acidly. "Kids'll always lie to protect their father. You don't think the authorities know that? Like I said, it would be your daddy's word against mine, a well-respected businessman from an old, well-respected family. What they call a pillar of society. That's me."

An edgy lull follows. Songbirds high in the branches remind me where we are, in the midst of a mountain forest after a hard rain. The crisp air smells sweet enough to drink. Golden rays of sunlight slant through gaps in the treetops. A place so peaceful and perfect is totally wasted on a jerk like Baxter.

"If you two are smart," he says, "you'll have a long talk with your old man. Explain the situation. Make him understand that the best thing to do is forget he ever knew my name. Now, speaking of yours truly, I am outta here. . . ."

Then, as if somebody flipped a switch, the birds quit singing. Lincoln Baxter halts in mid-stride, turns back slowly, and pulls his gun close to his chest.

"Hear that?" he whispers.

How could we *not*?

Something heavy is advancing toward us through the woods. It's not trying to be sneaky, either, which indicates a total lack of fear. Branches snap, bushes thrash, and dead logs crack under the weight of whatever is coming.

"No way that's a deer," Baxter murmurs anxiously. "Or even an elk."

"It's not a moose, either," says Summer. "Moose are quiet."

I'd say we've narrowed the list.

As the animal draws closer, it lets loose a deep chorus of nerve-wracking sounds—huffing, snorting, grunting, growling. I try to sing the go-away-bear chant, but the words die in my throat. Summer's fingernails are digging into my arm. Crouched nearby, Baxter seems to have forgotten we're here.

As the oncoming uproar grows louder, the saplings and bushes begin to part in front of us. Baxter raises his rifle to his shoulder, while I reach for the pocket where I put Dad's can of bear spray.

At the same moment Baxter takes aims at the fierce commotion, I take aim, too.

Blasting the poacher point-blank in the face.

The main ingredient in bear spray is called capsaicin. It comes from hot cayenne peppers. This isn't necessary information if you live a quiet normal life, but I did a little research. I wanted to be sure I'd be carrying enough firepower.

Propelled by an aerosol burst, capsaicin doesn't blind predators, but it makes their eyes and mouth burn like the devil. A faceful of pepper mist is so painful that a charging grizzly often wheels around and flees, which is the whole point.

Bear spray won't blind humans, either, but the experience is pure agony. Lincoln Baxter crumples to the ground screaming. The gun drops from his hands.

With a growl and a huff, Dad lurches out of a thicket. He shakes off a few loose ropes and looks down at the writhing poacher.

"Good shot, Billy," he says. "But how'd you know it was *me* coming at you?"

"Wild guess."

"You mean lucky guess."

Summer gasps, "You're bleeding!"

"Yes, I am," Dad replies.

He kneels beside the yowling, scarlet-faced Baxter, seizes him by the camo hood, and says, "Aren't you sorry you didn't take up golf?"

Then he calmly dumps the bullets from Baxter's rifle and hurls them downhill into a thorny thicket.

"We should get you to a doctor," I say. "Don't you think?"

TWENTY-TWO

It was Baxter's second shot that bounced off a rock and struck Dad in the thigh. He plugged the wound with a knotted bandanna to slow the bleeding. The team at the emergency room said that might have saved his life.

We had rushed Dad from the Tom Miner Basin to a fire station near the Pine Creek Lodge. Summer drove faster than the speed limit. The paramedics didn't ask to see her license. They loaded Dad into an ambulance and raced straight to Bozeman.

Mom flew in yesterday to make sure I was okay. I got a thirty-second hug and a thirty-minute lecture. Afterward, she agreed to come to the hospital, where my father spent the rest of the afternoon apologizing to her and Lil.

The poacher's bullet tore through some muscles and nicked his thigh bone, but Dad's going to be all right. A surgeon cut him open and fixed him up. The sheriff's department is keeping the crumpled slug for evidence.

Belinda has been texting me from Florida. She wants a photo of Dad in the hospital bed. So he poses for her, giving a halfhearted thumbs-up. His room has an amazing view of the Bridger Mountains, but he's still in a lousy mood, mad at himself for getting captured by Lincoln Baxter in the woods.

"Unbelievable," he grumbles. "I thought I was smarter than that."

Lil and Mom restrain themselves from stating the obvious.

"What did Baxter tell you?" I ask Dad.

"That he was sick and tired of me hassling him with the drone. While he was tying me up, he said, 'You like grizzly bears so much, now you're gonna see how much they like *you*.'"

The rope marks on his wrists are still pink and raw.

"The cops'll catch up with him soon," Lil says.

Dad stares listlessly out the window. "Maybe. Maybe not."

"Of course they will," says Mom.

Summer kisses his forehead. "You're still the craziest white man I ever saw."

Dad's roommate is a wheat farmer who broke his hip when an ATV flipped on top of him. He's not getting much rest, because Dad has lots of visitors.

Sheriff's deputies have been at the hospital two days in a row, along with officers from the Forest Service. Dad told them everything about his secret drone missions to stop Lincoln Baxter's poaching. I don't think they're ready to give him a medal, but they're acting like they believe him—at least for now. Dad is well aware that Baxter will spout a totally different story, if they find him.

Summer and I were questioned, too. They wanted to know everything Baxter said while he held us at gunpoint. One of the Forest Service officers took us to an empty hospital room and spread a topographical map of the Tom Miner Basin on the bed.

"Where was the last place you saw this man?" he asked.

I pointed to the ravine and said, "Afterward, he probably ran down to the creek to wash the bear spray off his face."

"We've already searched that area. Twice."

"Then maybe he's gone. All you've got to do is find that red helicopter."

"Oh, we've got the helicopter. It was tied down in the same place you saw it. Right *there*." The officer tapped his pen on a black X that had been drawn on the map.

"The door of the chopper was wide open," he added, "but there was no trace of Mr. Baxter."

Summer acted surprised. "So he could still be out there somewhere?"

"Possibly. We assumed he'd walk out to the dirt road and then hitchhike to the main highway, but his family in California hasn't heard from him."

Summer said, "I don't get why he didn't use the helicopter to escape."

"We believe something scared him out of the cockpit."

"Like what?"

"Like a rattlesnake," said the officer, "on the pilot's seat."

"Whoa!" Summer widened her eyes. "Was the snake alive?"

"Oh, extremely." The officer capped his pen. "Coiled up inside a pillowcase. Very weird."

My stepsister was trying her hardest not to look at me.

"Maybe Baxter's a snake collector," I said.

"No, his wife told us he's terrified of them." The officer rolled up the map. "Want to hear something else? The rattler's mouth was taped shut."

"Really?" I replied. "Now *that* is weird."

I know, I *know*.

I said I wouldn't do it again, but I did.

What I put on the snake's jaws wasn't regular tape. It was a Steri-Strip, a sticky piece of medical fabric designed to protect stitches or small wounds. They're available at any pharmacy, including the Western Drug store in Livingston, Montana, where Summer and I stopped on our way to Tom Miner.

Unlike ordinary surgical tape, Steri-Strips fall off by themselves after about ten days. That's exactly what I needed, because I didn't want the rattler to be crawling around too long with its mouth held shut. Usually they go about two weeks between meals.

Again, no normal person would need to know that.

You might be wondering: *How do you get a rattlesnake to hold still long enough so you can tape its mouth?*

I'm not telling. It's too dangerous—and I mean, insanely, ridiculously dangerous.

I'll never do it again. This time I'm serious. And if you're foolish enough to imagine it might be fun, I encourage you to google "rattlesnake" and check out the fangs.

Here was the conversation that took place between me

and Summer shortly after we "borrowed" her cousin's old Subaru.

Me: "Where can I go to catch a rattler?"

Her: "Right now? What on earth for?"

Me: "For when we find Baxter's car at Tom Miner. A big loud snake on the seat might change his travel plans."

Her: "You mean if he does something bad to Dennis and tries to get away?"

Me: "I need to stop at a drugstore, too. Oh—and I borrowed a pillowcase from your house."

Her: "There's a rocky bluff near the gun range north of town. It's covered with rattlers. I hope you know what you're doing, Billy."

Summer was right about the bluff. Halfway up, I caught a chunky three-footer by pinning its neck with a juniper stick. I waited for the snake to quit squirming before attempting to secure its mouth. Summer's job was to hand me the Steri-Strip. She was also my ride to the ER, if I screwed up.

Once inside the pillowcase, the rattler balled up and chilled out. Gently I placed the sack in my backpack and closed the zipper. During our slow stormy hike to the grizzly meadow, I heard the snake vibrate its tail only two or three times.

As it turned out, the red helicopter presented the same opportunity as a car: an empty driver's seat in Baxter's getaway vehicle. No doubt he noticed the pillowcase right away, and picked it up out of curiosity. He might have even shaken it, or messed with the knot.

Obviously the rattler woke up grumpy, making a noise that Baxter would have recognized instantly—and run away from.

For once, what I'd hoped would happen actually did happen.

"Where's the snake now?" I asked the officer who was interviewing us.

"We turned it over to State Fish and Wildlife. They let it go someplace safe."

Summer said, "But first they peeled the tape off its jaws, right?"

"Yes, ma'am. Very carefully." The officer put the rolled-up map under his arm. "I've spent my whole life in the wild, and two things I never, *ever* fool around with are grizzly bears and rattlesnakes. But let me tell you, there's some crazy-ass people out there."

"Yeah," I said. "Scary crazy."

The next day, Dad was released from the hospital. They wanted him to take both crutches but he insisted he only needed one. Lil spent the afternoon making his favorite meal—lamb chops, garden veggies, and huckleberry pie. Belinda actually called to see how he was doing, which magically brightened his mood.

When all of us sit down at the table, the first thing he says is: "Did they find Baxter?"

"Not yet, Dennis," Lil answers patiently.

This is like the fiftieth time he's asked since he got out of surgery.

"Baxter doesn't want to be found," Summer says. "He knows we got to the cops first and told them everything. Hey, the dude's so rich he could be in Paris by now."

Dad's tracing little circles in the air with his fork. "I can't stop wondering how a bag holding a prairie rattlesnake got inside that chopper." His eyes drift in my direction. "Isn't that bizarre?"

So I need to invent a semi-believable theory, quick.

"Maybe the snake was Baxter's Plan B for getting rid of you," I say, "in case the bear thing didn't work out. He could have paid somebody to go catch him one."

"Billy, you wouldn't ever fool around with a live rattler, would you?"

"Dennis, your dinner's getting cold," says Mom, without so much as glancing at me. There is no doubt she's figured out what happened.

I'm also sure that Lil, who knows I'm not afraid of snakes, assumes I'm the one who put the rattler in the poacher's helicopter. In front of my parents, she's nice enough not to mention the pillowcase that's missing from the bed in the guest room.

Daisy Baxter called earlier. She and Dad talked for a long time. She'd already spoken with the sheriff and the rangers, but she wanted a firsthand account of what went down at Tom Miner. She was also baffled about the rattle-snake in the chopper, but mostly she was flat-out furious at her husband—and sick about the shooting. She still hadn't heard from Lincoln, and it didn't sound like she was waiting anxiously by the phone. She told my father she'd already hired a divorce lawyer.

"Another good reason for Mr. Baxter to keep hiding," Mom remarks.

Dad, who is now inhaling the lamb chops, pauses to say, "I bet *I* could find him."

The coldness of our collective stare draws an instant apology. "You're right, you're right, that's a terrible idea," he says. "I guess I'm still loopy from all the medicine they gave me."

Lil smiles. "Admit it, Dennis. You're just loopy, *period.*"

Summer asks Dad about the savage noises he was making while he clomped through the woods. "Exactly what kind of creature was that supposed to be?"

"Really? A bear, what else!"

"Because . . . ?"

"I was scared of running into that momma griz," he says. "Females with cubs always run from big male grizzlies, so that's what I was imitating."

"No offense, Dad," I say, "but you sounded like a gorilla with asthma."

"My son the comedian."

"Seriously. That's why I blasted Baxter with the pepper spray before he could fire his gun. I figured it had to be you crashing through those trees. No self-respecting bear would make so much racket."

Dad grins sheepishly before turning serious. "If it weren't for you, Billy, I wouldn't be sitting here right now."

"And if you had an ounce of sense, Dennis," Mom says, "*none* of us would be sitting here right now, talking about the stupid bullet hole in your leg. If it weren't for you, none of us would be nervous wrecks. We'd all be out on the river, enjoying this lovely summer day."

"That's right," says Lil, "looking for eagles."

Summer and I are sensible enough to stay out of this one. My father clears his throat and announces that he's ready for a slice of huckleberry pie.

TWENTY-THREE

This one kid, he never stayed in the same town more than a couple years.

His mother kept moving the family from place to place because she was obsessed with eagle nests, of all things. The kid didn't try to make friends when he started at a new school, because he knew he wouldn't be there long, so what was the point?

Still, he didn't feel lonely or left out. He spent all his free time outdoors in the woods and wetlands, fishing, hiking, catching snakes.

The kid was different, definitely. He'd be the first to admit it.

One summer he got to travel to Montana. *Twice*. He was visiting his father, whom he hadn't seen for many years.

It wasn't a simple situation. The kid's dad had a new family and a dangerous job he didn't want to talk about. Lots of sketchy stuff was going on, but in time it all worked out. The kid was glad he went.

He came back to Florida with a good story. The only problem was the ending. There was one loose strand, one big question that remained unanswered.

Until now, maybe.

* * *

Except for working at the supermarket, I'm grounded until school starts in August. I really want to hop on my bike and go check my favorite snake spots, but that's not happening. Mom says the subject is closed.

So I'm in my room, reading, trying not to go nuts.

She knocks on the door. "Billy, come out here. Someone sent you a package."

The box came from Livingston, Montana, the house on Geyser Street.

"What're you waiting for? Open it already," says Belinda, hovering.

College starts in a couple weeks, and she's still trying to decide what to pack. Her clothes are piled all over the house. And the shoes? Seriously—she'll need to rent a semi-truck to carry all her shoes.

Inside the box from Montana are three hand-wrapped items and a plain brown envelope addressed to "Billy Big Stick."

First the gifts:

Little Thunder-Sky sent my mother a real golden eagle feather she found on the banks of the Yellowstone River. The feather is creamy white with a coffee-brown tip, which means it came from the bird's tail. A prize, in other words. Mom is speechless.

Summer Chasing-Hawks sent my sister a pair of shell

earrings, the same ones that had belonged to her great-grandmother on the Crow reservation. I was afraid Belinda would make some snarky comment about Summer's present, but she reacted as if they were diamonds. The earrings look good on her, I've got to admit.

My father sent me something solid, taped in Bubble Wrap. It's the engraved pocketknife that Chin had given me, the one that walloped Dad in a highly sensitive region when it dropped from the drone.

Dear B.A.D., says a neatly penned note inside the Bubble Wrap, *please aim higher next time!*

P.S. Thanks for saving my life, in more ways than one.

I open the envelope and unfold an article clipped from the Bozeman newspaper. Above the headline, somebody using a red Sharpie has jotted: *Nature always gets the last word!*

It's Summer's handwriting. I recognize it from the checks she mails to Mom.

Here's the headline on the article: FEW CLUES IN SEARCH FOR MISSING SPORTSMAN.

I'm thinking: *"Sportsman"? Give me a break.*

According to the news story, the whereabouts of Lincoln Chumley Baxter IV, a prominent California businessman and avid outdoorsman, remain unknown. A spokesperson for his family's real-estate company said Baxter piloted his helicopter to the Tom Miner Basin to scout for elk in advance of the fall hunting season—a weak excuse that nobody in Paradise Valley would believe.

Searchers found Baxter's empty rifle discarded on a thorny embankment. The weapon had been fired twice, raising the possibility that Baxter's true intention was to poach wild game. Three hikers—that would be me, Summer, and Dad—reported a "violent encounter" with the hunter.

Apparently the sheriff didn't give the details (or our names) to the newspaper, which is probably a good thing. Meanwhile Mrs. Daisy Baxter is directing all questions to her attorney, who won't comment.

Summer had underlined the last two paragraphs of the article:

> In addition to the rifle, searchers found a half-smoked cigar in a large mound of bear scat. A female grizzly with two young cubs has been seen in the area.
>
> Although Baxter is known to favor the same brand of cigar, authorities say it's too soon to draw any conclusions from this disturbing discovery.

Summer already drew her conclusion, obviously. She thinks the stogie in the bear poop means Nature got the last word. I'd say that's a definite possibility.

The next morning is Sunday, so we pack our binoculars, sunblock, and patience. Mom parks behind the same bait shop where we always leave the car. From there it's a short walk to the lagoon. For two hours we stand in the broiling heat staring up at the sky, waiting for the bald eagles. Belinda says her neck hurts. Mine does, too.

"That nest is just a mess," Mom mutters.

"They'll fix it up," I say.

Eagle parents usually begin to tidy their nests toward the end of September. The female lays her eggs in December or January.

"But what if they're gone, Billy?"

"The birds aren't gone, Mom."

"I read where there's a new pair in Sarasota. They built their nest on top of a cell-phone tower."

"I don't want to move to Sarasota."

Belinda says she can't wait to be at college, far away from all this craziness.

"That isn't very nice," Mom says. "You think I'm crazy?"

Major groan from Belinda. "That is not what I said."

My phone rings. It's such a rare event that my mother and sister stop arguing to stare in surprise.

Before answering, I check the name on the caller ID.

"So who is it?" Mom asks.

"It's Dad."

Belinda says, "You're kidding."

He sounds pretty good, for a guy who just got shot.

"Billy, did you get the package with the knife?"

"I did, thanks. How's your leg?"

"I'm a rock star at rehab. Yesterday I threw away my crutch!"

He asks to say hi to Mom and Belinda, so I pass the

phone along. Overhead I can see pelicans, gulls, and the occasional heron—but no baldies.

When I get back on the line, my father says, "They still haven't caught Lincoln Baxter. What do you suppose that means?"

"It's too late."

"You think he left the state?"

"No, Dad. I think he left this world. I think he made a wrong turn in the deep timber, and ran into that momma grizzly."

"Then why didn't they find more than a cigar butt?"

"There's miles of big country out there. Baxter could be anywhere—what's left of him."

"So Billy Big Stick believes in karma."

"More like justice, Dad."

He says, "You should see my new drone. I named it Sophie."

"Why do you need a new drone? You promised Lil no more secret missions."

"Summer didn't tell you? I lined up a job with the Montana tourism office, making aerial videos for their TV commercials."

"Wait—you're officially done chasing poachers?"

"Absolutely. All my future drone trips will be strictly scenic—mountains and rivers, sunrises and sunsets. 'Video postcards' are what they want."

"You'll crush it, Dad," I say, though I don't believe his

story for a minute. He'd be bored out of his skull doing video commercials, and I'll bet my bicycle there's nobody named Dennis Dickens on the payroll of the Montana tourism board.

"I'll talk to you later this week, Billy."

"You will?"

"On Thursday. From now on, I'll be calling every Thursday."

"Okay. That'll work," I say.

"Unless your mom doesn't want me to."

"I'm pretty sure she won't mind."

On the flight home, Mom had apologized for cutting up the envelopes that arrived every month from Montana. She said she didn't want me and Belinda seeing Dad's address and then writing to him, because that would let him off the hook. She wanted him to be the one to reach out, as any decent father should. It was the principle of the thing, she said.

When I asked if it was weird seeing him in a new place with a new family, Mom smiled and said it wasn't as awkward as she expected. She told me she admired what he was doing with his life now, but then quickly added: "He's still impossible, Billy. All over the map, as they say. Lil's got a thousand times more patience than I ever did."

Gray clouds are sneaking in, and soon a warm rain begins to fall on the lagoon. Our eagle lookout point is a picnic area near the water's edge, a small clearing away from the trees. Mom flings a waterproof jacket over her head. She looks restless and bummed. Belinda wants to walk back to the car.

"Ten more minutes," I say.

"Five," snaps Belinda. "My hair's getting drenched."

Mom peeks out at me. "I saw where there's a new magnet school near that nest in Sarasota."

"Too bad I'm not a magnetic person."

"Don't be a smart-ass, Billy."

I dry the lenses of my binoculars and make another slow sweep of the treetops.

"Well, hey there," I say.

Mom's head pops out from under the jacket. "What is it? You see something?"

I point. She looks up.

"Where, Billy? Show me!"

"Right there. Three pines north of the nest."

The eagles are perched on the same branch, raindrops glistening on their dark feathers. Both snowy faces are looking our way.

Belinda says, "Okay, now I see 'em."

My mother clenches her binoculars. "Oh my God, look at that! Have they been up there this whole time watching us?"

"It wouldn't surprise me," I say. "We're pretty amusing."

"Look how close together they're sitting. I love that!"

"I told you they weren't gone, Mom. They like this place."

"I guess they do."

Belinda asks if we can go home now.

"Not just yet," my mother says in a hushed, happy voice.

It feels nice out here. The rain won't last long, but I wouldn't mind if it poured all day.

When Wahoo Cray's dad—a professional animal wrangler—
takes a job with a reality-TV survival show, Wahoo figures
he'll have to do a bit of wrangling himself to keep his father
from killing the show's inept and egotistical star. But the job
keeps getting more complicated—and it isn't just the animals
who are ready to chomp.

ONE

Mickey Cray had been out of work ever since a dead iguana fell from a palm tree and hit him on the head.

The iguana, which had died during a hard freeze, was stiff as a board and weighed seven and a half pounds. Mickey's son had measured the lifeless lizard on a fishing scale, then packed it on ice with the turtle veggies, in the cooler behind the garage.

This was after the ambulance had hauled Mickey off to the hospital, where the doctors said he had a serious concussion and ordered him to take it easy.

And to everyone's surprise, Mickey did take it easy. That's because the injury left him with double vision and terrible headaches. He lost his appetite and dropped nineteen pounds and lay around on the couch all day, watching nature programs on television.

"I'll never be the same," he told his son.

"Knock it off, Pop," said Wahoo, Mickey's boy.

Mickey had named him after Wahoo McDaniel, a professional wrestler who'd once played linebacker for the Dolphins. Mickey's son often wished he'd been called Mickey Jr. or Joe or even Rupert—anything but Wahoo, which was also a species of saltwater fish.

It was a name that was hard to live up to. People naturally

expected somebody called Wahoo to act loud and crazy, but that wasn't Wahoo's style. Apparently nothing could be done about the name until he was all grown up, at which point he intended to go to the Cutler Ridge courthouse and tell a judge he wanted to be called something normal.

"Pop, you're gonna be okay," Wahoo would tell his father every morning. "Just hang in there."

Looking up with hound-dog eyes from the couch, Mickey Cray would say, "Whatever happens, I'm glad we ate that bleeping lizard."

On the day his dad had come home from the hospital, Wahoo had defrosted the dead iguana and made a peppercorn stew, which his mom had wisely refused to touch. Mickey had insisted that eating the critter that had dented his skull would be a spiritual remedy. "Big medicine," he'd predicted.

But the iguana had tasted awful, and Mickey Cray's headaches only got worse. Wahoo's mother was so concerned that she wanted Mickey to see a brain specialist in Miami, but Mickey refused to go.

Meanwhile, people kept calling up with new jobs, and Wahoo was forced to send them to other wranglers. His father was in no condition to work.

After school, Wahoo would feed the animals and clean out the pens and cages. The backyard was literally a zoo—gators, snakes, parrots, mynah birds, rats, mice, monkeys, raccoons, tortoises and even a bald eagle, which Mickey had raised from a fledgling after its mother was killed.

"Treat 'em like royalty," Mickey would instruct Wahoo, because the animals were quite valuable. Without them, Mickey would be unemployed.

It disturbed Wahoo to see his father so ill because Mickey was the toughest guy he'd ever known.

One morning, with summer approaching, Wahoo's mother took him aside and told him that the family's savings account was almost drained. "I'm going to China," she said.

Wahoo nodded, like it was no big deal.

"For two months," she said.

"That's a long time," said Wahoo.

"Sorry, big guy, but we really need the money."

Wahoo's mother taught Mandarin Chinese, an extremely difficult language. Big American companies that had offices in China would hire Mrs. Cray to tutor their top executives, but usually these companies flew their employees to South Florida for Mrs. Cray's lessons.

"This time they want me to go to Shanghai," she explained to her son. "They have, like, fifty people over there who learned Mandarin from some cheap audiotape. The other day, one of the big shots was trying to say 'Nice shoes!' and he accidentally told a government minister that his face looked like a butt wart. Not good."

"Did you tell Pop you're going?"

"That's next."

Wahoo slipped outside to clean Alice's pond. Alice the alligator was one of Mickey Cray's stars. She was twelve feet long and as tame as a guppy, but she looked truly ferocious. Over the years Alice had appeared often in front of a camera. Her credits included nine feature films, two National Geographic documentaries, a three-part Disney special about the Everglades and a TV commercial for a fancy French skin lotion.

She lay sunning on the mudbank while Wahoo skimmed the dead leaves and sticks from the water. Her eyes were closed, but Wahoo knew she was listening.

"Hungry, girl?" he asked.

The gator's mouth opened wide, the inside as white as spun cotton. Some of her teeth were snaggled and chipped. The tips were green from pond algae.

"You forgot to floss," Wahoo said.

Alice hissed. He went to get her some food. When she heard the squeaking of the wheelbarrow, she cracked her eyelids and turned her huge armored head.

Wahoo tossed a whole plucked chicken into the alligator's gaping jaws. The sound of her crunching on the thawed bird obscured the voices coming from the house—Wahoo's mother and father "discussing" the China trip.

Wahoo fed Alice two more dead chickens, locked the gate to the pond and took a walk. When he returned, his father was upright on the sofa and his mother was in the kitchen fixing bologna sandwiches for lunch.

"You believe this?" Mickey said to Wahoo. "She's bugging out on us!"

"Pop, we're broke."

Mickey's shoulders slumped. "Not *that* broke."

"You want the animals to starve?" Wahoo asked.

They ate their sandwiches barely speaking a word. When they were done, Mrs. Cray stood up and said: "I'm going to miss you guys. I wish I didn't have to go."

Then she went into the bedroom and shut the door.

Mickey seemed dazed. "I used to like iguanas."

"We'll be okay."

"My head hurts."

"Take your medicine," said Wahoo.

"I threw it away."

"What?"

"Those yellow pills, they made me constipated."

Wahoo shook his head. "Unbelievable."

"Seriously. I haven't had a satisfactory bowel movement since Easter."

"Thanks for sharing," said Wahoo. He started loading the dishwasher, trying to keep his mind off the fact that his mom was about to fly away to the far side of the world.

Mickey got up and apologized to his son.

"I'm just being selfish. I don't want her to go."

"Me neither."

The following Sunday, they all rose before dawn. Wahoo lugged his mother's suitcases to the waiting taxi. She had tears in her eyes when she kissed him goodbye.

"Take care of your dad," she whispered.

Then, to Mickey, she said: "I want you to get better. That's an order, mister."

Watching the cab speed off, Wahoo's father looked forlorn. "It's like she's leaving us twice," he remarked.

"What are you talking about, Pop?"

"I'm seein' double, remember? There she goes—and there she goes again."

Wahoo was in no mood for that. "You want eggs for breakfast?"

Afterward he went out in the backyard to deal with a troublesome howler monkey named Jocko, who'd picked the lock on his cage and was now leaping around, pestering the parrots and macaws. Wahoo had to be careful because Jocko was mean. He used a tangerine to lure the surly primate back to his cage, but Jocko still managed to sink a dirty fang into one of Wahoo's hands.

"I told you to wear the canvas gloves," scolded Mickey when Wahoo was standing at the sink, cleaning the wound.

"*You* don't wear gloves," Wahoo pointed out.

"Yeah, but I don't get chomped like you do."

That was hogwash. Mickey got chomped all the time; it was an occupational hazard. His hands were so scarred that they looked fake, like rubber Halloween props.

The phone rang and Wahoo picked it up. His father weaved back to the couch and flipped through the TV stations until he found the Rain Forest Channel.

"Who was it that called?" he asked when Wahoo came out of the kitchen.

"Another job, Pop."

"You send 'em to Stiggy?"

Jimmy Stigmore was an animal wrangler who had a ranch up in west Davie. Mickey Cray wasn't crazy about Stiggy.

"No, I didn't," Wahoo said.

His father frowned. "Then who'd you send 'em to? Not Dander!"

Donny Dander had lost his wildlife-importing license after he got caught smuggling thirty-eight rare tree frogs from South America. The frogs had been cleverly hidden in his underwear, but the adventure ended in embarrassment at the Miami airport when a customs officer noticed that Donny's pants were cheeping.

Wahoo said, "I didn't send 'em to Dander, either. I didn't send 'em anywhere."

"Okay. Now you lost me," said Mickey Cray.

"I said we'd take the job. I said we could start next week."

"Are you crazy, boy? Look at me, I can't see straight, I can't hardly walk, my skull's 'bout to split open like a rotten pumpkin—"

"Pop!"

"What?"

"I said *we*," Wahoo reminded him. "You and I together."

"But what about school?"

"Friday's the last day. Then I'm done for the summer."

"Already?" Wahoo's dad didn't keep up with Wahoo's academic schedule as closely as his mother did. "So who called about the job?"

Wahoo told him the name of the TV show.

"Not him!" Mickey Cray snorted. "I've heard stories about that jerk."

"Well, how does a thousand bucks sound?" Wahoo asked.

"Pretty darned sweet."

"That's one thousand a *day*." Wahoo let that sink in. "If you want, I'll call 'em back and give him Stiggy's number."

"Don't be a knucklehead." Wahoo's father rose off the sofa and gave him a hug. "You did good, son. We'll make this work."

"Absolutely," said Wahoo, trying to sound confident.

TWO

Hundreds of iguanas had died and tumbled from the treetops during the big freeze in southern Florida. As far as Wahoo knew, his dad was the only person who'd been seriously hurt by one of the falling reptiles.

Mickey Cray had been standing with a cup of hot cocoa beneath a coconut palm in the backyard when the dead lizard had knocked him stiff. Later, after he was brought home from the hospital, Mickey had ordered Wahoo to search the property, capture any iguanas that had survived the frigid weather and relocate them to an abandoned orchid farm half a mile away.

Wahoo hadn't searched very hard. It wasn't the fault of the iguanas that they'd frozen to death. They weren't meant to be living so far north, but Miami pet dealers had been importing baby specimens from the tropics for decades. The customers who bought them had no idea they would grow six feet long, eat all the flowers in the garden and then leap into the swimming pool to poop. When that rude reality set in, the unhappy owners would drive their pet lizards to the nearest park and set them free. Before long, South Florida was crawling with hordes of big wild iguanas that were producing hordes of little wild iguanas.

The cold snap had put an end to that, at least temporarily.

On the first morning of summer vacation, Wahoo found his father in the backyard scanning the trees.

"See any, Pop?"

"All clear," Mickey Cray reported.

Although months had passed since the accident, he was still paranoid about getting clobbered with another falling lizard.

"You must be feeling better," Wahoo remarked. He was pleased to see his dad up and moving around so early.

"My headache's gone!" Mickey announced.

Wahoo said, "No way."

"All those pills the doctors made me swallow, they didn't do a darn thing. Then all of a sudden I wake up and, boom, it's like a miracle." Mickey shrugged. "Some things just can't be explained, son."

But Wahoo had a theory that his father had been cured by five simple words: *one thousand dollars a day.*

Mickey said, "Go fetch some lettuce for Gary and Gail."

Gary and Gail were two ancient Galápagos tortoises that Wahoo's dad had purchased from a zoo in Sarasota many years earlier, when he was new to the wildlife business. These days there wasn't much demand from the TV nature shows for Gary and Gail, because tortoises were not exactly dynamic performers. Mickey Cray kept them around mainly for sentimental reasons. Each of the animals was more than a century old, and he didn't trust any of the other wranglers to treat them properly. The night before the big freeze, Mickey had gone out back and carefully cloaked Gail and Gary with heavy quilts so they wouldn't die. Wahoo had watched from his bedroom window.

"I don't suppose he's interested in these two," Mickey muttered while the tortoises munched loudly on their lettuce.

"No, they said he wants Alice," said Wahoo, "and a major python."

They were talking about their famous new client, Derek Badger. He was the star of *Expedition Survival!*, one of the most popular shows on cable. Every week, Derek would parachute into some gnarly wilderness teeming with fierce animals, venomous snakes and disease-carrying insects. Armed with only a Swiss army knife and a straw, he would hike, climb, crawl, paddle or swim back to civilization—or until he was "rescued." Along the way, he'd eat bugs, rodents, worms, even the fungus on tree bark—the grosser it looked, the happier Derek Badger was to stuff it into his cheeks.

Wahoo and his dad had watched *Expedition Survival!* often enough to know that most of the wildlife scenes were faked. They were also aware that at no time was Derek's life in actual danger, since he was always accompanied by a camera crew packing food, candy, sunblock, water, first-aid supplies and, most likely, a large gun.

"Derek's never done a show in the Everglades," Wahoo said to his father.

"They say he's a humongous pain in the butt, this guy."

"Just be nice, Pop. It's a lot of money."

Mickey promised to behave. "So, when do we get to meet the man himself?"

"His assistant is supposed to stop by later."

"What kind of python do they want—Burmese? African rock?"

Wahoo said, "Honestly, I don't think it matters."

They set to work building a pen for a young bobcat that was being delivered from a ranch up in Highlands County. The cat had been struck by a Jeep and suffered a broken leg that wouldn't mend, so it could never be released back into the wild. Mickey Cray had agreed to raise the animal, and he hoped to make it tame enough for TV work.

Bobcats were strong, meaning the pen had to be sturdy. Wahoo knew that a person with double vision shouldn't be using a nail gun, so he put his dad in charge of measuring and cutting the chicken wire. By noon Mickey's headache came roaring back, and he was in misery. Wahoo steered him to the house and made him lie on the couch and fed him four aspirins.

Minutes later, somebody started knocking on the front door. Mickey raised up and said, "That's probably the guy with the bobcat."

Wahoo looked out the window and saw a woman with a shining stack of red hair. She wore tan shorts and jeweled sandals, and she was carrying a leather briefcase.

"No cat," he said to his father.

"Well, open the darn door."

"But what if she's from the bank?" Wahoo whispered. The Crays were months behind on their mortgage payments.

Mickey peeked out the window. "She is definitely *not* from the bank."

Wahoo invited the woman inside. She introduced herself as Raven Stark.

"I'm Derek Badger's production assistant," she said. "I brought your contract."

"Excellent," said Mickey.

Wahoo noticed that Raven Stark had a strong accent. He tried not to stare at her hairdo, which looked like a sculpture made of red chrome.

She asked, "May I take a look around?"

"Nope," said Wahoo's father.

Raven Stark seemed surprised.

"First you've got to sign a release form," Mickey said. "I don't want to get sued if you fall into the gator pond and get bit."

She laughed. "I've been doing this a long time, Mr. Cray."

"You sign the release, my son will be happy to give you the grand tour."

A few years earlier, Mickey Cray had invited Wahoo's elementary school class to come see his wild animals. A boy named Tingley had ignored Wahoo's warning and reached into one of the cages to tug the tail of a grumpy raccoon, which had spun around and clawed the kid's arm so badly that it looked like a road map of Hialeah. Mickey paid for

Tingley's doctor bills, though not before telling his parents that their boy was dumb as a box of rocks. Ever since then, Mickey's insurance company insisted that everyone who came on the property had to fill out a legal form saying it wasn't Mickey's fault if they got hurt.

While Raven Stark signed the release, Mickey signed the contract from *Expedition Survival!* Wahoo noticed that he scrawled his name crookedly below the line where it was supposed to go, which meant his eyesight was still jumbled.

"How long is the shoot going to take?" Mickey asked.

Raven Stark said, "Until we get it right."

Wahoo's dad looked pleased. "So it's one thousand a day, plus location fees and the animal rentals."

"Correct." She took an envelope from her purse and handed it to him. "Here's eight hundred dollars as a deposit."

Mickey counted the cash and then turned to Wahoo. "Son, go show this fine lady whatever she wants to see."

Because it was going to be an Everglades show, Raven Stark was keenly interested in Alice the alligator. Wahoo led her to the pond and unlocked the gate.

Raven whistled. "That's a monster, eh?"

"Twelve feet," said Wahoo.

"How much?"

"One hundred and fifty dollars a foot, so that's . . ."

"Eighteen hundred even," Raven said. "No problem."

Wahoo couldn't wait to tell his father.

"Do you have another one that's smaller?" asked Raven.

"Yes, ma'am."

"Something Derek could wrestle?"

"Wrestle?"

"Maybe a four-footer," Raven said. "Five feet, max."

"I'll have to check with Pop." Wahoo foresaw trouble. His father didn't like anybody messing with the animals.

"Where are your pythons?" Raven asked.

Wahoo led her to the heavy glass tanks where the constrictors were kept. South Florida had become infested with huge exotic snakes that, like the iguanas, had been imported for the pet trade. Hurricane Andrew had blown apart several large reptile farms and scattered baby pythons and boa constrictors all over the place.

"Derek wants a beast," Raven stated.

Wahoo showed her a fourteen-footer that had been captured while devouring an opossum in a Dumpster behind the Dadeland Mall. The man who'd found the snake was supposed to turn it over to state game officers, but instead he'd sold it to Mickey Cray for three hundred bucks.

Raven agreed it was an impressive specimen. "But can he be handled safely?"

"It's a she," Wahoo said, "and she's a biter."

"Oh."

"Pop can work with her. She'll be okay."

"I hope so," said Raven Stark. "How much?"

"Seven hundred for the day." Wahoo tried to sound steady and businesslike. He wasn't used to handling the negotiations. The standard rental rate for pythons was fifty dollars a foot.

"Okay, fine. What did you say your name was?"

He told her.

"Is that 'Wahoo,' like the fish?"

Everybody made that assumption. "My dad named me after a wrestler," the boy explained.

"How interesting."

"Not really," said Wahoo.

"Can I ask what happened?" She pointed at the white bump on Wahoo's right hand, where a thumb should have been.

"Yes, ma'am. Alice got it."

"You're serious, aren't you?"

Quickly Wahoo said, "It wasn't her fault, it was mine."

One day he'd been showing off for a girl who had come over after school to see the animals. Wahoo had brought her down to the gator pond for a feeding, but he stepped way too close to Alice, who jumped up and snapped the thawed chicken out of his grasp, taking his thumb along with it. The girl's name was Paulette, and she'd fainted on the spot.

Changing the subject, Wahoo asked, "Where is Mr. Badger?"

"Paris," Raven said.

Wahoo had never heard of any dangerous jungles or swamps in Paris, so he assumed the famous survivalist was taking a vacation.

Mickey Cray came outside and joined them at the snake

tanks. Wahoo told him that Ms. Stark was interested in using Beulah, the big Burmese.

"Good choice," said Mickey. He appeared to be feeling better.

"You've seen the program, of course," Raven said.

"Sure," said Wahoo. "It's on Thursday nights."

"And rerun every Sunday morning," she said. "So you already know that we're all about verisimilitude."

Wahoo didn't even pretend to understand what the word meant. His father just looked at him and shrugged.

"Making it real," Raven explained. "On *Expedition Survival!*, we're all about making it real. Derek considers that his sacred mission, a bond of trust with our viewers."

Wahoo glanced at the massive snakes, coiled in their tanks. They were real enough; they just weren't wild and free.

The production assistant turned to Wahoo's father. "Any questions?"

Mickey smiled. "We put our animals on TV all the time. That's what we do."

Raven Stark bent down and tapped a scarlet fingernail on the glass panel that separated her from Beulah the python.

"Well, Mr. Cray," she said, "I promise you've never done a show like Derek's."

"Yes, it *is* a hoot." —*The Washington Post*

Everybody loves Mother Paula's pancakes. Everybody, that is, except the cute endangered owls that live on the building site of the new restaurant. Can the awkward new kid and his feral friend prank the pancake people out of town? Either way, it's sure to be a hoot.

"It's about greedy developers, corrupt politicians, clueless cops, and middle-school screwballs of all persuasions."
—*The New York Times Book Review*